THE PERFECT COED

Judy Alter

Alter Ego Publishing

Alter Ego Publishing
Fort Worth, TX 76110

ISBN 978-0-9960131-1-6 (digital)
ISBN 978-0-9960131-0-9 (trade paperback)

Editors: Mary Dulle and Lourdes Venard
Cover Art Design: Lyn Stanzione
Interior Book Design: Jennifer Zaczek

Release Date: May 2014

Disclaimer
Oak Grove University is purely a creation of the author's imagination.
Although set within easy distance of the Dallas/Fort Worth Metroplex,
it is not meant to be any specific school within the North or Central
Texas regions. Naturally, my knowledge of various schools in the area
went into the creation of Oak Grove but to make specific connections
between it and a real university would be a mistake. And to place the
murder herein on a specific campus would be a total mistake.

Similarly, the characters in this book bear no relation to any
real people, on or off Texas campuses.

For Bobbie Simms, who would have liked this book and been proud of me. I miss you yet, Bobbie.

Chapter One

Susan Hogan drove around Oak Grove, Texas, for two days before she realized there was a dead body in the trunk of her car. And it was another three days before she knew that someone was trying to kill her.

On the second day, she noticed a slightly unpleasant, sweet-but-foul odor in the car as she drove south on Main Street, headed for the Oak Grove State University campus and her eight o'clock American lit class. Susan's 1998 Honda Civic often had mysterious odors that were all her own fault. Her mind ranged over the possibilities—leftover spaghetti and meatballs that she'd put in an icebox dish to bring to school for lunch, maybe a to-go box from her favorite Thai restaurant in Fort Worth, spilled coffee since she drank hers with cream.

No matter. She was late for her class, so she opened the windows to let the cool air of the October morning blow through the car as she passed through the town. Oak Grove was one of those towns kept alive and even attractive by the presence of a small university. Main Street was landscaped with trees, benches, and some brick paving. Boutiques and small cafes sat next to a bookstore, a lawyer's office, and the traditional old brick-and-stone bank. Just before the campus, the street curved uphill through a city park. It was, Susan always thought, a perfect place to live and teach. She didn't really care if the university was second-tier, not as prestigious as some of the bigger schools in the state. She'd been here almost eight years, and Oak Grove was home by now.

"I'll clean the car tonight," she told herself, "before Jake sees it or smells it."

Her thoughts wandered to Jake Phillips. He was the police chief on the Oak Grove campus but more than that, he had been Susan's lover for two years. That he loved her, she had no doubt; that he might get tired of her high jinks and stubbornness was a thought that lingered in the back of her mind. Sometimes she wondered if she kept the relationship because it irritated her department chair, John Scott, that she was involved with someone with no more than a community college two-year degree. Well, maybe at first, but she knew now she was hooked. She needed Jake in her life.

As she drove onto campus, Susan looked at the seemingly endless construction, adding new imitations to the lovely old red-brick, red-tiled roofs of the original buildings. The administration had been on a construction jag in the last few years, adding buildings so fast it made the head spin, a few with ornate, out-of-places arches. But for the most part there was an attempt at consistency. For all her sometime rebellion at academic restrictions and prejudices, Susan always felt a sense of being home when she arrived on campus.

She was late, she reminded herself. Parking in the faculty lot behind Baker Hall, the liberal arts class building, she sprinted to her class. Her twenty or so college juniors looked ready to bolt for the door. Casually, she walked in, said good morning, and began her lecture on Emily Dickinson. As usual, the girls were interested, scribbling frantic notes; the boys glanced out the windows and chewed their fingernails in boredom. Susan was as happy as they were when the hour ended. Next time she'd cater to the boys and talk about Walt Whitman.

Caught up in a departmental meeting, at which Scott lectured on the importance of faculty maintaining their dignity, among other things, as well as planning for her afternoon graduate seminar and keeping office hours, Susan forgot about the smell in her car. During office hours, three students had to see her privately to explain why it was absolutely impossible for them to turn their papers in that day. Another boy came to explain the plagiarism in his paper about Nathaniel Hawthorne.

"My mother helped me write it," he said.

"Then your mother stole from one of the leading Hawthorne scholars," Susan said icily. The boy's grade remained an F.

Then Brandy Perkins appeared in tears to report that she had missed Susan's noon class on women's lit because her roommate, Missy Jackson, hadn't come home the night before and she was too worried to concentrate.

Susan wanted to suggest that she call the roommate's boyfriend's apartment, where she'd probably find the girl. Staying out at night wasn't all that unusual for coeds these days. But instead she asked, "If you're that worried, have you called her parents?"

A shake of the head. "I didn't want to scare them."

Susan doubted the Jacksons scared easily. They had been one of about six parents who called to complain about Susan's ideas in the women's lit class she taught last spring. She was, according to the Jacksons, corrupting young minds and turning them away from their faith. She had lectured on Carolyn Heilbrun, women's activist, professor, free spirit, and author of the Amanda Cross academic mysteries, and as she recalled, Missy had been one of those particularly taken by Heilbrun's life story and her book, *Writing a Woman's Life*.

Dark circles under Brandy's eyes suggested that she had indeed spent a sleepless night, and Susan somehow suspected there was more going on here than a roommate who spent the night with her boyfriend. Brandy's manner—secretive and yet scared—sounded an alarm to Susan.

"Have you called the campus police?"

Another shake of the head. "If she's okay, think how embarrassing that would be."

And if she's not? "I think your roommate is probably fine, and I think you should come to class from now on. It'll keep your mind off worrying, and you might get more out of it than you think."

She was in the midst of her afternoon seminar, listening to a senior defend her paper on Edith Wharton, when Mildred, the department secretary, stuck her head in the classroom door.

"Dr. Hogan, I'm sorry to interrupt . . . "

It was an unwritten rule that no class was ever interrupted, except perhaps in case of fire. Susan whirled on Mildred. "Yes?" Her tone barely hid her surprise—and a bit of indignation.

"Mr. Phillips, the chief . . . " Mildred began to stammer, and Susan wanted to urge her along. "He's on the phone. Says . . .

well, he says he has to talk to you now. It can't wait twenty minutes until class is out." She looked a little brighter. "I asked him to wait, but he said no."

Jake calling her out of class? Susan didn't know whether to be angry or worried. She gave the class a reading assignment from Wharton and dismissed them.

Running to the office, she knew that she was at least a little bit scared. When she picked up the phone, she demanded, "What is it?"

Jake was businesslike and clearly impatient. "Susan, when did you bash the trunk of your car? I can't open it with my key."

"Why are you trying to open my trunk?" she asked, relieved that he wasn't telling her that her house had burned down or some equally major catastrophe had happened.

"Because," he said with ice in his tone, "we've had four complaints of a really foul odor coming from your car. I got a thousand problems this morning—someone reported a missing coed, someone's parked in the dean's parking space. I don't have time to pry open your trunk and discover a five-day-old takeout order of Thai food." Now he was really impatient.

Susan could see him, his blue eyes that icy color they got when he was angry or upset. He'd be running his hand across his burr haircut. That wonderful lopsided grin, under the nose bent by too many breaks in high school football, would be missing, and his mouth would be in a grim straight line.

"I didn't leave any food in the trunk!" she responded indignantly, her fear turning to anger. "Want me to come pry it open? Just give me a crowbar and watch me go."

"What happened to the trunk?" he asked again.

"I don't know. I noticed a couple of nights ago when I came out of the library that it had a new dent, but I didn't need to get into the trunk, and I sort of forgot about it. I suppose someone backed into it." Susan's car had several dents, which always made Jake nervous because he drove a Toyota pickup in perfect condition.

"Just give me permission to open it. I'll call you back. But, Susan, if it's Thai food . . . " His voice drifted off.

"Okay. You have my permission."

She thought she'd just go back to her office, collect her things, and head for her car. But Ernie Westin stopped her. Susan and Westin were locked in a race for tenure, a race he periodically tried to prove to her that she was losing. Westin had almost convinced her that the tenure committee would not approve all eligible candidates because that might indicate a lack of credibility on their part. And the automatic pay raise that comes with tenure would stretch the department's budget. She wasn't sure she believed him but she was working as hard as she could on her publication record, which now consisted only of articles. Tenure review committees always looked for an academic book, and she was working on a book about Zane Grey, hoping to prove that his novels were not potboiler westerns but carefully constructed works, filled with sexual tension and symbolism. Ernie was working on a study of Greek tragedies.

"I have a contract for my book," he said. "Do you?"

He stood, trying to look casual by leaning in the doorway, his eyes darting toward her and then away again. Susan often thought he resembled a toad, with his round belly, prominent eyes, and raspy voice. He was rapidly going to both fat and middle age and had that kind of gray complexion associated with ivory-tower academics who never let the sun shine on them. He was also a whiner. She bet he read all his class lectures, in a monotone, from his notes and then wondered why there were no questions. Who cared? Susan thought tenure committees should sit in on classes rather than just review publications, but the world didn't always go Susan's way.

She moved past him toward her desk. "No, Ernie," she said with as much patience as she could muster. She really wanted to wipe the smirk off his face. "I've been too busy preparing for classes to work much on it." There it was, that old academic dilemma, publish or perish, which didn't encourage great classroom preparation.

"Probably," he said nastily, "because you spend too much time with that Jake Phillips. You could do better than a cop."

Susan considered decking him with a well-placed fist. For an instant, his snide reference to Jake made her wonder about Ernie's sexual orientation, but she figured that was none of her business. As far as she knew, Ernie lived alone in a one-room apartment in a house in town, and any sort of nasty comment would, she thought, be beneath her.

But cross me one more time, Ernie Westin, and I'll give you something to whine about.

"Ernie," she said, "I just don't have time to talk about your book or tenure or anything right now. There's a problem with my car—"

"Oh, well," he said loftily. "That beat-up car you drive . . . I'm sure it has many problems." Ernie drove a dull Chevrolet with no character.

"Leave my car out of this," she said angrily. *Why, am I arguing with Ernie Westin when Jake's breaking into the trunk of my car?*

Her cell phone startled her. It was Jake. "Susan, get over here now. To your car." He spoke in the low, measured tones that Susan knew indicated a major problem, not just the impatience she'd heard in his voice a few minutes ago.

"Jake, I was—"

"Susan, for God's sake, would you just do what I tell you for once?"

Jake's tone alarmed her. She bolted down the three flights of the liberal arts hall, grateful that she had decided on jeans and Reeboks that day, in spite of Ernie Westin's disapproving looks. Jogging toward her car, she saw a crowd of people in the parking lot.

They were mostly students, and they stood behind an area roped off with yellow police-scene tape. Her car stood in the middle of the tape. Around her she could hear voices, "What's happened? What's in that car? Whose car is it?"

Just then two city police cars roared into the parking lot, sirens blaring. An ambulance followed them. Susan saw a knot of men gathered about her car. The battered trunk lid was raised, and they were all staring inside.

She lifted the tape to scoot under it.

"Pardon, ma'am, but no one can go past. This is a crime scene."

She didn't know if she was angrier at being stopped or being called "ma'am" by a deputy who was at best five years younger than she was. "It's my car," she shouted. "They told me to get over here right away. Ask Jake Phillips."

"No need, ma'am," he said, holding the tape for her. "Phillips told us you'd be coming. I just . . . well, I expected a teacher."

Susan looked down at her jeans and running shoes and ignored the deputy.

As she started toward the car, Jake came toward her. "Stop here, Susan. Don't go up there."

"Why not?" she demanded. "First you tell me to get over here—then you stop me." She started to pull away from him, but he held firmly to her arm.

"We found the missing coed," he said. "In the trunk of your car. Someone beat her to death, really bashed in her head."

For a moment, Susan staggered. Her mind's eye saw another body, a young girl, curled in a ball on a cold, tile floor. But that was a long time ago, something she'd worked hard to put behind her—the death, the murder accusation, the anger. She shook her head to clear her thoughts, but she felt momentarily remote, removed from whatever was happening around her. *This can't happen to me twice. At least I didn't know this girl well. I knew Shelley— oh, boy, did I know Shelley.*

"You okay, Susan?" Jake asked. His voice jerked her back to reality. "Did you hear me? Someone put a body in your car. When did you first notice that dent in the trunk?"

"Night before last," she muttered. "I was in the library, doing research on Zane Grey, and when I came out I thought I saw a dent that hadn't been there before."

"But you didn't do anything about it?" Jake asked, his tone angry again. "Why am I not surprised?"

"I was going to. I just hadn't had time. Besides, it's not the only dent in my car."

She had the uncomfortable feeling that she was going to break down and cry.

And right there, in front of everyone, Jake Phillips put his arms around her and held her tightly, pulling her head down onto his shoulder and running his hands through her hair, as though he were comforting a child. He was tall enough that she fit easily against him and found comfort.

"I just want to go home," Susan said, tears running down her face. "Can you take me home?"

"Not yet," Jake said softly.

* * *

Neither of them noticed Brandy Perkins standing on the edge of the crowd. Her face was strained, and her hands were clenched into tight fists. When the buzz went from one person to the next that a body had been found in the trunk of a teacher's car, she asked of no one in particular, "A guy?"

"Nah," came the answer, "a girl."

A small sound escaped her mouth. And then Brandy Perkins turned and ran. Only one student, a dark-haired, good-looking boy about twenty-one, turned away from the scene at the car to watch Brandy run away. And he watched with an intense, brooding expression on his face that would have added to Brandy's terror if she had seen it. When she was out of sight, he turned slowly toward the car.

Brandy ran past Baker, the building she'd just left, and the business school and the administration building, headed for the patio outside the student center. She slowed when she found the patio empty and sat down on one of the iron chairs that were bolted to the textured concrete patio. With shaking hands she pulled out a cell phone and punched in numbers.

"They found Missy," she whispered. A pause and then, "In the trunk of a car. Dr. Hogan's car. She's dead."

Another pause. "Of course, that's what I think. We have to be sure not to tell anyone, not anyone." She tried to be firm but there was a quaver in her voice.

Then, "Oh, God, will I have to talk to the police?" Whoever was on the other end of the line must have said she would, because Brandy said, "I don't know if I can do it."

One last pause, and Brandy whispered partly into the phone and partly to herself, "I'm scared. I'm so scared."

She hit the "end" button, put the phone in her book bag, and ran into the union. Only once she was safely locked into a stall in the restroom did she give in to the tears that had been building. Then she sobbed and sobbed, not even trying to muffle her cries.

* * *

A plainclothes policeman approached Susan, who still stood clutching Jake's arm. "Dr. Hogan? If you'll just come with me . . . "

With horror Susan realized he meant to take her away from Jake. She sent a look of panic toward Jake, who said to the officer, "Listen, Jordan, that's not necessary. I'll take responsibility for her and bring her downtown."

Jordan, whoever he was, did not look like a man who bent the rules. "It's irregular," he said. "We need to question her. At this point, she's not under arrest."

Susan thought he stressed the "at this point" a little too heavily. Later she found out his first name was Dirk. It rhymed with jerk.

"Come on," Jake protested. "I know you have to question her, but Susan's upset, and you and I both know she didn't do this."

"I don't know any such thing," Jordan said. "It'll take me about another hour out here. I'll send an officer to escort her downtown. You can come on your own. And get your people to do something about this crowd." He stalked away.

Jake looked amused, whereas Susan thought he should be angry. "He giving you orders," she protested.

"He just thinks he is," Jake said wryly. "Not much we can do about the crowd, except keep 'em at a good distance, and we're doing that."

As the officer arrived to escort her downtown, Susan said, "Jake, my purse, my books . . . in my office."

He nodded.

* * *

Susan huddled in the back seat of the squad car, as much as she could, sure that every student was staring at her. The day had warmed considerably, but she was shaking and chilled. Above all, she was scared. All thoughts of tenure and classes and John Scott flew out of her mind as she relived the past, the day she'd found Shelley's body and ended up at the police station, accused of murder.

Questions raced through her mind. *Why my car? It must be Missy Jackson, Brandy Perkins' roommate.* "Who is she?" she asked the officer, though she knew all along it would be Missy Jackson. She harbored a faint hope it was someone else, though she didn't know how that would make the situation better.

The officer drove, eyes straight ahead. "Not at liberty to tell you, ma'am."

Susan considered throwing something at him, but she had nothing to throw. And wouldn't really have done it anyway. It was just a comforting thought. She shivered again.

* * *

Brandy Perkins lay on the bed in her room at the sorority house, but sleep was the last thing on her mind. She had finally pulled herself together in that bathroom stall, splashed water on her face, and hurried to her room—the room she had shared with Missy. Bolting up the stairs, she ignored the girls who sat in the lounge and nearly knocked one girl down the steps in her blind haste. Now she tossed and turned and her thoughts raced. Missy's face appeared in front of her, and then that of a young man with outrageous red hair. Every time she saw him, she covered her eyes to make the image disappear. She couldn't bear to look at Missy's half of the room, and questions about Missy's family haunted her. Would they come to Oak Grove? Would they expect her to know something?

When the phone rang, she almost didn't answer it. When she did, her fingers tightened around it. "Kenny?"

Whatever he asked, she turned pale. "No, Kenny, not tonight. I can't."

A little anger crept into her voice. "I can't, Kenny. I'm worried about Missy." Then she had a thought and added, "She's sick. She's real sick."

Kenny either didn't know about Missy's death or was pretending not to know, because he asked Brandy to have Missy call him. "Okay, I'll tell her."

A pause and then Brandy said, "Yeah, sure, Kenny, next time."

She hung up the phone and began to sob again. Two hours later, when she woke up from a drug-like sleep, she thought,

"I've got to get out of here. NOW!" Applying a hasty dab of lipstick and running a comb through her hair, she headed downstairs.

News of Missy's death had reached the sorority house. Girls stood in clusters in the hall and the lounge. For a moment when Brandy rounded the last landing on the staircase, all eyes turned toward her, but no one said a word and no one moved. Then, one by one, they came over to hug her, tears on their faces, empty words coming from their mouths. Brandy tried to thank them and to hug back, and suddenly it hit her again.

"I've got to get out of here!" She bolted for the door, and the next thing she knew she was at the Green Lizard Lounge, an off-campus and supposedly off-limits place where students hung out. A smoky bar, the place catered to old men from the town in the daytime and the college crowd at night—high school kids too if they could sneak in. Nobody much checked IDs, just as they didn't count how many beers any old man drank during the morning.

Kids were just beginning to arrive, and Brandy chose a booth in the back where she could watch. She ordered a Coors Light and sat sipping it, trying not to think.

Suddenly a young man appeared at the booth. He was tall and thin, with dark brown hair that hung in a shank over his eyes. "Hey, Brandy," he said.

Startled, she barely managed to answer, "Hey, Eric."

Uninvited he sat down. "You okay?"

"Yeah, I guess. I think I'm numb. Are you?"

He shrugged. "I can't believe it. Nobody told me. I just heard it on the radio. I can't believe no one told me." He didn't mention that he'd been in the crowd around Susan Hogan's car or that he'd watched Brandy bolt from the scene. His hand fingered a gold ring on a chain around his neck. It was the promise ring that Missy had given him.

"Oh, God," Brandy said. Then, with desperation, she realized she had to put on an act for Missy's boyfriend. "I . . . I don't know why anyone would do this to Missy. It had to be mistaken identity . . . or a random act. Nobody could be that mad at Missy." She thought she might cry again.

"And why Dr. Hogan's car?" Eric asked, an intense look making his eyes shine. "I feel like I'm supposed to solve this."

Brandy shrugged. "Dr. Hogan's a great teacher, nice person. Who would do that to her?"

"I hear she's sort of, well, a feminist and all that," Eric said. "I never had her for class. Missy used to talk about what she learned in her . . . what was it? Women's lit class?"

"Yeah," Brandy said. "Missy was impressed with her. I'm taking her women's lit class now, and I like her a lot."

Eric rose suddenly. "I got to go. Missy's parents are supposed to arrive early in the morning. Got to get myself together so I can help them."

"See you," Brandy said and took a long pull at her beer. She hoped Kenny wouldn't come looking for her.

Chapter Two

Susan's interview with Dirk Jordan was predictable. He thought she was hiding something—and was probably guilty—and she resented that he assumed she was guilty when she was a victim. She slowly realized that the only way she could convince this detective that she was innocent was to find the real killer herself.

The non-speaking officer had delivered her to the basement police headquarters. All she saw were cubicles with the liberal use of wallboard and small rooms with closed doors. Susan knew the jail was upstairs. A few uniformed police officers wandered in and out of various cubbyhole offices, their faces serious. Some clutched sheaves of paper, and others looked like they didn't know what to do with their empty hands.

She glimpsed at least four desperate criminals, until she reminded herself that desperate criminals were fairly rare in a quiet town like Oak Grove. But in the narrow hall she had brushed against a man in an orange jumpsuit, his hands cuffed in front of him. Her already testy stomach lurched at the smell of him.

The policeman escorted her to a small room badly in need of new paint and fresh air. The smell of stale smoke mixed with the mustiness that hung over the whole area. The room validated every detective show she'd ever seen on TV. A scarred, wooden table with four metal chairs around it. A window that made her wish she'd tried to look in from the outside to see if it was one-way glass.

Dirk Jordan came in shortly and greeted her warmly enough. "Dr. Hogan, thanks for coming in. I'm truly sorry about what's happened."

"So am I," Susan said, as she took his outstretched hand. *Thanks for coming? As if she'd had a choice.* She looked into eyes that were cold and distant. Then she studied him a minute. He was maybe ten years older and an inch or two taller than Jake. His nose didn't turn sideways in his face, but she noticed that he held his left hand in an awkward position by his side.

"Coffee?" he asked, but Susan declined. She realized that she hadn't had lunch, and she didn't think it was smart to put caffeine into an empty stomach. Her hands still felt shaky.

"I'll pass too," he said, motioning for her to sit. He took a seat across the table from her. He meant to look casual, but she could see that the muscles in his neck were corded with tension. The hair on the back of Susan's neck prickled.

He wasted no more time on pleasantries. "We've identified the body as Missy Jackson, a senior. You knew her, I believe. How well?"

Startled, Susan almost jumped. "Not well at all. She was a student of mine last year. I didn't know her outside class."

"And what was your classroom relationship like?"

Susan pondered that for a moment. "The same as it is with most of my students. I tried to encourage her to be an independent thinker. Sometimes she was . . . ah . . . very independent and other times she seemed very traditional."

"Her reputation is, I believe, above reproach." Somehow his tone made it seem that he was questioning her evaluation of the dead girl.

"I didn't know her reputation or accomplishments when she was in my class."

"I don't understand why her body was in your car," he said, his eyes challenging her.

"Neither do I." Susan's voice flared in anger.

"The medical examiner tells me as a preliminary finding that the girl was killed Monday night. Where were you?"

"In the library, until it closed at ten."

"Anyone see you? Anyone that knows you?"

"Of course. The librarians know me."

"That can be checked." He tried another tack. "Do you know Eric Lindler?"

"Who?"

"The dead girl's boyfriend."

She shook her head in the negative. "But I wish I knew why he chose my car to put her body in," she said.

"We have no proof that it was Eric Lindler. We haven't interviewed him yet."

She wanted to scream, "Don't you think he should be first on your list, ahead of me?"

"Whoever it was," Jordan said slowly, "wanted the body found. That's why it was in your car. Otherwise, anyone with half a brain would have dumped the body way out in the country someplace."

"Then that should rule me out," she replied quickly. "If I wanted a body found, I wouldn't be so dumb as to put it in my own car."

"Not necessarily," he said, dismissing her protest. "If you don't know why your car was chosen, have you considered it was because of your relationship with Jake Phillips?" His cold eyes stared, watching her every reaction.

What else does this man know? "Why would that matter?"

"If . . . " He paused to let that word sink it. "If you didn't put the body in your car, perhaps someone else knew you would get instant attention from the campus police because of your relationship with Phillips."

"I don't believe the campus police treat me any differently than anyone else at the school," she said firmly.

The questioning went on, always coming back to the question of why the body was in her car. Finally, Jordan said, "Dr. Hogan, your story has too many holes in it for my comfort. One more thing: have you ever been involved in a criminal investigation before?"

Susan shook her head in the negative, but visions of Shelley lying curled in a ball blurred in front of her until she raised a hand as though to wipe the image away.

"That can be checked. We'll have to impound your car indefinitely. Here's my card, in case you remember anything else. Please assure me that you won't leave Oak Grove. I have no authority to order you to stay here, but it would look suspicious if you left," Jordan said.

Stunned, Susan managed to mutter, "Yes, sir." She wanted to scream.

Jake was waiting to take her home, and she fell into his arms gratefully. "He didn't believe me," she told him once in the car. "He thinks I know something I'm not telling." She thought a minute and then asked, "What's wrong with his left hand?"

"Shot," Jake said. "Way I hear it was the bullet severed some nerves. Jordan won't talk about it, but they say it's made him a tougher cop. It's probably also why he's in a small town and not on a big city force."

"Well, he thinks that somebody probably crashed into my car to pop the trunk open and then pounded it shut once they put . . . ah, her . . . inside."

"I'm not a detective," Jake said dryly, "but they could have just opened the trunk from inside your car. I know it wasn't locked, never is. So why would they crash into it?"

"Nothing else makes sense," she said, "so why should that?"

Jake turned into the town square. "You hungry?"

"Ravenous." She'd have thought all that had happened would have killed any appetite she had, but she realized she hadn't eaten anything since an early-morning bowl of cereal.

They went to Subie's Café on the square. It had the usual plastic-covered chairs with chrome and vinyl tables covered with oilcloth—what her mother used to refer to proudly as her "dinette set" when Susan was young. The salt and pepper sat next to a container of sugar and sweetener, with the ever-present bottle of ketchup that always made Susan wonder why restaurants didn't feel the need to refrigerate ketchup like she did at home.

What Susan loved about Subie's was the collection of old pictures, maps, and memorabilia that hung on its walls—pictures of Gary Cooper and John Wayne, an ornate and aged sombrero, a 1950s map of Oak Grove. Overhead, an old porch swing was suspended from the ceiling and next to it was a tumbleweed. She always imagined they were all dusty, sifting bits of dirt onto her food, but it never bothered her.

Neither Jake nor Susan looked at the menu. He would have chicken-fried steak, and she would have a hamburger with fries.

The waitress came over, pad in hand. "The usual?" she asked.

"Thanks, Margie," Jake said.

She turned toward the kitchen, then stopped and faced Jake, hands on her hips. "Is it true about them finding a body in a car on campus?" Indignation was written all over her face.

"I'm afraid it is," Jake said, and Susan held her breath for fear that it would come out whose car it was.

"I tell you, Mr. Phillips," Marge said, her voice rising shrilly, "them college students, they're gonna ruin this town. Look at the way they hang out in them bars up on the edge of town of a Saturday night. Used to be a body was safe in her own bed, but now . . . I don't know."

"I don't think it's a sign of a crime spree," Jake said, fighting to keep a smile from his face and avoiding looking at Susan. "We'll find out, I'm sure, that it was someone who knew this poor girl."

"What kind of a friend would do that?" She finally went away, shaking her head in despair.

"Not going to be easy for the university," Jake said. "The communications office is going to have a real PR job on its hands."

"So am I," Susan said, "when word gets around it was my car."

Jake reached across the table and covered her hand with his. "I'm as sorry as I can be, Susan, you got mixed up in this. I'll do everything I can to get you out of it, but . . . " He shrugged, and Susan felt a sense of inevitability about everything that had happened and a helplessness about whatever would happen next.

The chicken-fried steak was fork tender—wasn't it always? Susan thought—and the hamburger thick and the good kind of greasy. Every time they ate at the café, they vowed never again because they were so stuffed and satisfied when they finished eating. But they ate there once a week or more. Sometimes, Susan tried to tell Jake about how her Aunt Jenny could cook chicken-fried steak that was as good as what he had just eaten, but he always said, "Don't fool me, Susan. No one in your family could cook, or they'd have taught you."

"My Aunt Jenny can," she said defensively.

Jake pushed his plate away from him. "You ready?" he asked. "It's been a long day."

"You think you've had a long day!" Susan exploded. "I feel, oh, I don't know how I feel. Like I could cry one minute and bang my fist into a wall the next."

"Come on. I'll take you home. You got bourbon?"

"Yeah." She thought maybe she needed two fingers of bourbon instead of wine.

Jake paid the bill, and they chatted with Margie for a minute. It made Susan itch to talk about inanities with all that was on her mind, and she could barely keep from tugging at Jake's arm to get him out of there. But he was Jake, ever sociable, ever ready for a little casual conversation, as though nothing in the world was worrying him.

Susan was only halfway out the door that Jake held when she screamed—a long, high-pitched scream that mixed surprise and anger and fright. Behind her, Jake let out a passionate, "Goddamn!"

Jake's university-owned Jeep had four flat tires and a broken windshield. "Go inside," he said to her, his voice calm and controlling, "and call my office. Then call the police."

Two cars of Jake's patrolmen arrived just before the city police car. The police car had sirens blaring and lights flashing. Lt. Jordan was the first one out of the car.

"Who did this?" he demanded.

"You tell us," Susan said, but Jake raised a hand for her to be quiet. In his other hand he held a large red rock with a note tied to it with brown twine.

"What's that?" Jordan demanded.

"A rock with a note," Jake said, repeating the obvious. "I haven't read it yet."

"Get me some evidence gloves," Jordan barked over his shoulder at one of the other officers. As soon as his hands were protected, so they would neither destroy nor add fingerprints, he undid the twine and smoothed out the note. It was awkward because he could only use one hand, and Susan itched to reach out and help him. Jake would really slap her then. Finally, he read the note aloud:

"You're next, Dr. Hogan. You cannot continue to corrupt young women's minds."

Jake grabbed Susan just as her knees buckled. "Steady," he said. "It's just a threat, not a loaded gun."

"No," she said weakly, "that probably comes next."

"Probably a prank," Jordan said. "News about that girl is all over town and the campus, and everyone knows you were involved"—he jerked his head toward Susan but didn't do her the courtesy of calling her by name. "Probably some kid who's gotten too many parking tickets saw this as a good way to get at you, Phillips."

"By threatening my life?" Susan was incredulous at the logic—or lack of it—in the lieutenant's reasoning.

"Everyone knows he, ah, cares about you," Jordan said. "What would worry him more than a threat to you?"

"I have to get Susan home," Jake said, feeling the tremor in her legs as she stood pressed next to him. "Grady, you guys take care of my Jeep and give me one of your cars. Jordan, if you need me I'll be at Susan's."

"All night, I presume," the lieutenant said.

Jake didn't answer him.

They drove in silence, Susan wondering if she would ever stop shaking or if she had developed a permanent palsy. When they reached her house, she wanted to leave books and everything in the car and flee to the sanctuary of home, but Jake put a restraining arm on hers.

"Wait here."

Home for Susan Hogan was a sixties ranch-style house on the outskirts of town. The front, she always thought, was bland and plain, a red brick low and long, distinguished only by its tin roof, landscaped with bushes and a curving walkway. But the driveway led to the back yard, where she had a large deck filled with flowering plants and herbs, both on the deck and on a wide railing around it. The backyard was landscaped to her taste—with curving beds and lots of southwestern, xeriscape plants—Mexican hat, coneflowers which would bloom in the spring, coreopsis, butterfly plant, all things that bloomed at various times and kept her yard a jungle of color much of the year. Behind them were the taller photinas, and to one side a carefully tended garden of antique roses. There was little lawn, but Susan still battled crab grass and pampered her St. Augustine. The deck was where Susan and Jake barbecued, sat sipping drinks, and generally lived from spring until late fall. A sliding glass patio door offered entry into the family room.

Jake made her wait in the locked car while he did a search. Then he motioned her in and went to the front door to scoop the contents out of the mailbox.

Inside, Susan breathed a deep sigh of relief at being in the place she considered a safe haven. The house had a typical ranch-style layout—living room, dining room, kitchen, family room, and three bedrooms branching off to one end. The floors were hardwood, albeit in need of refinishing, and the kitchen had been redone long enough ago that it needed updating again. But someone had turned the back of the house into a kind of common room, by opening the wall between the kitchen and the family room, creating a large open area divided only by a counter. From the kitchen, Susan could visit with whoever sat around her pedestal oak table or lounged on the couch. Not that she ever cooked much. But Jake often cooked, and she sat on the couch or at the counter and admired him as he put together one gourmet dinner after another.

Jake poured drinks for them—bourbon for him and white wine for her. "You don't need bourbon," he said, as though he was reading her mind.

As they sat on the deck, Jake asked Susan what she knew about Missy Jackson.

She shrugged. "Not much. She was in my women's lit class last spring. She was fairly typical at the beginning of the semester. All the values that her mother probably had, like she wasn't in touch with the modern world. I try to encourage students to break out of the old roles, and I did that with Missy. So one minute she was Miss Goody Two-Shoes and the next she was in rebellion."

"Against what?"

Susan shrugged. "Society. The way women are treated. The way we're expected to act."

"And I supposed you encouraged her to be a feminist?" Jake's voice had an ironic twist.

"I encouraged her to think for herself," Susan said. "But she was sort of mixed up. There was something going on that I didn't understand."

Susan paused a minute. "Her roommate is taking the class now. Brandy Perkins. She's the one who told me she couldn't come to class because her roommate was missing and told me who it was. Frankly, I didn't take it very seriously."

After a long silence that Jake let drag on, Susan spoke again. "You think there's a real threat to me, don't you?"

"Let's say I'm not willing to take the chance of not believing it," he said. "It doesn't make sense, but it could be real. Yeah, I'm going to act like I believe it."

"Thanks," she said. She asked the questions she would repeat over and over again in the coming days. "Why would anyone kill a coed? Especially a coed like this one? And why would they put her in my car? What does it mean about my corrupting young girls?"

Jake shook his head. "That part's so crazy I can't think about it. I'm afraid there's a bigger story here. I think once we get to unraveling it, we're going to be like a kitten with a ball of twine, always finding another loose end."

"Aren't you glad it's not your responsibility? You're the one who told me it's out of your jurisdiction now."

"Susan, if you're involved—and particularly if you're in danger—it's always my jurisdiction. And"—he leaned closer to her—"I'm in love with you, which means I want to get it over with quickly and get your car back to you and our lives back to normal."

Jake spent the night at her house, teasing her worries away with his magical hands, urging her to lose herself in lovemaking and forget about death. When at last she cried out in satisfaction, he covered her face with kisses and finally, still panting, asked, "Feel better?"

"Yeah," she admitted.

She didn't tell him the next morning that she was glad to have slept the night wrapped in his protective arms. Instead, grumbling when the alarm went off, she said, "If you'd gone home last night like you should have, we wouldn't be getting up at the crack of dawn."

Undaunted, he leaned over her, kissed her nose, and said, "Be grateful, or I'll attack you again." They made love quickly, fiercely, and found themselves fighting over the shower at six-thirty in the morning.

"I'll have to drop you at school and go home for clean clothes," Jake said, standing before her with a towel wrapped around his middle and water glistening on the curly hair on his chest.

"Good. I can stand to be there early and collect my thoughts." She was blow-drying her hair, impatient with the time it took.

"We've got to figure out a car for you."

"Ummm," she agreed. "You can't spend the night all the time."

He snapped his fingers as though to say, "Damn," and turned to find his clothes. Then, more seriously, he said, "I don't want you here alone."

Susan shuddered. She'd almost been able to forget that someone was apparently stalking her and held a big-time grudge.

In the end, she went home with Jake and borrowed his moped, one of the larger Honda models—an Aero, he'd told her in superior tones. He'd ridden it in high school and kept it in his garage ever since, taking it out often enough to keep it in running condition. He said he was sentimentally attached to it and couldn't bear to sell it. Susan never told him that mopeds had seen their day and no one would buy it now.

"I'm not sure you're safe on this," he protested.

"Jake Phillips, I can ride this thing as well as you can!"

"That's not what I meant," he said. "It makes you a sitting target."

She felt a sudden surge of bravado. "I can't stop living my life because some nutcase puts a body in my car and writes me a scary note." *But it's a temptation to hide in my house and never come out.*

Jake shook his head. "I guess you can't, but you can be careful. Besides, how do you think it will look for Assistant Professor Hogan to arrive on campus on a moped?"

"It suits my style." She kissed him lightly and roared off, books packed in a side compartment, huge sunglasses protecting her eyes, and her short hair flying in all directions.

Jake shook his head as he watched.

Susan was watchful on the fifteen-minute ride between Jake's house and the campus. What was it self-protection classes taught? Always be aware of your surroundings? She was—and particularly of cars around her. But nothing alarmed her, and she reached her office with a feeling of relief.

Susan was called to the English office before she even got her first cup of coffee from the lounge. Mildred called to say, "Dr. Scott wants to see you in his office right now."

Susan knew John Worthington Scott, as he signed his name, when he was just another faculty member, teaching mostly sophomore world lit classes because there wasn't that much interest in Renaissance literature. No wonder both he and his pal Ernie Westin resented her. Ernie's love was Greek literature, and his classes often didn't make their enrollment quota. There was even less interest in Greek literature than Renaissance. Yet students flocked to Susan's American lit and women's lit classes.

She entered the chair's office. Like most offices in the older Baker Hall, it was small. Unlike most faculty offices, it was not filled with bookshelves so jammed in that books were piled every which way and papers were stacked high on the desk and even the floor. In John Scott's office, everything was neat, every book aligned.

"Ah, Dr. Hogan," Dr. Scott said, staring at his hands and not looking at her. "I heard about the, ah, unfortunate incident last night. How did you get to school this morning?" Dr. Scott sat behind the protection of his desk, drumming his fingers on the large blotter that covered the center part of his desk's immaculately clean surface. Two even stacks of books, an old-fashioned penholder, and a telephone were aligned on the desk. Susan wondered if he ever did any work. No pictures revealed that he had a family, but she knew he had a wife and two daughters.

"I rode Jake Phillips' moped," Susan answered without hesitation. "You probably know that I don't have my car." Ernie Westin told him, she thought. It was just the kind of news Ernie couldn't wait to share, because it would ingratiate him with Scott while running her further down.

"Yes, yes. Unfortunate." Scott stared off into space. "We need to talk about that, Dr. Hogan. But first let me say I hope you will find more suitable means of transportation."

Someone's threatening me and the police think I'm a murderer, but you're worried about appearances! She spoke more calmly than she had thought she could. "I can't afford to rent a car, sir, and there's no telling how long my car will be impounded. And then it has to be repaired." She paused a moment and then said, "Dr. Frank in psychology drives a battered old Jeep. I can't see that a moped is any worse."

He acted as though he hadn't heard her. "We must talk," he said again.

"About what, sir?" Susan thought it was probably a good thing she'd worn rayon pants and her good loafers today instead of her usual jeans and running shoes.

"The unfortunate matter of your car . . . and that coed. It, ah, reflects poorly on your record." He seemed to like the word "unfortunate" this morning.

Susan fought an urge to leap to her feet and scream at him that she'd had enough trouble in the last twenty-four hours without his adding to it and she knew he'd love to find a reason to fire her, but he wasn't going to do it in this mess. Forcing herself to speak slowly, she said, "Are you referring to the tenure review, Dr. Scott?"

"Ah, well . . . yes." His eyes were fixed slightly over her left shoulder as he deliberately avoided looking at her.

Here she was on solid ground. "Until it is proven—which it won't be—that I had anything to do with putting that un . . . uh, poor girl's body in the trunk of my car, I am an innocent victim. If you try to use that against me, Dr. Scott, I'll make a large and legal fuss that will make you wish for early retirement." Okay, she'd lost her cool at the end of it, but her point was well taken. She almost grinned when she realized that she'd started to use the word "unfortunate" herself, in reference to Missy Jackson, as though she were mimicking Dr. Scott.

"We just want to see this matter cleared up as quickly and quietly as possible," Scott said nervously.

"Nobody wants that more than I do. The death of any young girl is a great tragedy, especially one of such promise and especially in these circumstances." Susan felt like she was lecturing, but she plowed on. "It has nothing to do with my tenure review or with me." Remembering the note on the rock thrown through Jake's windshield, Susan fervently hoped that the last statement was true.

"We'll see," he said, rising and turning his back to her as he looked out the window. "I don't believe in coincidences. There must be a reason that body was in your car."

Ernie gave him that idea, too, Susan thought. He's really out to get me, so he can get tenure without any complication. Maybe he's out to get me out of just plain meanness. Nothing like academic competition. Ernie the worm!

Susan knew dismissal when it hit her over the head. She left his office without another word.

Chapter Three

Susan promised Jake she wouldn't be on campus alone after dark, so she dutifully headed for the library about four o'clock. But she found some new research on Zane Grey and stayed longer than she intended. It was dusk when she walked into the parking lot and then remembered that the moped was in her faculty parking spot behind Baker Hall. Darn, a long walk! And she was tired and wanted a glass of wine. She wondered if Jake was looking for her. If so, he'd be mad—again! Trying to keep Jake Phillips happy was on her mind almost as much as solving Missy Jackson's murder. In fact, she was surprised she'd put both things out of her mind so thoroughly in the library.

She cut through the library parking lot, headed toward the faculty lot, her thoughts on Jake. But when she heard a car gun its motor behind her, she froze for just an instant and then turned to look. She couldn't tell what make or model the car was, except that it was small and dark and it could go like hell when gunned. And it was headed straight toward her.

With a yelp and a loud curse, Susan made a sideways leap between parked cars and landed in a heap. Her purse and book bag scattered behind her. She felt the car go by her and heard its engine next to her ear. Then it roared out of the parking lot, lights off. She lay perfectly still for a moment, afraid to move because the car might come back—and because she wasn't sure she hadn't broken every bone in her body. Then slowly, carefully, she began to move, feeling her arms and legs, trying to see how badly she was hurt. She was mostly okay. Her rayon pants were torn on the left side where she landed, and she thought she could feel a large scrape under the torn pant leg. Her silk blouse was torn on the left sleeve, and her arm stung. Her left shoulder hurt like hell, and her hands were scraped and raw. Even the left side of her face hurt, and she wondered if she'd sprout a good-sized bruise there. But she could stand and, after a few tentative steps, she found she could walk.

She gathered up her purse and books and fished for the cell phone. Then she called campus police.

"Security," a bored voice said. It was Melba, the night dispatcher.

"This is Susan Hogan," she said, trying hard to keep her voice calm and low yet recognizing that it skittered into the high tones of anxiety. "Someone just tried to run over me in the library parking lot."

The voice became amazingly alert. "Are you hurt, Dr. Hogan?"

"No, I think I'm all right. Just bruised."

"I'll call Mr. Phillips right away."

Why didn't I call him myself? Now he'll be mad about that too. He would have come and gotten me, and I could have just gone on home. But, she realized, then she'd have no documentation of the attack.

"You stay right there," Melba said. "Well, maybe you should go back inside the library."

Susan hated the thought of climbing those stairs and sitting in the library foyer in her torn and dirty clothes. "I'm all right here," she said. "The car's gone. I'll tell you what. I'll sit in that patio, by the fountain."

"Okay," Melba said, with some doubt in her voice.

Susan gathered her purse and her books and walked the half-block to the patio. A through street had been dead-ended, the area paved with old bricks, and wooden benches scattered around. Trees arched overhead, and the soft sound of the fountain was comforting. Susan didn't even notice the traffic on Main, not yards from where she sat in her own private sanctuary.

Pleasant as her surroundings were, her thoughts were far from serene. *Somebody tried to kill me!* That thought kept singing over and over in her mind. It made no sense. It was bad enough that someone had dumped a body in her car, but she'd been willing to believe that was coincidence. Now, it didn't seem so. The two incidents were clearly connected. Was some student so angry at her that harassment was going way too far? Surely no one was

that pissed off over an F. She remembered the boy who had pla-
giarized in his essay about Hawthorne. But surely he had no
relation to Missy Jackson, and the threat on her life must be connected to the murder.

"Susan!" Jake's voice interrupted her thoughts, and she was
almost grateful until she saw the look on his face. "I thought you
promised not to be on campus alone after dark!" It was, by then,
as dark as the evening was going to get.

She was too angry and too scared to apologize. Instead, her
voice flared indignantly, "I lost track of time in the library. And it
wasn't really dark when I left, just sort of . . . well, the end of
dusk."

Jake threw her a withering glance. "Then you saw the car
that tried to run you down."

Just then a campus patrol car pulled up, with Spencer Grady,
the night patrolman, at the wheel. He started toward them, saw
the exchange going on, and kept his distance. "You need me,
chief?" he asked from several yards away.

"Yeah, I need you to file a report," Jake barked. "Susan will
give you the details."

Susan repeated her story for both of them, identifying the car
as small and dark but, no, she didn't know the make, and, no,
she couldn't identify the driver, hadn't even seen him clearly,
wasn't positive it was a male. She was too busy throwing herself
out of the path of the car.

"Got enough?" Jake asked Grady. "I want to get her home
and see how badly she's really hurt."

Even Susan blushed at that, and she wasn't unaware of the
grin on Grady's face as he stood behind Jake. Clearly, Jake intended to take off her torn clothes to examine the damage to her
person.

"I think this is okay, sir. Want me to report it to the city?"

Jake, usually easygoing and affable, regarded Grady as
though he were an idiot. "Of course," he said. "Susan, get in my
truck."

"The moped . . . " she said, "it's in my parking spot."

"And it'll stay there until tomorrow," he said. "You need
help?"

She gritted her teeth. She could feel her muscles tightening and knew soreness would be hers in the morning, but she wasn't about to tell Jake Phillips. "No."

He followed her as she made her way slowly to the car. *I should help her,* he thought, *but she's so damn stubborn.*

They drove to her house in silence. Susan, staring out the window, was thinking over and over, *Someone really tried to kill me.* Once again Jake made Susan stay in the truck while he checked the house, then motioned for her to come in. When she was settled on the sofa, he brought her a glass of wine and said, "Take off your clothes."

"You've asked that in nicer tones," she said, trying for lightness.

"I'm not going to seduce you. I want to see how badly you're hurt. You didn't break anything or you'd know it, but some of the scrapes may be pretty deep."

Susan stood up and shed a now-ruined silk blouse and an equally destroyed pair of rayon pants. "Might as well throw these right in the trash," she said. "What a day to decide not to wear jeans for once."

"Let me look first," he said.

Susan wanted to yell that it was her body and she wanted to look first, but she stood while he placed gentle fingers on her face, her arm, and her side and stared long at her leg, where the skin appeared to be scraped away in patches. "You'll heal," he finally said, "but we've got to clean all those places."

He went to his truck for a first-aid kit. Then he sat Susan on a bar stool and with incredible gentleness sponged away bits of dirt, dried blood, tiny bits of torn fabric. "This'll sting," he warned as he put antiseptic on the worst scrapes.

"Sting is an understatement," she said through gritted teeth.

"Go ahead and yell. Probably do you good."

"Neighbors might think you were attacking me and rush to my rescue," she replied.

Jake left her alone long enough to go buy salmon filets and salad makings. He grilled the salmon with soy sauce, tossed the salad with olive oil and balsamic vinegar, and threw in some blue cheese. They ate at the table on the deck without talking, still wrapped in their own thoughts. Susan was in bed and asleep by nine-thirty.

When she woke in the morning, Jake was sound asleep on the couch, still wearing his clothes from the day before. "Morning," he muttered. "How are you?"

"Stiff as an old lady," she said. "I don't have a muscle that doesn't hurt. A shower will help." She looked at him a minute. "You could have slept in the bed," she said.

"Didn't want to disturb you. You needed the sleep." He looked up at her, standing over him, and commented, "We should have put ice on your face right away. You've got a beaut of a bruise."

"Thanks."

He drove her to class and then went home to change. "Jordan will want to talk to you," he warned as she pulled herself gingerly out of the truck.

"Well," she said tartly, "he can just come to me this time."

"I don't think Scott would like that," he said with a grin. "Maybe he'll settle for a phone call."

"I doubt that," she muttered. "Wait a minute." She walked around the truck to the driver's side, leaned in the open window, and kissed Jake Phillips on the mouth, hard. "Thank you," she said.

Jake grinned. "Anytime."

* * *

Susan dropped her books in her office and went straight to the English department lounge for coffee. The lounge was strangely empty for that hour of the morning. None of her colleagues lingered over the day's newspaper, and even Ernie Westin wasn't there to carry on about tenure. Someone she didn't know—a graduate student?—peered across the room at her over the top of a newspaper and quickly lowered his eyes when he saw her glance his way.

Susan poured her coffee, left a quarter in the money jar, and took the coffee back upstairs to her office. Two minutes later, Ellen Peck appeared, carrying the morning's city newspaper.

She took one look at Susan and said, "You look like hell!"

"Thanks. Someone tried to run me down in the library parking lot last night. I jumped into the paving."

"Ouch," Ellen said. "You okay?"

"Physically. I'm just sore and stiff. But, Ellen, I'm mad as hell at being accused of murder, and I'm scared."

"What's Jake say?"

"We didn't really talk about it. He just keeps saying I have to be careful. I imagine that detective will have more to say."

"You see yesterday's paper?" Ellen seated herself in the student chair opposite Susan's desk. She was thirty-five and looked fifteen, with shoulder-length blonde hair, bright blue eyes, and an easy smile. Today she wore a print wraparound skirt and a matching T-shirt, neither of which did much to distinguish her from the coed population. Sometimes Ellen made Susan think of Shelley before . . . but then she batted that thought away. She had to put Shelley in the past and concentrate on Missy and the present.

Susan shook her head. "I've been avoiding the newspaper."

"You better read this," Ellen said, handing her the *Oak Grove News.*

"COED'S BODY FOUND IN ENGLISH PROF'S CAR," the headline blared. Beneath it was a large picture of Missy Jackson and an article whose text wrapped around a smaller picture of Susan herself. "I think they used my passport photo," she moaned.

But she wasn't really looking at her own photo. She studied Missy Jackson's photo, which was in color, albeit slightly out of register. Missy's blonde hair showed fine red and blue lines at the edge, and her eyes had a blurry quality that made them all the more poignant. Susan studied the face, trying to reconcile the fact that two days ago this girl had been alive, vibrant, a part of the campus, and now she lay in a funeral home somewhere in town.

Missy Jackson had wide blue eyes, a smile which showed teeth obviously carefully straightened by orthodontic care. She wore her hair shoulder length, a little longer toward the face and curling under ever so slightly—a fashionable cut for a girl from Uvalde, Texas, the city identified in the cutline under the picture as her hometown. For what must have been a yearbook picture, she appeared to be wearing a cheerleader's outfit.

"She looks like you," Susan said slowly, raising her eyes from the photo to look at Ellen.

"Thanks," Ellen said dryly.

"Well, I mean, your hair is the same and you look about the same age . . . "

"And she's dead," Ellen said flatly. "Read the article."

Susan read, her anxiety mounting with each line because the story echoed what she'd heard from Jordan and Scott: if the body was in her car, she must know something about the murder. Oh, it didn't come out and say that but it dwelt too little on Missy's background and too long on Susan's. "This is not Dr. Hogan's first brush with the law." Susan could feel her stomach knot as she read further: "In 1987, Dr. Hogan's college roommate was found dead in the apartment they shared. The death was later pronounced a suicide." *So much for putting Shelley in the past.*

She raised her eyes to Ellen. "Can they do that? Can they say that about Shelley? Who would have told them?"

"I'm guessing at who Shelley is . . . or was," Ellen said, "but whether they can or can't, they just have. It's a matter of public record. How they found out is another question, but law enforcement has an amazing network of databases. Wouldn't have been hard."

Why did I ever think Shelley wouldn't follow me everywhere? "Jordan must have found out about it. Damn!" Susan hurled the paper on the desk. "That was a long time ago, and I wasn't involved, though at first I was under suspicion. I . . . I thought I'd put it way behind me."

"You want to talk about it?" Ellen asked gently.

"No, not really. She took too much cocaine. That's all there was to it." She paused a moment. "Now I suppose that means I was a dopehead too."

"Not necessarily, but Scott will try to assume that," Ellen said, her voice soft. "I'm sorry, Susan."

Susan smiled ruefully at her. "Thanks. So am I. Wonder what Jake will think if he reads this?"

"That you haven't been honest with him," Ellen supplied helpfully.

"Great," Susan said. "He's not alone. That police officer, Jordan, and Scott both think I'm not being honest about this coed's body in my car. Why would I be dishonest? What do I have to hide?" She shifted her attention back to the newspaper. "A dead roommate, apparently. Jordan will be calling about it."

The story also said that the police had interviewed her at length about Missy Jackson's death and announced that she was not at this point a suspect.

"At this point!" she exploded. "That's what they say about everyone they're sure is guilty as sin! Ellen, I . . . do I need a lawyer?"

Ellen shook her head. "I don't think so. That might make you look really nervous. But ask Jake what he thinks."

Susan found it hard, to say the least, to concentrate on preparing for her classes that day. She went to lunch at the faculty center, an add-on to the old liberal arts building. The room was cheerful enough with windows on two sides and tables for four or eight. Since it was in Baker Hall, the science and math people didn't use it much, probably eating at the fast-food joints on Main. But the liberal arts people tended to sit by departments at the larger tables. Susan went through the buffet line and then noticed several of her colleagues at one of the large table, so she joined them. One by one they melted away as she settled herself, some with a nod in her direction and "Got to go" and others without a word. Faculty from other departments stared openly. Depressed by the lack of support from her colleagues, she was about to take her lunch back to her office when Ellen appeared.

"Sit right there," she ordered.

"Can't. I feel like an exhibit at the zoo."

"If you leave, they'll talk about you."

"They'll do that anyway. Are you going to eat with me?"

"Sure." Ellen went to the buffet table and returned shortly with a plate piled high with salad makings.

Susan looked ruefully at her own plate of lasagna, which now tasted like sawdust. "I'm not hungry," she said, pushing the plate away.

Ellen calmly poured low-cal ranch dressing on her salad. "Susan, you've got to act normal or people will really think you know something you don't—or did something you didn't."

"If you'd written that sentence in a paper, I'd have given you an F," Susan said.

Ellen smiled. "That's more like it. Get your spirit back."

"How can I get my spirit back when someone's trying to kill me?"

Ellen shook her head, as though to make the very idea go away. "I can't believe anyone would try to kill you. Surely, they were just trying to scare you."

Susan thought that Ellen couldn't believe it because she didn't want to. Denial is always safer.

"Maybe you need to separate the murder from the fact that it was your car. We are all devastated about this girl's death, and rightly so. But her death is one thing, and the part about her being in your car is something else. An accident. Nothing to do with you."

"Then why did that car take out after me? Besides, you're the only one who thinks her being in my car has nothing to do with me," Susan said bitterly. "And," she went on, "I'm the only one who doesn't think Missy Jackson was the perfect coed. I think, thought last semester, that she couldn't decide if she wanted to be the perfect coed or a rebelling young feminist. And she didn't know any middle ground."

* * *

Lt. Jordan called in the early afternoon. "Ah, I understand you've had an accident."

Susan wanted to tell him to quit pussyfooting around and get to the point. "Right. I'm a little stiff and sore."

He did get right to the point. "I need to talk to you about that . . . and about your college roommate. But I don't want to ask you to come downtown, feeling as you do. Phillips suggested it might cause trouble if I came to your office. He suggested your home tonight at five-thirty."

Rage threatened to explode in Susan. How could Jake invite this man into her home? But instead of anger, she replied with a surprised, "He did?"

"Yes. Said he'd be there. I'll only come with your permission, but I thought you might think it the best alternative to coming downtown."

"I guess so," she said reluctantly. Probably it was the best plan. She'd be on home turf, and Jake would be with her. "Sure, that's fine. I'll see you there. Did he tell you where I live?"

"It's on file. 2115 Greenbriar Lane. Almost out in the country."

"Okay." Susan hung up and sat staring at the phone for a long time, as though it were an enemy. She felt like Big Brother was watching her. He even knew where she lived. Well, of course he did.

* * *

Susan rode the moped home—in spite of Jake's protests—and got there a little before five. Jake arrived just minutes later, with steaks for the grill, potatoes that he immediately put in to bake, and fresh green beans.

Susan greeted him with a demanding question. "Why hasn't there been anything in the paper about Eric Lindler?"

"The boyfriend? They interviewed him today, and they've checked his car. Jordan says they found no trace evidence at all. Clean as a whistle. It'll probably be in the paper tomorrow."

"What kind of a car?" she asked.

"Big old clunker of a '78 Ford."

"So it wasn't his car that tried to run me down?"

Jake shook his head. "No, but that doesn't rule out the possibility, however slim, that he was driving that car. But, Susan, if Missy Jackson was the perfect coed, so is this kid. He's studying to be a minister, for Pete's sake, and his grades are excellent. He belongs to Brothers in Christ and a bunch of other church-related things, doesn't seem to have a life apart from religion . . . and Missy."

Jake was cleaning green beans when Dirk Jordan arrived, a sight that made Jordan break into an unexpected grin.

"He likes to cook," Susan said defensively.

"And she's no good at it," Jake added cheerfully. "Want a drink?"

Jordan declined because his was a business call. He asked the predictable questions about Susan's near-encounter with a car the night before, and she repeated what she had told Jake. Then she asked, "I hear it wasn't Eric's car. His is an old clunker."

"And clean of any evidence," Jordan said. "In your car, however, they found fibers, blood, and wood slivers. The blood belonged to the girl, the slivers probably came from the baseball bat that killed her, and the fibers . . . some from her clothing were in the front seat of your car."

"The front seat?" she echoed.

"Means she was in the front seat before she was in the trunk. We don't know if she was alive or dead at that point. She may have been moved from the place she was killed."

Susan thought she might never drive the damn car again because she'd always see Missy Jackson sitting next to her. "Moved in my car? Impossible! It was in the parking lot all day, and I had the keys with me."

"Did you actually see it?" Jordan asked. "Every second person knows how to wire a car, so where the keys were doesn't matter."

Susan looked at Jake and was grateful that he didn't chime in with a comment about her habit of not locking her car.

"What about Missy's roommate? What kind of car does she drive?"

Jordan stood up and began to pace around the family room. "I couldn't find her today—not in her room, not in class. If she doesn't turn up tomorrow, I'll put out a missing persons bulletin."

Then he turned serious. "Dr. Hogan, you've got to tell me about this roommate of yours."

She saw Jake staring at her wordlessly.

"What about her? We roomed together for two years. We were . . . oh shit, soul mates sounds corny, but we really clicked. We liked the same things, dated the same kind of guys, had a real picnic all through that part of college." She hesitated. "Then she fell for a creep."

"A creep?" Jordan asked.

"Yeah. He did drugs, and he started Shelley on them, and I lost her. Lost her like we'd never been friends. I wasn't any Goody Two-Shoes, but I knew how wrong it was. Shelley'd just brush me off when I'd try to talk to her, and pretty soon we weren't talking at all. We just sort of lived in the same space without being together. And I hated it, I really hated it. She was one of the few people I'd loved in my life or who'd ever loved me, and I lost her.

"And then I came home one day, and there she was, curled up on the bathroom floor like a newborn baby. Clutching herself.

I never knew if she died in pain, but I hoped not. They . . . they wouldn't talk to me about it."

"There was an investigation, and you were questioned?" Jordan asked. It wasn't a question on his part, and Susan knew he already knew all about it . . . except her version.

"Yeah. I had to go to police headquarters and testify, and they grilled me about having given her the cocaine. I told them to go after the creep, but they were convinced they could at least charge me with possession or whatever. Maybe it was just how my head was right then. Finally they said it was an OD, and I was supposed to just wipe it out of my life like it never happened."

"Was Missy Jackson doing drugs?"

Susan saw the connection he was making, and she flared in anger. "I have no idea! If she was, I had nothing to do with it. I didn't do drugs back then, and I don't have anything to do with them now."

"Most people . . . ," Jordan began tentatively, then seemed to gain speed, "go through life without ever being associated with a suspicious death. You now have been associated with two."

Susan reached her boiling point. "You want to add my mother, who committed suicide when I was four?" she roared.

Jake came and took her in his arms. "Dirk," he said, "I think you've got all you're going to get here today. Would you just let yourself out the front door?"

Jordan left without another word, and Jake stood holding a trembling Susan for a long time. Susan never ate her steak that night. She threw down two fingers of bourbon, straight, and fell into bed.

Jake grilled himself a steak and enjoyed a good, if lonely, meal. Then he went in, gently undressed Susan, and finally crawled into bed next to her.

Susan woke in the middle of the night, Jake's arms protectively around her. "Jake?"

When he didn't respond, she yelled, "Jake!"

"What is it?" He came sleepily to consciousness. "You hear something?"

"Who reported Missy Jackson missing to your office?" Susan demanded.

"What? You woke me up to ask that?"

"It's important," she insisted. "The roommate wouldn't talk about it, wouldn't call the girl's parents. So it wasn't Brandy Perkins. Who was it?"

He shook his head. "I haven't any idea. I'll check the log in the morning. Can we go back to sleep now?"

She was wide awake, and she knew she couldn't go back to sleep. When Jake turned his back to her, she reached over him and began slowly to stroke him, starting at his chest and working her way down. Finally, he turned toward her. "Damn! Will you never let a man sleep?"

Afterward, they both slept soundly.

Chapter Four

Missy Jackson's parents came to the campus early in the morning for the memorial service to be held later in the day.

Jake met with them before he took them downtown to talk with Dirk Jordan. "I . . . I hope you know how truly upset we all are here at the university," he said as he ushered them into his office.

Mrs. Jackson's face was tear-stained, her eyes red and puffy. Her husband was sullen, angry, and bewildered.

"If she had died in an automobile accident," Mrs. Jackson sobbed, "we could accept it as God's will. But this . . . " According to Jake's later description, she was maybe forty-five, with once-pretty blondness that had now faded into a sort of nondescript paleness and probably forty more pounds than she should have carried at her height of five-foot-six. Jake thought she must have looked like Missy when she was a bride.

"She was the perfect daughter," Mr. Jackson said angrily, his tone at variance with his words, "the light of our lives." He was tall and squarely built, with a belly that spoke of too much chicken-fried steak and, perhaps, too much beer. His hands were roughened by work—he owned and operated a gas station and mechanic shop in Uvalde. "We never put no pressure on her, but she did everything just right." He looked directly at Jake, challenge in his eyes. "Why would anybody kill our little girl?"

Jake wanted to squirm and forced himself to sit straight and still. "It was probably a random thing, Mr. Jackson. I can't believe that anyone deliberately targeted your daughter"—it seemed too personal to call her Missy at that point—"for murder. She may simply have been in the wrong place at the wrong time." He paused, feeling the need to say something more, something to comfort them. Speaking slowly, he said, "I'm sure she was the perfect daughter. She was an outstanding student here and very much admired by other students and the faculty. You should be very proud in the midst of your grief."

"God wouldn't have taken Missy that way, just because she was in the wrong place at the wrong time," Mrs. Jackson said, totally ignoring Jake's words of comfort. "This was part of the devil's plan . . . and somebody is responsible."

Jake, at a loss for a reply to that kind of thinking, sat in silence.

"You find out who it is," Mrs. Jackson said, her voice rising in near-hysteria. "Beginning with that teacher whose car she was in. She must know! She tried to corrupt Missy with her feminist thinking."

Now Jake was appalled. He could see that neither reason nor sympathy were going to help with Mrs. Jackson. And her words made him think of the note thrown through his Jeep window, the note that said Susan had to stop corrupting young women. Surely the Jacksons had nothing to do with that. The puzzle of it all made his head ache.

Mr. Jackson reached over and patted his wife's hand softly. "Now, Mother . . . "

"Don't ever call me that again," she said fiercely. "I'm not a mother any longer."

Jake decided it was time to take them to see Jordan. The police detective later reported to Jake that he'd gotten much the same response and no helpful information.

"We don't find out who killed that girl soon, there may be a lynch mob from Uvalde after your lady friend," he told Jake.

* * *

At the memorial service, Susan, Jake, and Ellen sat near the back—Susan wanted to be able to view the participants and, besides, they were late arriving. The Jacksons sat in the front pew. Mrs. Jackson wore a black crepe dress and a small black hat with a veil that covered her face—obviously new purchases for the occasion. Her husband kept his head bowed while the minister commended unto God the unblemished soul of this their child, Melissa Ann Jackson. Next to them sat a young man Susan presumed was Eric Lindler. From where Susan sat he appeared to be good-looking but with nothing to mark him from dozens of other handsome, brown-haired, brown-eyed young men on the campus. He kept his head down, apparently staring at his shoes, except that every once in a while he raised his eyes and looked at Mrs. Jackson. He didn't seem to have the support of either his own family or friends.

Susan suddenly noticed that Brandy Perkins sat on the other side of Mr. Jackson. *So she's reappeared. I bet Dirk Jordan is relieved, but I wonder where she was.*

The campus chapel was filled to overflowing. Tearful young girls clutched Kleenexes that they frequently had to use to blot their eyes, and young men in dark blue suits sat looking stoic. The faculty had almost all appeared, as though on command, even John Scott and Ernie Westin, who sat together. The president of the university spoke a few words about "this tragedy that has befallen all of us." Craig Bishop, the university minister, conducted the service. The campus choir sang "Amazing Grace" and "How Great Thou Art." Craig Bishop spoke in generalities about the comfort of God's love in times of trial and grief, and Brandy Perkins gave a moving if tearful tribute to the girl who was, she said, "the best friend I'll ever have in my life." Susan had the feeling Brandy had not quite finished her prepared remarks when tears forced her off the stage. She too wore black, but hers was a miniskirt, tight at the hips and cut off well above the knees. Susan couldn't see her feet but she bet she wore those big, clunky shoes that were so fashionable and looked so awful with tiny dresses.

Afterward, students and faculty milled around outside the chapel. The mourners obviously couldn't go back to the family's home to gather, talk, and eat, as they would if they were in Uvalde, and no reception had been planned on campus. Nobody knew quite what to do. To walk away seemed callous; to stay, uncomfortable.

Craig Bishop stood by the Jacksons, his hand resting lightly on Mrs. Jackson's shoulder. Both parents seemed indecisive, confused, and Craig Bishop was apparently little help to them. Brandy Perkins and Eric Lindler, both of whom might have been expected to stay by their friend's parents, had vanished.

Susan, on impulse, decided she must speak to the Jacksons. She moved quickly, just dodging the restraining arm Jake put out when he realized her intention. She also moved too quickly to hear his groan. Susan had no idea she was about to do the very last thing she should have done, either for the Jacksons or for herself.

"Mrs. Jackson? I'm Susan Hogan. I'm so terribly upset about what happened to your daughter, and I just want you to know that I'll do everything I can to find out who did this awful thing."

Mrs. Jackson drew herself out of the foggy, uncertain state which enveloped her. "You're the one whose car she was in!" she said in an accusatory tone.

"Yes, ma'am," Susan muttered, "I'm afraid it was mine." She was just beginning to understand that she'd made a mistake, a huge mistake. Grief was unpredictable, and her credibility was not at all helped by her shiner or the bruises visible on her arm.

"Then you know who killed my baby!" The woman's voice rose until, to Susan, it screamed out to the crowd.

Susan reached a tentative, placating hand toward the other woman. "No, ma'am, I have no idea."

"But it was your car! You've got to know!" Neither her husband's rough pull on her arm nor Craig Bishop's quiet "there, there," had any effect on the distraught woman. By now, bystanders who had begun to wander away had turned to stare.

"I'm sorry," Susan said, "I don't. But I will. I promise you, Mrs. Jackson, I will find out what happened to your daughter, who did this awful thing."

Even as she spoke, Susan felt Jake pulling her backward, so that her last words were spoken from too great a distance to be heard unless she shouted. Jake turned her around and without a word marched her away, but Susan took one quick look over her shoulder: Missy Jackson's mother had collapsed into the arms of her husband and was sobbing uncontrollably, while Craig Bishop stood by uncomfortably, literally wringing his hands.

"I'm walking you back to your office," Jake said firmly, his hand on her shoulder guiding her.

She stopped in protect. "You don't have to. I know I did the wrong thing again, and I won't go anywhere near the Jacksons."

"Hey," he said, "you had good intentions." This time he gave her shoulders an affectionate squeeze.

"But you would have stopped me."

"Yeah, I would have."

"I wish you had," she said fervently.

"Well, that's not why I'm walking you back. I haven't had time to tell you, but I checked into who reported the girl missing. It was a man who refused to leave his name."

"A man?" Susan voice rose in curiosity.

"Well, maybe a boy . . . the operator who took the call said he sounded young."

"What else did she say?"

"He didn't sound upset. He was sort of matter-of-fact about it. Sort of 'just the facts, ma'am.'"

"Do you have a recording of it?"

"Susan, we're not the FBI. No, we don't record calls." He was wishing she'd get off her detective kick and leave these things to him.

"Damn," she said. "You could use voice prints to match it."

"Susan, forget it! You're not the detective. I am!"

Susan's next class was a disaster. It was a two-hour graduate seminar in which one student was supposed to lead a discussion of *The Great Gatsby*, but this day it degenerated into an awkward silence, with students casting sidelong glances at the instructor.

"Have you read the book?" she finally demanded.

Eight heads bobbed up and down. Yes, they had read the assignment.

"Then why aren't you talking to Elizabeth when she asks you questions?"

"Because," one bold soul ventured, "we're distracted by what's happened. By the fact that the girl's body was in your car and someone tried to run you down last night."

Susan resisted the urge to ask how he knew about last night. The story of Missy Jackson's body was in the city and campus newspapers and all over town, but last night . . .

Instead, she snapped, "I'm distracted too. Class dismissed. By a week from today, I want from each of you a twenty-page paper on the importance of this particular novel in the Fitzgerald canon."

There was a universal groan, followed by the shuffling of chairs and sound of books being gathered. Alone in the seminar room, Susan put her head in her hands and willed herself not to weep. She couldn't believe she had taken her anger out on graduate students. And now she'd have to read those damn papers. *Wait until Scott hears she'd lost her cool in a seminar!*

Susan went by her office, gathered up papers for some studying that night, and roared off campus on the moped. Jake had offered to drive it, but she insisted, and now she felt her energy returning as she balanced the small machine and guided it toward her country home.

She pulled up to the back of her driveway, unloaded books and papers from the side pockets, fished for her keys, and then headed for the sliding glass door. It never occurred to her to look down, and she nearly tripped on a shoebox in front of the door.

"What the . . . ?" She dumped her stuff on the deck table and reached for the box, all the time hearing Jake say, "Never open an unexpected package. Letter and package bombs have turned up in stranger places than Oak Grove."

Surely not, she thought. *Maybe Aunt Jenny has sent me something.* It didn't occur to her that if the package had come from Aunt Jenny, there'd have been a postmark and a label. She tore off the lid, looked inside, and screamed. Hands to her face, she kept screaming . . . and staring inside the box. A kitten lay in a bed of white satin. It was gray, fluffy, small, and very dead. A note lay next to the pitiful creature.

Gingerly, she picked up the note and started to unfold it. Then she remembered how careful Jordan had been with that note on the rock that went through Jake's windshield. Almost too rattled to think, she unlocked her door, crossed the kitchen to prowl under the sink for rubber gloves, and went back to the note. It held the same message as the last one: "Die, Susan Hogan, before you ruin any more lives."

"Susan, are you all right?" It was Mrs. Whitley, the elderly widow who lived next door to her and whose usual reaction to Susan's shenanigans was to shake her head and make a noise that sounded like "Tsk, tsk, tsk." Next door, where she lived, wasn't really that close, but Mrs. Whitley made it seem like the distance between their houses was feet, not yards.

Susan drew herself together. "I'm fine, thanks, Mrs. Whitley. It was a snake . . . a plain old garden snake, but it scared me for a minute."

Mrs. Whitley chuckled. "Many times I've been scared by those critters. Well, I'm glad you're all right." She turned back down the driveway, and Susan called after her, "Thanks for checking."

It was comforting to know that Mrs. Whitley was aware of what went on at her house. But Susan realized she was probably also aware of the nights that Jake didn't go home till morning.

Susan used her foot to shove the box away from the door and with a gloved hand she put the lid back on it. Then she went inside and poured herself a finger of bourbon. *Jake's going to start wondering why his bourbon disappears so fast,* she thought wryly. Then she realized that her books and papers were still outside, and to get them, she'd have to walk by that damn box again. She took another sip of bourbon, strode deliberately out the door, eyes avoiding the box, retrieved her belongings, and retreated inside. Then she sat on the couch and had a good cry.

* * *

Susan waited in the growing dusk for Jake, who was later than usual. Any other night, she would have been hungry and hoping he'd bring takeout something, anything. Tonight, she had no appetite. The ringing of the phone startled her, and she almost didn't answer. But then she picked it up and uttered a curt, "Susan Hogan."

"Susan? It's Aunt Jenny. How are you, dear? You don't sound well at all." She listened to reassurances that Susan was fine and busy and then said, "I'm coming to see you. You need me right now."

Jenny Hogan was Susan's seventy-something-year-old aunt. Susan would have told anyone—including Aunt Jenny—that her aunt was the person she most loved in the world. Susan's parents had divorced when she was three, and then her mother, frightened by the responsibility of a child and the prospect of being alone, took a successful dose of sleeping pills. Susan's father, on hearing the news, had thrown Susan's clothes in a suitcase, grabbed her and the suitcase, and taken the whole kit and caboodle to his sister Jenny, the maiden schoolteacher who lived in Wichita Falls. Thereafter, he appeared at Christmas with toy trains that bored Susan and on her birthday with gifts equally inappropriate. Ten years later, he died himself, worn out by drink and gambling and—Aunt Jenny never said the word, but Susan knew—womanizing.

Aunt Jenny, fluttery, distracted, loving beyond measure, had been Susan's world.

"Aunt Jenny, I'd love to see you. But there's a lot going on right now. Maybe Christmas?"

"No, Susan, I read the newspaper, and I know you're as good as accused of murder. I need to be there with you. And, besides, I haven't met this man—what's his name? Jake?"

Susan was at a loss. "Uh, yeah, Jake. But Aunt Jenny I really can't be a good hostess right now."

"Yes, yes, dear, I understand, and I won't be any trouble. I'll be there in time to cook Sunday supper for you."

"What time is your plane? Jake and I will come get you."

"Plane? Oh, no, I'll drive. Far too much trouble to get to the airport, go through all that check-in security. I can be there faster if I drive. Yes, dear, I know how to find Oak Grove. Just go to Fort Worth and turn southwest—what's the road again? I bet I can even find your house. Susan, stop worrying so much about things. That's why I have to be there to help you."

"Aunt Jenny, I love you. But it worries me to have you drive all this way. I'll be all right. Really. Jake will see to it." Well, she hoped he would.

"Yes, Susan dear, I love you too. I'll see you Sunday. And I can't wait to meet Jake. Buy the makings for chicken and dumplings."

Susan hung up the phone and held her head in her hands. She loved Aunt Jenny more than she could ever say, but she didn't need her underfoot right now. And here it was Thursday already, and she'd have to have her house sparkling by Sunday. Wearily, she called Jake.

"I need you," she said without saying hello or asking where he was and why he hadn't started cooking her dinner.

He was still at the office. "Susan? Is this an invitation? I didn't think we parted on the best of terms at the memorial service." He was laughing at her.

If only you knew, she thought. "Yeah," she said, keeping her voice light, "it's an invitation for Sunday night supper. My Aunt

Jenny says she'll be here in time to cook."

"Aunt Jenny! I've been wondering when I'd be invited to meet her."

"Jake, what am I going to do with a seventy-plus dither-head sharing my house with me?"

"I guess," he said, "you're going to learn a lesson in patience. And the two of us are going to learn a lesson in stolen moments of passion—you won't let me spend the night, will you?"

"Aunt Jenny would be horrified."

He sighed. "I was afraid of that. How long's she staying?"

"She didn't say. She knows all about Missy Jackson being found in my car, and she's worried about me." As she talked, Susan paced as far as the long phone cord would let her, traveling toward the kitchen bar and back again as many as ten times.

"Well, let me go with you to meet her plane."

"She's driving," Susan said flatly.

He was amazed and indignant. "From what you've told me, she's too old to drive here from Wichita Falls. Susan, how could you let her do that?"

"Wait till you meet Aunt Jenny, and then you'll wonder how I could have stopped her."

He chuckled. "I'll be glad to meet the person who can stymie you, Susan. Meantime, I do have a couple of things to report on the murder. Want to forgive and forget over dinner?"

"Yes." Her answer came so quickly that she heard Jake chuckle again, but she wanted him to come and comfort her and bury the poor kitten. "What time will you be here?"

"Not your place but mine," he said. "I've got beer and wine and hamburger meat, buns, tomatoes and onion, dill pickles—all the makings of your kind of meal."

Susan rarely went to Jake's house, and it was a source of argument between them. "It's not that I mind coming to your house," he'd told her once, "but I think we ought to share."

"In Scott's eyes, it's bad enough you spend the night at my house, but if I were to spend the night there . . . " She had thrown her hands up in the air.

"He probably wouldn't even know," Jake said, "as far away from campus as I am."

"Don't bet on it," she'd told him.

Tonight, she was about to say, "Jake, I need you here," when she realized that she wanted to be away from her own house for a while.

"I'll pick you up, so you don't have to go home late on the moped."

She drew her own personal line in the sand. "I'll ride the moped," she said with determination. Maybe, she thought, the ride will get rid of whatever I'm feeling. What? Stress? Tension? Fear? That was it—good old-fashioned scared-to-death. "I'll be there before dark, and I'll spend the night," she said.

"I'll be waiting with open arms." When he hung up, Jake shook his head in exasperation. Sometimes Susan was so hard to help that it frustrated him and made him wonder about their relationship. Where he came from a man protected a woman, and yet Susan seemed to reject protection—even when she needed it most.

* * *

Jake lived in the country, beyond where Susan lived. Outside, his was the perfunctory ranch-style house with red brick, evenly spaced windows, ordinary landscaping—lots of nandinas—and not much to distinguish it from most suburban houses except that it sat on its own two acres of land. But inside it was totally, well, Jake. For several years, Jake had been gradually fixing it up, beginning with a complete redo of the kitchen. He'd installed a gas cook top, a Jenn-Air indoor grill, a convection oven, a dishwasher, and garbage compactor—Susan laughed at the latter as absolutely useless. He'd used gray tiles on the counters, backsplash, and floor to complement the white walls. The appliances had brushed steel finishes. The result was a clean, streamlined look that spoke of serious dedication to cooking.

Following the standard plan for 1960s houses, his front door opened into a hall with a living room to the right and a dining room beyond that. Straight ahead lay the ubiquitous paneled family room, only Jake had painted the paneling a soft off-white that lightened the room. The bedroom wing was off the hall to the left, but to get to the kitchen you had to go through either the dining room or the family room. A bar-height counter connected family room and kitchen. The front bedroom served as a sort of television room, though Jake read more than he watched the tube, and the room's walls were lined with bookcases. Several shelves held popular paperbacks, everything from John Grisham and John LeCarré to Louis L'Amour. The middle bedroom was a guest room—maybe Aunt Jenny should stay there, Susan thought—and the larger back bedroom was Jake's, done in dark green with tan accents. Unlike the other bedrooms, it had its own master bath.

Susan left her house a little after six, after going around locking all the windows and turning on all the lights. She locked the door behind her and even went back once to try it. *I'm turning into a nervous Nellie,* she thought unhappily. *Once my house becomes a threat instead of a safe haven, I've had it.* And then it occurred to her that was exactly what this crazy person was trying to accomplish— make her afraid in the places where she felt most safe. Defiantly she strode across her deck, keeping her eyes averted from that damn shoebox. Gunning the moped into action, she whirled past Mrs. Whitley's house and saw that lady peeking out through discreetly parted curtains.

She headed south on Main, which soon turned into FM 1161, to where Jake lived. Always uneasy now, she looked in the rearview mirror and saw a small, dark car close on her tail. She sped up as much as she could, pushing the moped to forty, a speed that made her feel giddily dangerous. The dark car stayed close behind.

I wish I were smarter about cars. I have no idea if that's the car that tried to kill me before or not. They look the same, but . . . If the driver of that car wants to kill me, he's got a perfect shot on this empty country road. Her heart was pounding, and she had a hard time concentrating on keeping the speeding moped on course. Suddenly, the car behind her veered to the left, gunned its motor, and passed, quickly leaving her behind.

Damn my imagination, Susan said to herself. If I'd been thinking, I'd have known that even a sociopath wouldn't go to all the elaborate trouble of leaving a dead kitten at my door only to kill me within the hour.

Jake greeted her with open arms, as he'd promised. His words of welcome were less comforting. "You look like hell," he said. "What happened?"

She pulled herself from his arms, avoiding looking at him. "Nothing," she said. "It's just been a long day."

"The memorial service?" he asked.

Well, it wasn't a lie. It was just another instance where she wasn't telling the whole truth. "Yeah," she said. "That upset me."

His arms went around her again. "You meant well, Susan. I never doubted that. It's just . . . well, you hadn't met the parents, and I had. I should have warned you. Come on, I'll get you a glass of wine."

She didn't tell him she'd already had bourbon. That drink seemed long ago and far away, and he might have scolded her for riding the moped after she'd had a drink. By now, Susan had decided she wanted a comforting evening, not one spoiled by the news of the gift at her door.

He poured her a glass of Chardonnay and opened a Shiner Bock for himself. Watching him prepare their dinner, Susan realized he was as efficient in his own kitchen as he was in hers, chopping lettuce for the sandwiches, slicing tomatoes and onions into the thinnest of pieces.

Jake grilled on the Jenn-Air, preferring it, he said, to an outdoor grill. Susan sat at the kitchen table while he cooked the hamburgers, his medium well and hers rare.

"What's your news?" she asked.

"I got reports from Jordan today about his interviews with Missy Jackson's parents and with the boyfriend, Eric Lindler. Which do you want to hear first?"

"The boyfriend," Susan said unhesitatingly, her attention perking up quickly. *Even if he doesn't own a small, dark car, maybe something came out of that.*

"He's Mister Squeaky-Clean, like I told you before. Was in the library studying the night of the murder . . . "

"Who saw him?" Susan asked sharply.

Jake laughed. "What're you? The master detective? Jordan will check that out. But he says the boy is so obviously grieving and so obviously Mr. College America that he's not a suspect. He had no reason to kill her."

Susan stood up impatiently. "Great! The person closest to her is not a suspect, and yet I am, just because her body was found in my car! And because I didn't think she was perfect, like everyone else does!" She thought for a minute. "How do we know that she didn't break off the relationship, or that she wasn't two-timing him . . . or that something hadn't happened between them?" As an afterthought, she added, "I assume she wasn't pregnant."

Jake shook his head. "No, she wasn't. First thing I asked too. And we don't know for sure about what was between them, but we'll keep digging. Lindler showed Jordan the engagement ring he had planned to give her at homecoming."

"How touching," Susan said sarcastically. "It doesn't mean he didn't kill her."

He shrugged. "Makes it unlikely."

"Okay. What about the parents?" She was getting snappish, and she knew it. Maybe food would help. Meantime she poured another glass of wine for herself and saw Jake grin ever so slightly as he watched her out of the corner of his eye.

"Nothing much," he said, turning quickly back to the hamburgers. "She was a wonderful child, the daughter every parent should have, and so on, everything they said to me, except . . . "

"Except what?" Susan interrupted impatiently.

"They said she paid all her expenses—clothes, meals outside the dorm, that kind of stuff—from her work-study job."

"What kind of work-study job lets a kid earn that much?" Susan asked.

"She didn't have one," Jake said. "I checked."

Susan didn't say it aloud to Jake, who would have forbidden her, but she needed to talk to the Lindler boy.

She couldn't bring up the kitten now.

The hamburgers were delicious and the wine plentiful enough that Susan fell asleep as soon as she hit the bed.

"Great," Jake muttered, "I've wanted you to stay over here for a long time, and look what you do when it finally happens. You fall asleep!"

She woke around two, when the wine wore off, and reached for Jake, stroking his chest. He neither grumbled nor pushed her away, but he did ask, "Are you sure this isn't just a ploy to talk about some aspect of the murder that just occurred to you?"

"It might be," she said. "I . . . " Suddenly she sat straight up. "When I got home today, someone had left a dead kitten in a shoebox at my door."

"What?" Jake had been nibbling her ear and now came close to biting it off in his surprise. "Why didn't you tell me hours ago?"

She shrugged. "At first I couldn't wait to tell you, and then I just wanted to get away from it and forget it. But, Jake, I . . . I can't go back there and dispose of it."

He wrapped his arms around her. "I'll do that, Susan. But why, who? I don't understand it at all."

"There was a note—I wore rubber gloves when I looked at it and put it back in the box with the cat. It said pretty much what the other one did, only something about not ruining other lives."

He shook his head. "Rubber gloves just make it worse—you blur whatever prints are on there. They're not the same as evidence gloves. But never mind. It makes no sense, no sense at all. Somebody out there is warped. So warped that I'm scared for you. It's someone who wants you dead."

"Maybe," she said, "they just want me scared to death. I locked the house before I left." She was glad now she hadn't told him about the small, dark car that scared her on her ride out to his house. She had to be able to separate real threats from imaginary ones.

"Swell," he said. "You're not to be alone in that house again. I'm glad your aunt is coming."

"Some protection she'd be," Susan said. "Wait till you meet her."

"At least you won't be alone. And until then, I'm staying with you."

She shrugged, relieved but too proud to tell him. Instead, she leaned forward and kissed him. He lay down, pulling her next to him. "Sleep now, Susan, you're safe. I promise you that."

* * *

In the morning, they had to get up early so Susan could ride the moped home and change clothes.

"I'll have to follow you in the truck," Jake said. "You're not going in that house alone."

Morning always made her feel brave. "Nothing will happen," she said. "I'm going alone. You come along when you can and dispose of that box for me, okay?" It was what she had to do to keep from being a prisoner of fear.

"I can't dispose of it. I'll take it to Jordan."

She threw her hands up in the air. "Swell, he'll think I put it there myself."

"Susan, Susan, he's a law enforcement officer. Surely he'll see the pattern here, the danger."

"Don't count on it," she said bitterly.

"Wait till I take a quick shower, and I'll follow you home," he said.

Susan sneaked out while Jake was in the shower. To her surprise, she enjoyed the ride home. There was little traffic, nothing to scare her, and the breeze blew through her hair and made her thankful for the sunglasses she wore even though the sun was barely up.

At her house, nothing had changed. The box still sat pushed to one side, the door was still locked. Feeling almost normal, she took a shower, dressed, and roared off on the moped—a quiet roar.

Chapter Five

Friday morning, Susan dropped her books on her desk and headed not for the lounge but for the registrar's office in the administration building.

"Hi, Dr. Hogan!" The young black girl behind the counter greeted her enthusiastically, and Susan remembered that she'd been in her women's lit class last year—the same class Missy Jackson had been in. Jamie had been interested in Toni Morrison's work.

"Tina, how are you?"

"Doin' just fine, thank you. I'll graduate in June."

"June? A year ahead of time?" Susan was truly impressed, and Tina beamed with pride.

"Yes, ma'am. I went to summer school two summers."

"You should be proud," Susan said, reaching to touch the girl's arm. "Most kids take five years to get out of school, and you'll have done it in three."

"I am proud," Tina said, "and so's my family. What can I do for you this morning, Dr. Hogan?"

Susan slid a piece of paper toward the girl with the name "Eric Lindler" written on it. "Can you give me his schedule?"

Jamie lowered her eyes. "You know I can't do that. It's against the privacy laws. Dr. Hogan, I'd do anything I could for you, but I can't risk my job."

"No, no, Jamie. I wouldn't want you to do that. Sorry I asked." Susan had known it was against the law but hoped she'd run into some student who didn't know that. "I'll find him some other way," she said.

"He's Missy Jackson's boyfriend," Tina said. "You really think you should be talking to him?"

Startled, Susan said, "Why shouldn't I?"

The girl shrugged. "Police might not like it. I mean, it's none of my business, Dr. Hogan, but, aren't you more mixed up in this already than you should be?"

"Yeah, Jamie, I am," she said as she left the office.

She couldn't call Jake. He could probably find out the boy's schedule, but he would forbid her to talk to him. Besides, he was probably furious at her now for sneaking out of the house. Discouraged already at eight-thirty, Susan went back to her office.

Jake called almost the minute she got in the door. "That wasn't funny, Susan. Dammit, how can a person protect you when you're so goddamned stubborn?"

"I'm sorry," she said and really meant it. "But, Jake, I can't have a bodyguard every minute—even if he is the most handsome man in Oak Grove and the best lover and—"

"Cut it out, Susan. I'm serious."

"So am I. Jake, I watched to see that I wasn't followed"—she didn't say that she didn't know what she'd have done if someone followed her—"and I checked out the house carefully before I went in."

"I'm going to get you a gun," he said.

"I'm scared of guns."

"I don't care. You'll have to take a class and after that, you won't be scared."

"I don't have time to take a class," she protested.

"You'll make time," he said, his voice grim. "This morning I'll send someone over to take that cat to Jordan."

"It deserves to be buried, Jake, not thrown into a Dumpster. Jordan doesn't need the box and the cat—he just needs the note."

"He needs to see the whole thing. Then, by God, I'll bury it. But Susan, you try a man's patience."

"I'm sorry," she said again.

She longed for coffee but was reluctant to face the lounge. While she contemplated that dilemma, Ellen appeared at her door.

"You need coffee," she said, and there was no question in her voice. Ellen had apparently decided to go casual this day too, for she wore denim pants and a denim shirt, a concho belt looped below her waist—very southwestern looking. Her hair was in a ponytail—well, not in the teenage style but one of those that sat low at the neck.

"Yeah," Susan said, "I do."

"If I go get you some and bring it back here, will you listen to something weird that happened to me?"

"Sure." Susan's attention perked up a bit. Something weird happening to someone else would be a relief.

Ellen was back in minutes. "You could have gone yourself. Place is deserted. Ever since the, ah, the murder, no one seems to hang out at the department lounge."

"It's because they don't want to meet me," Susan said.

"Oh, go feel sorry for yourself, why don't you?"

It was enough to startle Susan. "Okay, what weird happened to you?"

"Well, yesterday, I just couldn't face the faculty center—okay, okay, I feel the same way you do, I just usually don't admit it. Anyway, I went to the cafeteria in the Union, got my salad, and decided to eat it right there. Found a table in the corner and thought it was great. I'd eat in peaceful solitude, even in the midst of all those noisy students."

"Sounds good," Susan said. "So what's weird?"

"Well, I'm sitting there, and this guy comes up and says, 'You really remind me of someone.' I wanted to say, 'Listen, sonny, that's the oldest line in the world and you're ten years too young.'"

"He couldn't tell that by looking at you," Susan said.

"Is that a slap because I dress like the kids?" Ellen was just the least bit indignant.

Susan laughed a little. "No, it's an honest compliment. Nobody will mistake me for twenty-one ever again."

"You laughed," Ellen whispered. "I'm glad I'm telling you this story." Then her voice grew stronger again. "Anyway, he sat down without so much as a 'May I?' or 'Do you mind?'"

"Did he have food?"

She shook her head. "No. It was like he was looking around the cafeteria, seeing who he could spot. But wait till you hear what he said."

Somewhere in the back of Susan's brain a warning bell was going off. "Okay, what did he say?" She leaned her elbows on the desk and, face propped in her hands, stared at Ellen.

"He said, 'Want to make some extra money after class? I'll give you my card.'"

"He offered you a job? Doing what?"

"We never got that far," Ellen admitted. "I was so astounded I just said, 'No, thanks.'" Ellen gestured as she spoke, her eyes sometimes growing wide with the puzzle of the story she was telling. "I told him, 'I'm a teacher,' and he bolted."

"You should have taken the card," Susan said.

Ellen nodded. "I suppose so, but I was so taken back . . . "

Susan felt herself falling into a detective mode. "What did he look like? Was he a, what do they call them? Not older, but non-traditional student?"

Ellen shook her head. "I don't know all ten-thousand students on this campus, but I swear I've never seen him before. He had red hair—that kind of real bright red that there's no suspicion it's anything but natural. And it, well, it held to his head in waves, like it had been marcelled."

"What the hell is marcelled?" Susan asked.

Ellen rolled her eyes. "You know, those waves they used to create with a special machine. My grandmother had her hair marcelled."

"Aunt Jenny just has hers permed," Susan said. "I can't imagine what you're talking about."

"You would if you saw it," Ellen said. "And his waves were natural. Nobody marcells hair anymore."

"Thank heaven," Susan said, and they both laughed. Susan thought Ellen was right—it was good to laugh again.

"Enjoying yourselves, ladies?" Dr. Scott stuck his head in the door. "Just passing by, and I couldn't help hearing your jocularity."

Susan hoped he hadn't also heard their conversation. If he disapproved of Susan for her unconventional ways, he also disapproved of Ellen for her youthful appearance. "Too young to teach," he had once been overheard to say. At least Ellen did not come up for tenure review until the next year.

"Just a light moment in a serious discussion about teaching methods," Susan said.

"I'm sure." His head withdrew.

"If he heard . . . " Ellen's voice trailed off.

"I don't think he did, Ellen. But there's something in that story, something I can't put my finger on. But it has to do with Missy Jackson."

"Missy Jackson? Susan, you're getting tunnel vision. It was just a weird case of mistaken identity or whatever."

"Okay, but if you see that guy again, get his card."

"Yes, sir!" Ellen saluted and marched out of the office, whistling, "This is the Army, Mr. Jones!"

When Ellen was gone, Susan realized she hadn't told her about the cat. Maybe if she had, Ellen wouldn't have accused her of tunnel vision. Then again, maybe she ought not broadcast around campus everything that frightened her. If whoever did all this was on campus, it would only provide fuel for his crazy fire. She began to wonder if Missy Jackson's murder had nothing to do with it, and Ernie Westin was trying to distract her from getting her book far enough along to seek a contract for publication.

Susan couldn't concentrate. She sharpened pencils, read her grade book twice, checked her notes for today's two classes, and got not one bit of new work done. But at ten o'clock, something popped into her mind that made her realize why she was so interested in Ellen's story: Missy Jackson had lied about having a work-study job, and yet she had earned money somehow. What did that have to do with the red-haired stranger with funny waves in his hair who offered coeds ways to make money after class?

If she could answer that question, she might know who was framing her for murder—and trying to kill her at the same time.

John Scott had called a departmental meeting for four that afternoon, which kept Susan on campus much later than she normally would have stayed on a Friday afternoon. It would, she knew, be boring as always. Ellen stopped by her office and they went together, slinking into seats near the door. Susan vowed if it went past five, she was leaving. Ernie Westin sat right in the front row, and when Dr. Scott (as he preferred to be called) strode into the room, Westin called out, "Want me to take minutes, John?"

Scott looked first surprised and then disapproving. "No, that won't be necessary. This will be brief."

Scott droned on for a few minutes about mid-semester break, attendance records (not all teachers kept them) and the importance of a level grading system—all things they'd heard before. Then he turned, almost happily, to his main subject.

"As you all know we've had a tragic death on campus, and one of our own has been accused of murder." At least he had the grace to refrain from either naming Susan or looking directly at her. "We must all work together to solve this crime and free the English department from any stigma that hangs over it at present. I will be issuing some memoranda on curriculum, since I understand a curriculum problem may have contributed to this sad situation."

Susan sat stunned. She saw no point in telling him, here and now, that she hadn't been accused. He hadn't named her, but he didn't need to. What bothered her more was the curriculum reference—he meant her class on women's lit. Would he drop it from the schedule? It was the most useful and satisfactory—and popular—class she taught, and for a minute she saw white with fury. Ellen grabbed her hand, just as Westin said, "We all know, sir, that our job is to teach them about literature, not to encourage new ways of thinking."

Toad! Susan rushed from the room, not caring what impression she left behind.

* * *

Susan spent Friday night in a frenzy of cleaning that left her exhausted but did much to distract her from that awful department meeting. It wasn't so much cleaning as it was straightening, sorting, hiding—this stack of books could go back to the library, that pile of papers should be in her office at school, the dirty socks and underwear she fished from under the couch needed to go in the washing machine. She washed sheets, put clean ones on the guest bed, hung fresh towels in the bath for Aunt Jenny.

The frantic work made her forget about dead coeds and dead cats and fear, until the phone rang. It was Jake. "You all right?"

"Of course I'm all right," she said, her voice sharper than she meant it to be. "I'm all locked in, and I'm in the cleanest house you ever saw."

"And you're not scared?"

"Haven't even thought about it." Silently she added, *until this minute.* "What did Jordan say about the kitten?"

Jake paused. "Uh, well, he's got a theory."

Susan rolled her eyes heavenward. She could tell from Jake's voice that the "theory" was going to make her angry. "What's his theory?"

"That you've angered some student, and that kid is taking advantage of the Missy Jackson case to harass you. He, well, he thinks the incident with the Jeep and the kitten are related to each other but completely separate from the murder case."

Susan yelped. "Doesn't he see it as an awfully strange coincidence that I'm involved in both? Especially in a town where nothing like any of this ever happens?"

Jake tried to choose his words carefully. "I think he sees the one reflecting the other."

"What the hell does that mean, Jake? Could you speak English?"

"He thinks the fact that a student is angry enough at you to do these things says something about your character, something that makes it more likely that you're involved in the murder."

She didn't know whether to laugh or cry. "What school of crime detection did he go to?" she asked incredulously.

"I'm on my way to get dinner and bring it over. What do you want?"

"Nothing," she said too harshly. "I just need to be alone." Even as she said the words, she knew she wanted to tell him about the department meeting.

He kept his voice firm. "Susan, I will not—repeat, will not— let you stay alone in that house tonight."

"Well, that's what I'm going to do," she said and slammed down the phone. *Talk about cutting off your nose to spite your face.*

Susan ate cold cereal for supper. The milk in the refrigerator had soured, so she mixed the powdered cream she kept for Jake's coffee with a little ice water and poured it over the cereal. The result was barely passable, and she gave up.

She managed to keep busy all evening—and thereby keep the demons away from her—by cleaning the refrigerator. She threw away the remnants of beef bourguignon—dinner Jake made sometime before the murder?—two pieces of moldy cheese, some lunch meat she no longer trusted, and the carton of milk that had soured. Then she washed the shelves and put an open dish of baking soda in the fridge. Aunt Jenny had a thing about clean refrigerators.

Ellen called to sympathize about the department meeting, but Susan was in no mood for sympathy. She was still angry. "My curriculum did not cause a murder. That's the most ridiculous thing I ever heard."

"I agree," Ellen said, "but could you please not shout in my ear?"

"Sorry. I'm in a mood. Turned Jake away tonight too. Let me talk to you tomorrow."

"Are you sure you're okay? Will you call if you need me . . . or need a sympathetic ear?"

Susan promised and hung up the phone.

Finally, she settled down to read one of the few Zane Grey novels she hadn't read. *The Shepherd of Guadalupe*, about a rancher who returns from the Civil War to find his New Mexico land occupied by a nester, was so far removed from Susan's own troubles that she was able to lose herself in the book and forget anything else. There was a love story—Grey always wove them in—and lots of violence and melodrama. It was good escape reading.

About eleven, after she'd finished the book, she drank a glass of wine and decided it was time to go to bed. *Hah! And Jake thought I'd be afraid alone!* Knowing they were locked but just to be sure, she checked the doors and windows and then fell into bed in her jeans and T-shirt.

She woke at three-thirty in a cold sweat. Was that a noise she heard? She lay motionless, afraid to move. Around her everything was pitch dark and absolutely silent. Finally, as her eyes adjusted, the glow from the night light helped her to see. Shakily, she stumbled from her bed and began to prowl the house, turning on lights in the guest bedroom and then the bath and finally making her way into the kitchen. From the kitchen window she peered out toward the parking area by her deck.

There sat Jake's truck. When she looked closely she could see him sitting sprawled across the front seat. Opening the sliding glass doors, she called out, "What are you doing?"

He kicked open a door with his feet and slid out of the truck. "Watching you," he said. Then with a hand on his back, he moaned, "I'm getting too old for a stakeout. Makes me stiff and sore."

Susan couldn't stifle a laugh. "Why are you watching me?" she asked.

He shrugged. "I told you I wasn't going to let you be alone here at night. And it's a good thing. You got scared."

She opened her mouth to protest, but he raised his hand. "Don't deny it, Susan. Why else did you go from room to room turning lights on and off?"

"I thought I heard a noise," she muttered, chagrined at having been caught in her moment of fear.

"Probably your own snoring woke you," he said. "I kind of circled the house about midnight, and you were really lettin' it go. How much wine you drink last night?"

"Not that much!" she said indignantly.

"Well," Jake said, "I'm glad nobody with evil on his mind came by. You were out like . . . what's that phrase?"

"Lottie's eye," she supplied. "I've no idea where it came from." She looked at him a long minute. "You going to come in?"

"Yeah. I'd really rather spend the rest of the night in your bed than in this truck."

"This is your last chance," she said teasingly, as he brushed past her. "When Aunt Jenny's here, you're banished."

He grabbed her and pulled her to the bedroom. "Then let's not waste time!" He was laughing as he said it, but once in the bedroom they made a ritual of undressing each other, dancing to a tune only they heard, and then slowly, ever so slowly, leading each other to the bed.

It was nearing morning before they slept, and Susan later remembered murmuring, "It's a good thing no one tried to kill me. You wouldn't have heard them and wouldn't have been able to protect me."

"Umm," he murmured sleepily, "you're right."

* * *

After Jake left about eleven on Saturday morning, Susan settled down to make notes on *The Shepherd of Guadalupe*. Maybe it was Jake, who promised—threatened? insisted?—he'd be back for one more night before Aunt Jenny's arrival, or maybe it was the sunny, pleasant day, but Susan felt better than she had since the day before Missy Jackson's murder. She even took her book and laptop out on the deck to work. The notion that anyone thought her a bad influence was far from her mind, and nothing seemed out of order in her world.

When the phone rang, she went impatiently to answer it, resentful of the interruption of her work.

It was Brandy Perkins, Missy Jackson's roommate. "I've got to see you," she said, her voice tense.

"What about?" Susan asked, her attention having jumped immediately from Zane Grey to Missy Jackson.

"Missy," came the reply.

"I don't know any more than you do," Susan protested.

"I've got to see you," the girl repeated, and then her voice faltered as she said, "It's real important."

Susan couldn't tell what she detected in the girl's voice, but she was suddenly alarmed, worried about Brandy. "Can we meet somewhere, maybe have some lunch? I'm famished."

"I won't eat," Brandy said, "but I'll meet you at Subway in thirty minutes."

"Okay," Susan said.

She was in the bathroom, running a comb through her hair and dabbing powder on her shiny nose, when the phone rang again. Expecting it to be Brandy canceling their meeting, she answered it with, "Why can't you meet me?"

"I can, I can," Jake said laughing. "Just tell me where and when."

"Oh, Jake, I thought you were someone else."

"Obviously. Want to tell me who?"

"No." Jake would tell her in no uncertain terms not to meet Brandy. No, Susan did not want to tell him who she was meeting.

"Susan, you aren't about to do something that would disturb me, are you?"

"No," she lied.

Jake Phillips was no dummy, and he knew Susan well enough that he could read her tone of voice. But he figured there was no sense making a fuss about this. He wouldn't win anyway. "I didn't call to give you the third degree," he said. "I called to invite you to dinner."

"Subie's Cafe?" she asked.

"Nope. The City Restaurant. I figure your aunt may stay a while, and . . . well, things between us may be distant while she's here, so I thought we ought to have a big blowout."

The City Restaurant in Fort Worth was the most expensive restaurant Susan had ever eaten in. Jake had taken her once before, and while she never saw the bill, she knew it was high. They had steak and au gratin potatoes and spinach casserole, a wonderful Chardonnay (at her insistence, even with red meat), and the most unobtrusive but efficient service Susan had ever seen in a restaurant. She had savored it as one of the few moments of luxury in her life.

"Are you sure you can afford it?" she asked. "I can't." She immediately wanted to kick herself. Why did she always insult him?

"Thanks, Susan. I wouldn't have asked if I couldn't afford it. And you're worth it."

"I'm sorry," she said, with true contrition in her voice. "I'd love to. What time?"

"Pick you up at six. I made reservations for seven-thirty. If we get there early we'll have an extra glass of wine."

"I'll be ready," she said, "and, Jake, thanks. I need an evening like this."

"You're worth it," he repeated.

Susan grabbed her purse and left to meet Brandy. The girl was ten minutes late for their meeting. Susan had ordered and almost consumed a six-inch tuna-salad sandwich and was drumming her fingers on the table, thinking *I could be home doing . . . doing what? More work on that damn manuscript? More cleaning? More scaring myself to death?* She settled down to wait and filled the time with anticipation of dinner that night.

When Brandy arrived, she looked a mess. Her hair badly needed washing, and she had pulled it back and caught it with a ponytail holder from which stray clumps escaped. Her eyes had dark circles under them, and yet her cheeks had an unnatural bright pink tone. Susan noticed that unkempt as she was Brandy wore an unusual pair of earrings—silver dangles with just a bit of turquoise.

Brandy ordered a Coke and brought it to the table where Susan sat over the remnants of her sandwich.

"Sorry I'm late. I have a hard time getting myself together these days," she said, but there was no real apology in her tone.

"Sure," Susan said. "What can I do for you?"

"I hear you've been trying to find Eric Lindler."

"Yes, I have. I'm determined to find out what happened to your roommate, mostly because people think I was involved." She deliberately didn't add, *and mostly because someone's trying to kill me or at least scare me to death.*

"No one thinks you were involved," Brandy said, almost pleading with Susan to believe her. "But Eric won't know either. Can't you just leave the whole thing alone?"

"You're the only one who doesn't think I'm involved—and that goes from my department chair to the police officer who's leading the investigation to Missy's parents. I've got to defend myself. Besides, it can't hurt if I find that boy, express my sympathy and talk to him."

"Dr. Hogan, just stay away from Eric Lindler. Leave the whole thing to the authorities."

Convenient for Brandy, Susan thought, that the authorities are sure Eric Lindler isn't the murderer. If I let the authorities handle it, everyone will stay away from Eric Lindler, which is what this girl wants. She's terrified of something. Susan realized now that it had been fear in Brandy's voice the day after Missy's disappearance, when she refused to call her roommate's parents. That fear was even more pronounced today. Brandy wasn't as much upset about Missy and desperate to find out what happened to her as she was scared for herself. Susan wanted to tell her that they had something in common—she was terrified too.

Instead, she said slowly, "Brandy, what are you afraid of? Finding out who killed Missy? Surely you would want to know that."

The girl's eyes roamed around the restaurant, looking everywhere but at Susan, and she shrugged. "I do. Of course I do. I guess I just have that 'it could be me next' feeling."

"Well," Susan said, "so do I." She told a wide-eyed Brandy about the car trying to run her down in the parking lot but didn't go on to the incidents of the Jeep with the flat tires or the dead kitten, though even now the that memory made her shudder.

Brandy saw the shudder. "You really are afraid, aren't you?" she asked. When Susan nodded, the girl said, "I tell you, Dr. Hogan, we've got to just leave this all alone."

"No," Susan said firmly. "I can't live my life scared. I've got to find out who's behind this." She thought a minute. "Has anyone threatened you? Why do you think you could be next?"

Brandy shrugged, and Susan pressed. "Is there something you and Missy had in common that I should know about?"

"We were roommates, best friends, we double-dated a lot, did lots of things together. But she was from Uvalde, and I'm from Oklahoma City. And she was pre-med. Me? I'm an English major because I love to read, not because I burn to teach English to a bunch of little kids." Cynicism was evident in her voice. There was something flip or studied about the answer, as though Brandy had rehearsed it in her mind.

Trying to be casual, Susan said, "I'll tell you one thing, Brandy. English majors never make the money doctors do."

"I'll never be poor," Brandy said with determination.

Susan noticed that even in jeans and a T-shirt, the girl carried a Bottega Veneta hobo bag and wore expensive boots. She wondered curiously if Brandy's family had money. Were they rich professionals who let hired help raise their daughter? Aloud, she said idly, "What about Missy? Did she want to be a doctor to make a lot of money?"

"Oh," Brandy said hastily, "I don't know that I'd say that exactly. But she had expensive tastes."

Susan had found a kernel, the small beginning of a clue to the truth about Missy Jackson. "Expensive tastes?" she asked casually.

"Oh, you know, Ferragamo shoes. She liked to shop at Neiman's." She paused a minute. "Her mom is . . . well, she's like a throwback to the fifties, someone who has had nothing in her life but taking care of her husband and daughter. Missy vowed she'd never be like her mother."

"Missy's parents," Susan said slowly, "say she bought all her own clothes. How could she afford that?"

"She worked a lot," Brandy said, and Susan noticed that the girl again avoided looking directly at her.

"Doing what?" There was a terse demand in Susan's voice.

Brandy simply shrugged. "Don't know. I gotta be going now."

"Tell me about Eric Lindler."

Susan's tone was so commanding that Brandy, halfway out of the booth, sat back down. She shifted in her seat, tried to smooth her hair, turned to look out the window.

"Tell me about him, what kind of a person he is," Susan insisted.

For once, Brandy looked her straight in the eye and said in a clear voice, "Dull."

Startled, Susan sat back in the booth to contemplate that answer. And in the moment she did that, Brandy was up and headed for the door. "Stay away from him, Dr. Hogan," she said over her shoulder. "Don't make it worse for me . . . or for you."

Stunned, Susan watched the girl leave the fast-food shop. Then she sat in the booth a good five minutes, mulling over the strange conversation she'd just had and Brandy's final parting shot that had raised Shelley's ghost again. As if this whole murder case weren't bad enough in itself, it was bringing Shelley back into sharp focus.

Chapter Six

When he picked her up for dinner that night Jake wore a navy blazer over a pale blue shirt, a red-and-tan tie, and tan slacks. He looked terrific. Susan thought she looked pretty terrific too in a velour drop-waist dress she had ordered from Eddie Bauer and clunky brown shoes that she'd bought on sale at DSW shoe warehouse. She could wear those ugly things as well as the young girls could, and they looked better with long skirts than mini-short things.

"Golly gee, Miss Susan, a dress!" Jake whistled through his teeth.

"Shut up or I'll go put on jeans," she said.

"I'll be quiet all night, dumbstruck by your beauty," he replied.

He drove the pickup truck that night, and when Susan asked why they weren't taking the Jeep, he said, "Not university business."

"Never know what will turn into university business," she said with a laugh.

Jake liked back roads, but there wasn't much choice. A two-lane highway took them to Granbury, but from then on they were on four-lane until he reached a point where he could skirt the suburban business district that put several stoplights in their way. Then it was IH 20 to Hulen and Forest Park to downtown. At least that route circled along the river and was a lot more scenic than the interstate. As he drove, Jake looked at her and asked, "Have a good day?"

Susan knew he was fishing to find out who she'd met for lunch. "Uh, well, sort of," she said innocently. "The house is clean, and I worked on my Zane Grey thing a lot." Well, it was only sort of a lie. She'd just left out the part she didn't want to tell him.

"Is it going well?" His interest was polite, no more.

"Okay. I can't seem to concentrate on it."

"Well, you've had a lot of distractions, and with Aunt Jenny about to arrive, it's no wonder." Then, again, so casual it was obvious, he asked, "Who'd you meet for lunch?"

Susan tried to divert him. "Do you think it was another man? Do I detect jealousy here?"

"No, Susan, you don't detect jealousy. You're hearing suspicion. I think you're meddling in things that you shouldn't be."

"I don't know what you mean." *Jake is going to push the issue and ruin the evening,* Susan thought. She stared out the window at the river, dark green but flowing swiftly, still swollen with fall rains. The trees in Trinity Park were beginning to lose their leaves and the grass still looked brown and burned from summer.

"Susan, look at me." Jake voice was a command.

She turned her head slowly and looked at him. "Jake Phillips, we're off to have a nice, relaxed evening—at your suggestion and, I might add, at your very generous invitation. Don't ruin it by asking me about things I don't want to tell you."

"Caught in my own trap," he said.

She turned back to the river and then decided that the evening was off to a rotten start, and it was partly her fault. "You'll like Aunt Jenny," she said, as though she were continuing a conversation instead of breaking a long silence. "She's dithery and opinionated and as good-hearted as they come. And the chicken and dumplings will be delicious."

"Good," he said, picking up her tone and going with it. "I need mothering and good cooking."

"You never want me to cook!" Susan said.

"That's because Aunt Jenny apparently never taught you how. You're the only grown woman I know whose idea of cooking is a Kraft macaroni dinner or who brags about the way you cook corn when all you do is open the can and add some butter and salt and pepper."

"You ate it," Susan said, laughing as her mood lightened. "And besides, I can make terrific beef Stroganoff."

"Yeah, but just like you can't live on love, you can't live on Stroganoff. Once every few months is plenty for me, thanks."

"Well," Susan said, pretending to be petulant, "I could learn other things. What do you like?"

"I like to cook," he said.

"You're being contradictory. You want Aunt Jenny to mother you, but you don't want me to cook for you—and then you accuse me of not doing it."

He laughed aloud. "I think you twisted my words."

He took the 7th Street exit to downtown and turned south on Main toward The City Restaurant. The valet took their car, the hostess said, "Right this way, Mr. Phillips" as though she thought he owned Phillips Petroleum Company, and they were soon seated at a cozy and private table in a corner of the main dining room. Their waiter was a middle-aged man with gray hair who greeted them with a simple, "Good evening" as he spread their napkins in their laps. Susan thought he was a welcome relief from young men who said, "Hi, I'm Colin . . . or Jamie or Brandon or Christian . . . and I'm your server tonight."

She ordered Pinot Grigio.

"Susan, we're going to eat steak. Can't you have a merlot or a Beaujolais?"

"No. I like white wine with steak."

He ordered a Scotch, and they studied the menu.

"I want the same steak I had last time," Susan said, "only I don't know what it was."

"New York strip. I think I'll have the lobster. Can we share?" He reached across the table and took her hand.

"You're trying to sweet talk me out of some of my steak," she said, but she was grinning and she held on to the offered hand. She knew she'd order it rare and he wanted his well done.

They talked of everything over their drinks—the lingering effect of the Boston Marathon bombings, the periodic worry over North Korea's unpredictable young dictator, the gun control issue (they differed on this one and didn't usually discuss it, though Susan was quick to point out the last school shootings), and what Susan called the "war on women," which made Jake mutter under his breath. What they didn't talk about—and what hung heavily in the air between them—was the death of Missy Jackson.

The steak was even better than the last time they had eaten at The City Restaurant. Susan savored it and reluctantly cut off two small chunks to give Jake in exchange for a good-sized piece of his lobster.

"Don't be too generous," he said dryly. Then, predictably, he exclaimed, "It's still raw."

"You're the one who wanted lobster," she said, and then, suddenly, she dropped her fork onto her plate with a clatter.

Startled, Jake followed her gaze to the bar. All he saw was a young woman and a young man, apparently enjoying a drink. The girl looked a little tense and seemed to avoid looking at the man, but it could have been an awkward blind date. The only other thing he noticed was that the young man had remarkable wavy red hair.

"Susan? What's the matter?"

She continued to stare, as though frozen.

He reached across the table and put his hand gently on her arm. "Calling Susan. Please come back to our table. What is it?"

"That's Brandy," she whispered.

"Brandy," he repeated dumbly. Then it dawned on him. "Missy Jackson's roommate?"

"Yeah, and she's made an amazing recovery since noon today. She looked awful when I met her—dirty hair, no makeup, circles under her eyes. Look at her now."

"I knew that's who you were meeting," Jake said slowly. "Why didn't you tell me the truth?"

"Because you would have made me promise not to see her," Susan said promptly.

Jake sighed aloud.

"Now look at her," Susan said, her voice almost a command.

Jake turned to look.

"No, don't turn. Don't be so obvious. They'll see us." Now Susan's voice was a controlled whisper.

"I can't look at her if I don't turn," he said.

"I'll describe. She's wearing a slinky black dress, her hair is curled around her face, her makeup is flawless. She looks like she's thirty, not nineteen."

"So she's trying to get on with her life," Jake said. "That doesn't mean she isn't upset about Missy. Besides, now that I know who you met for lunch, tell me what she wanted."

"Wait a minute, Jake. That man she's with—he's the one!"

Jake threw his hands up in the air and gave up, at least for the time being, on his dinner. "What one?" he asked impatiently.

"The one that asked Ellen if she wanted work in the student center."

"Why would Ellen want to work in the student center?"

"No, no, she was in the student center when he came up to her. Said she reminded him of someone else, and then asked her if she wanted to earn some extra money."

"How?"

"He didn't say, and she didn't ask."

Jake turned slowly toward the bar again and this time took a good, long look. Just then the couple at the bar were joined by a third man, one who appeared to be in his early forties and looked distinguished, sophisticated. The young red-haired man made obvious introductions between Brandy and the newcomer, chatted for a moment, and then left. Then Brandy and the older man were shown to a table at the opposite end of the dining room.

Susan lowered her eyes. "Thank heaven they didn't seat them near us," she said.

"I don't know," Jake said, "it might have been interesting." Then he returned his attention to his now-cold lobster. "Susan, this could all have a perfectly simple explanation."

"It doesn't," Susan said. "I know it doesn't."

"Okay. What do you think the explanation is?" This time he continued to eat.

"It looks like a dating service to me," Susan said.

"Oh, Susan, come on now. Oak Grove coeds as high-priced call girls? Give me a break."

Jake's disbelief angered her. "Why else would Missy Jackson have been able to shop at Neiman's? Why would that redhead ask Ellen if she wanted money? I'm sure he mistook her for a coed. And what else could Brandy be doing here?"

"Okay," Jake said, "you better tell me, in detail, about your lunch with Brandy. I'm going to have a brandy. And that's not a bad pun."

By the time she repeated Ellen Peck's story in detail and gave a blow-by-blow account of her meeting with Brandy, Jake was on his second brandy and Susan had asked for iced tea. It was eleven o'clock.

"You drive," Jake said. "I shouldn't have had that second brandy, but by God, Susan, I don't think I'd have believed your story without it." He shook his head.

"And do you believe it?"

"I don't know. I'll think about it in the cold light of day."

He fell asleep on the way home, and Susan welcomed the solitude. It gave her time to think about how to get the truth out of Brandy and how to trap the redheaded man. She'd start by tracking down Eric Lindler. But tomorrow—ah, tomorrow there was Aunt Jenny.

She drove straight to her own house, woke Jake, and led him into the bedroom, where he shed his clothes, fell into the bed, and was asleep again while Susan was still brushing her teeth. *And he,* she thought, *worried about our lack of privacy when Aunt Jenny's here.*

Jake woke her in the morning by rubbing her back, and they stayed in bed a long time, enjoying each other, concentrating on their bodies and totally oblivious to either Missy Jackson or Aunt Jenny. When Susan finally looked at the clock, it was nearly eleven.

"Good Lord," she said, jumping from the bed. "Aunt Jenny could be here any minute."

"I thought you said one-thirty at the earliest," he said, raising himself up lazily on one elbow and reaching for her with the other hand.

"Stay away from me, Jake Phillips, and get out of that bed. You know how old people are. They always start a trip at the crack of dawn."

He could see that Susan was really concerned, so he dressed rapidly, helped her straighten the bedroom, and gratefully accepted the cup of coffee she finally offered. He'd been up thirty minutes and felt like it was three hours. "Can I take a nap?" he asked.

"At your house," she said firmly. "It's time for you to go. You come back at suppertime, and we'll pretend it's the first time we've seen each other today."

"Susan," he said patiently, "you're thirty-what? Your aunt knows you're not an eighteen-year-old virgin."

"Not Aunt Jenny," she said forcefully.

He shrugged. "You sure you'll be all right alone?"

"Nothing's happened in forty-eight hours, has it?" she said lightly.

The minute the words "Nothing's happened" were out of her mouth, Susan regretted tempting fate. She knocked quickly on the wooden counter top.

"Superstitious?" Jake laughed. "I'd never have believed it of you." Then, giving her a quick kiss on the nose, he slid open the doors to the deck.

"Goddamn!" His voice echoed back into the kitchen, its tone sending a wave of fear through Susan.

"What?" she asked, throwing down the dishtowel she held and hurrying to the sliding glass doors.

Absolute disaster greeted her. Every plant drooped, lifeless— all her herbs, the mums she had planted for fall color, the pot of ferns and ivy which had been so lush and green. Color drained from her face, and she grabbed Jake to steady herself. "How?" she asked.

He shrugged. "Looks to me like someone poured acid or something on them. You'll have to throw out everything— potting soil, even the pots."

She knew better than to ask why. It was the next step in the war that began with the rock through the Jeep windshield and led then to the dead kitten. "Jake, this is no student with a grudge. This is . . . it's someone who wants me to know how close he can get to me without my knowing."

"Yeah," Jake said glumly. "Some protection I turned out to be. This happened between three-thirty and, oh, I'd say, day-break. I was right here, keeping you safe." He kicked angrily at a pot, knocking it over and spilling the contents on the deck.

"Don't pick that up with bare hands," she said practically. "Acid. I'll get gloves."

When she handed him the gloves, he began loading pots into the bed of his pickup. "Can't have Aunt Jenny see this," he explained. "I'll drive them to the landfill."

"Aunt Jenny! I hadn't even thought how this will look. What will she say when she sees a bare deck? She knows I garden, she's been here . . . she'll know something is really wrong."

"Susan, you're going to have to tell your aunt the truth."

"No, I'm not, Jake Phillips. I'm not going to worry that poor woman."

"If this keeps up"—he looked ruefully at the wilted plants—"you won't have to tell her. She'll find out for herself."

"I'll see that she doesn't."

Jake didn't want to tell her she was fooling herself. He took her in his arms, hugged her tight, and said, "Lock yourself in the house. Don't come out to sit on the deck."

"I have to sweep it up!" She was being stubborn.

"Okay, sweep quickly, while I stay here."

She swept not only quickly but angrily, vicious strokes pushing dirt into a pile for the dustpan. With each powerful thrust of the broom, she thought she was beating whoever it was that had done this. When she put the broom up, Jake asked her, "Scared?"

"No," she said, "angry. Madder than hell. And puzzled. Trying to run me down is one thing; dead kittens and plants are in a whole different category." Suddenly, she had a thought. "Maybe it's Brandy Perkins. She sure wanted to scare me away."

"I'll talk to Jordan," Jake said, "in the morning."

Susan shook her head. "No, don't tell him. It won't do any good."

"Okay, but then he'll get you for withholding evidence," he said grimly. "I've got to go. See you later."

Susan did as she was told and spent the rest of the morning and early afternoon behind locked doors. But she was restless—worrying about Aunt Jenny finding out about all that had gone on, trying to puzzle out why these things were being done, going from window to window to peer outside. By the time Jake came back at two o'clock, she felt like she'd been alone—and trapped—for days.

He didn't pull the truck up to the parking area as usual. Instead, he backed carefully up next to the deck. In the bed of his pickup were pots of ivy and ferns. For color, there were three pots of golden and rust mums. And two pots of rosemary and one each of oregano and thyme, all of which would winter over well.

She ran shrieking out the door. "Jake! You're wonderful. Where'd you get those?"

He beamed and opened his arms as she hurled herself toward him. "Nice to be appreciated," he murmured into her hair. "I went to the nursery out on the highway. Sorry, but you'll have to wait till spring to replace most of your herbs and native flowering plants. But these should winter over."

"Oh, they will. Jake, they're perfect. And Aunt Jenny will never know."

"Why do you think I did this?" he asked dryly. "Not for you, I hope."

She kissed him soundly and didn't care if Mrs. Whitley was looking out her back door.

They spent a half hour arranging plants, and when they were through Susan surveyed the result with obvious delight. "It looks better than it did before. I hate to admit it, Jake, but you're a plant man, after all."

"I'm a beer man right now," he said. "Those things are heavy."

Inside, Susan saw that it was nearly three o'clock. "Jake? She's not here yet."

"Aunt Jenny? She'll be along." He was unconcerned.

"She's two hours late, and I'm worried."

"Susan, contrary to what you think about old people—ah, elderly people—she may not have left first thing this morning. Maybe she hadn't finished packing, maybe she went to church. There are a thousand possibilities, and you haven't heard from the highway department, so no news is good news. May I please have that beer?"

Absently, she handed him the beer. "What if . . . what if whoever did that"—she nodded toward the deck—"knows she's my aunt and, you know, runs her off the road or something. I think we should call the highway department or the state patrol or whoever."

"What you think," he said, taking a swig of the beer, "is that I should call. I'll call the office, have them check accidents. But Susan, the idea that her being late is connected to this other stuff . . . that's crazy!"

"Thanks," she muttered.

* * *

Aunt Jenny arrived about four. She had gotten lost, gone to Dallas, even beyond that to Mesquite. She was flustered.

"My, I just don't know where I took a wrong turn," she said. "I was following the signs and next thing I knew . . . "

"Probably missed the I-35 West turnoff," Jake said to no one in particular.

Aunt Jenny collapsed on the couch, and Susan brought her a glass of iced tea. Sipping at it, she eyed Jake. "You're Susan's boyfriend?" The smile on her face indicated that she hoped he'd say "yes."

"I hope so," he said. "Most times I think you have to ask Susan that question."

"Oh," the aunt replied with a dismissing wave of her hand, "I've given up listening to her long ago. She's the silliest child."

Jake stole a glance at Susan and saw that she was standing, hands on her hips, staring at them.

"I . . . " he ventured into new territory for him, "I think she's pretty wonderful."

"Then you'll do," Aunt Jenny beamed, patting the seat on the couch beside her. "Come sit down and tell me all about yourself."

Jake thought he might fall in love all over again, this time with this unexpected treasure of an aunt who spoke her mind and was perhaps the only person he knew—and that included himself—who wasn't somewhat cowed by Susan Hogan.

"Aunt Jenny, if you're going to cook chicken and dumplings, it's already nearly five o'clock," Susan's voice was businesslike.

"Oh, my, did I tell you I'd do that?" she asked with complete innocence. "It takes me most of the day to cook chicken and dumplings. I'm afraid we wouldn't eat by ten, and that's past my bedtime."

"Not to worry," Jake said. "Susan, if you'd just run to the store while I visit with your aunt. Get chicken breasts, ah—some artichokes, and salad makings. Okay?" He hid a smile, knowing that it made Susan furious to run his errands and yet she wouldn't complain because he'd been practically ordered to visit with Aunt Jenny.

Thirty minutes later Susan stomped back into the house with the bag of groceries, in time to hear Jake giving a sort of "and then" account of his life—growing up in Canyon, Texas, being orphaned at the age of ten and raised by an older brother, running away at seventeen, tending bar to put himself through junior college in Fort Worth and the law enforcement program there, and finally ending up at Oak Grove.

Susan knew which fact Aunt Jenny would fix on.

"You're an orphan?" she said, her voice softening, her pudgy hand reaching to take his.

"Yes, ma'am, my parents died in an automobile crash. I think it's one reason I wanted to go into law enforcement. They were hit by a drunk driver."

Play it for all it's worth, Jake, Susan thought. You'll have her eating out of your hand any minute now.

"Well, son, I never had children of my own, but I had Susan, and she was a real joy to me. It will pleasure me to adopt you."

"Well, ma'am . . . "

Was it Susan's imagination or was he really drawling?

"I'd just be delighted to be adopted. But right now, you best let me get those chicken breasts to marinating, so I can grill them."

"He cooks too!" Aunt Jenny murmured, throwing Susan a look that clearly said she should not let this one get away.

"Jake's a very good cook, Aunt Jenny," Susan said and wondered why she hated herself for being mad at both of them.

Susan cut up a salad, steamed the artichokes, and set the table while Jake grilled the chicken and Aunt Jenny sat on the deck and filled his ears with stories of Susan's childhood. By the time dinner was ready, Jake knew that she'd taken violin but hadn't the ear for it and had done better at piano, that she'd been in Girl Scout plays but shyness often caused her to forget her lines, and that she'd been a gangly teenager, awkward around boys.

"But isn't she lovely now?" Aunt Jenny asked, her voice wafting through the patio doors to where Susan was working.

"Yes," Jake said, "she is. But I don't think she knows it."

Susan stopped, paring knife in midair, and stared through the door at him. She found him looking directly at her.

Looking around, Aunt Jenny called out, "Susan, your deck looks lovelier than ever. You have such a green thumb—and I know you didn't get it from me."

"Thanks, Aunt Jenny. I . . . I enjoy my plants." *Would God forgive a white lie?*

Jake was watching her again, this time with one eyebrow cocked, and she knew he was sending her a mental message: *You'll have to tell her sooner or later.*

Dinner was delicious, and Aunt Jenny was profuse in her compliments to Jake, until Susan wanted to say, "Wait a minute. I did the salad and the artichokes." She wouldn't have added that Jake had to do the hollandaise sauce because she didn't know how, even when it was that quick kind made in the blender.

After dinner, the three of them sat on the deck with coffee— decaffeinated for Jake and Aunt Jenny, the real thing for Susan. Aunt Jenny had protested that they must do the dishes, but Susan had been equally insistent that they would wait until tomorrow. Finally, Aunt Jenny gave in, and they sat in the cool but pleasant October night air.

Murders and dead cats and wilted plants seemed far away until, out of the blue, Aunt Jenny said, "All right. Tell me everything about this murdered coed."

Jake spilled coffee down his shirt front, and Susan choked on the hot swallow in her mouth. Finally, she muttered, "Now, Aunt Jenny, you don't want to hear about that gossip."

"Of course, I do, dear. It involves you, doesn't it?"

"Well, yes and no. I mean, it was my car, but beyond that, I'm not involved." *Okay, another white lie told, and this one a biggie by now.*

"But other people think you are," Aunt Jenny said.

It was not a question, though that's how Susan answered it. "Well, yes, some do—the police lieutenant in charge of the investigation for one, and my department chair for another."

"That awful Dr. Scott who doesn't want to give you tenure?" Aunt Jenny was indignant.

Jake hid a smile. He had no idea Aunt Jenny knew that much about either Susan's life or academic procedure. Then he wondered how much this aunt knew—or guessed—about his relationship with her niece.

"Then you best tell me every detail," Aunt Jenny said. "Start at the beginning."

So Susan told her, beginning with the body in the car. She told her about the memorial service and Missy's parents and about Eric Lindler and Brandy and Dr. Scott's accusations. Jake noticed, however, she did not tell her about nearly being run down by a car nor about the red-haired man, dinner at The City Restaurant, her suspicions about a coed call-girl ring, the dead kitten or the plants.

She may have told the biggest thing, he thought, but she's left out more than she's told.

"It was the boyfriend," Aunt Jenny said decisively.

"Oh, now, Aunt Jenny, you can't say that. He seems from what I've heard to be a nice enough young man." Jake answered this time.

"Have the police questioned him?"

"Sure. But they don't see him as a suspect at this time."

"Did they question Susan?" The old lady's voice became sharp.

"Well, yes, but they don't see her as a suspect either."

"At this time?" Aunt Jenny asked, and Jake shrugged.

"It was the boyfriend," she repeated.

"Well," Jake said heartily, "we'll have to leave that to the police to work out. And it's getting late enough I guess I better get along. Susan, can I help with the dishes?" What he really wanted was two minutes alone with Susan to ask if he couldn't sleep on the couch.

Susan, unfortunately, seemed oblivious of the meaningful looks he was throwing her way. "No, thanks. I'll do them in the morning. I don't have class until ten."

"Okay." Then he took Aunt Jenny's hand in his, bent to kiss it, and said, "It's been a real delight, Aunt Jenny. I'm looking forward to many more evenings together."

Aunt Jenny beamed. "So am I," she said, "so am I."

"Now I don't want you cooking a lot," Jake said. "We'll take you out to eat." He seemed to think a minute. "Susan, let's take her to Subie's Cafe."

Susan made a face. "I don't want to go there. Margie thinks she knows everything about Missy Jackson's murder, and I bet by now she thinks I did it."

"Subie's Cafe?" Aunt Jenny asked. "Where's that? And why would this Margie person be so convinced?"

Susan said, "It's on the square," just as Jake said, "Margie knows all the latest gossip in town."

Aunt Jenny made a mental note to find the café and talk to Margie.

"Susan? Walk me to the truck?"

Aunt Jenny got the hint even if Susan didn't. "I'll just go on inside," she said.

Once they alone, Jake said, "I'm not sure about leaving you two here alone."

Susan kicked at a pebble in the driveway. "I'm not going to assure you we'll be fine—that'd be tempting fate just like telling you this morning nothing had happened for forty-eight hours. But I don't think you should stay. Aunt Jenny would be alarmed that you thought the situation was that serious."

"But I do," he said. Reaching into the truck, he pulled out a small handgun. "Here. Take this."

She shook her head. "I'd just shoot myself in the foot. I'll keep the phone right by the bed."

He was reluctant, but he kissed her lightly and left.

Jake was barely out of the driveway, when Aunt Jenny turned on her niece and said, "Why don't you marry that wonderful man?"

"He hasn't asked me," Susan said. Then, "I think I'll do the dishes tonight." She turned and went into the kitchen.

Aunt Jenny followed her. "Dear," she said softly, "you mustn't be impatient with an old woman who just wants to see you happy. And who right now is terribly upset about this mess you're in."

Oh, if only you knew, Susan thought. She bit her lip to stop the tears and then went and put her arms around her aunt. "I know that, Aunt Jenny, and I'm sorry I'm so prickly. I just . . . well, I just always seem to be the worst with people that care about me. Like you and Jake."

"We know that, dear," her aunt said, "and we love you anyway."

Susan attacked the dishes with vigor, but Aunt Jenny said, "Run the sink full of soapy water and let them soak overnight. I'll do them tomorrow before I cook the chicken and dumplings. And you be sure Jake comes for supper tomorrow."

"Yes, ma'am," Susan said. In spite of her vow to Jake to be alert and watchful, Susan slept better that night than she had since the murder of Missy Jackson.

Chapter Seven

The first thing Susan did at school on Monday was to go in search of Ellen. Not unexpectedly, she found her in her office with her morning cup of coffee. Ellen, too, avoided the English department lounge these days. Whatever camaraderie might once have existed in the department had vanished.

"We've got to talk," Susan said tersely.

"Fine. Sit down." Ellen yawned up at her, missing the seriousness in Susan's tone. She was astounded to watch Susan close the door. "Remember," Susan asked, "when Scott came by just at the wrong time when you were describing that red-haired young man in the student center? I don't want that to happen again."

"What's this all about?" Ellen asked, curiosity making her more alert and awake.

"The red-haired young man. I saw him at The City Restaurant Saturday night. Jake took me there for dinner."

Ellen failed to grasp the significance of this. "You've never even seen him. How do you know it's the same red-haired man? They're not that common, but there's bound to be more than one around." She was almost smiling, which made Susan angry.

"He met Brandy, Missy Jackson's roommate," she said, as though that explained everything.

Now Ellen did really smile. "So? If it was the man I met in the Main, it wouldn't be impossible for him to know her. What's wrong with her meeting him for dinner?"

The whole story tumbled out of Susan, about the older man who'd actually had dinner with Brandy and how she was convinced it was a call-girl ring of college students.

"Susan, that's preposterous! Did you tell Jake this theory?"

"He didn't think it was preposterous," Susan said righteously. Then she added, "In fact, he was so intrigued by my theory he drank too much and I had to drive home."

"And when he was sober again, what did he say?"

"Never mind. I just thought you should know, and you should watch out for that man."

"Yeah, Susan, thanks. I'll watch. But I think this whole business is making you paranoid. Leave the detective work to the police."

"You wouldn't say that if everyone thought you'd committed a murder," Susan said angrily.

Ellen shrugged as Susan left her office.

Susan realized she hadn't even told Ellen about the plants or the kitten, but she doubted if that would have convinced her.

* * *

In spite of the registrar's office strict compliance to privacy laws, it wasn't hard for Susan to find Eric Lindler by asking first here, then there. When she found him in the library where he had a work-study job, he was shelving books in the stacks.

She watched silently for a few moments from the end of the row of shelves. Absorbed in his work, he didn't see her. He was taller than he'd seemed at the memorial service and lankier—maybe it was the jeans instead of a suit and tie. A shock of brown hair kept falling onto his forehead, and he'd swing his head to get it out of the way. She liked the way he handled the books, sometimes tracing his finger along the title on the spine. He was careful with each book, moving others to make room, easing it into place.

Finally she spoke softly, aware that they were in the quiet section of the library. "Eric?"

He gave a little startled jump and turned toward her voice. His voice was louder than he expected because of the suddenness of her appearance. "Yes, ma'am?"

Looking straight at him, Susan knew she'd never seen him except that once from a distance at the service. She also knew he didn't look like a killer. His politeness was instinctive. Now he stood attentively, waiting for her to speak. Too many young men would have lounged against the shelves, their body language offering a defiant challenge. Not this one.

"I'm Susan Hogan. May I talk to you?"

"Susan Hogan," he repeated slowly. "Missy was in your car."

"That's right." She walked slowly toward him and was relieved that he showed no inclination to bolt and run. Neither did he look angry at her.

"I'm sorry," he said. "That must have been hard for you."

"Do you think I know anything about it?" Susan stared straight at him.

He ducked his head but there was a certain charm about his gesture, as though he did it from shyness. "Why would you harm Missy? You didn't even know her, did you?"

"Yes," Susan said, "she was in one of my classes last spring. Women's lit."

"She's gone from my life," he said mournfully, as though he hadn't heard what Susan had said. "She was more than part of my life. She was everything . . . except school."

"I'm sure these days are difficult for you." She felt a rush of sympathy for this young man whom she'd expected to suspect of murder.

"Yes, ma'am," he lowered his eyes and looked at the floor. "I'm having a pretty hard time getting used to, well, to Missy not being around, and I guess most of all to how it happened. It's been a week today . . . tonight."

Susan took a deep breath. One week! Her life had been turned upside-down in one short week.

"What can I do for you, Dr. Hogan?" He turned back to the books and began peering at the numbers on the spine of one he now held in his hand.

"Tell me about Missy."

"Oh, you don't have all day. It would take me that long. Missy . . . she was the most unusual person I ever met. She and I . . . we were just perfect together. She was growing every day, finding herself, becoming more sure of herself and, well, of her faith." He had put the book back on the cart.

Did Missy start from behind in matters of faith? No one had ever said that Missy Jackson was not sure of herself—just the opposite. But "finding her faith"? What did he mean by that?

"She was religious, wasn't she?" she asked carefully.

"Yes, ma'am, we both were. But I was able to teach her, to help her grow in faith, because mine is so strong." He said it without self-consciousness or boasting. He was simply stating a fact, but she knew it was a rare college student who would talk openly about something called faith. And yet, he didn't look like what the kids called a "nerd." He was wholesome, clean cut, all-American but with a boyishness about him that was charming.

"How long did you know Missy?"

He looked at her and screwed his face up a little bit, as though in pain. "We dated since my, ah, our second year. We met in comparative religion class. We were going to get married. Missy would have made a wonderful minister's wife. You see, I intend to minister to a great big city church someday, and she, well, she had the manners and all that the wife of such a man would need."

"Sophistication," Susan supplied, remembering that she'd heard that word applied to Missy before.

"Oh, not too much sophistication. Churches want their leaders to be plain folk and yet . . . well, sophisticated in a way. Missy would have been just right." A tear slid down his cheek, and he turned his head. "I'll probably never marry now."

He was so naive and so straightforward in his answers, so open in his grief that Susan's heart went out to him. She liked this boy.

"Eric, it's important to me to solve this, to find out what happened to Missy. I haven't suffered as you and her parents have, but I'm a suspect according to the police. Somehow Missy's death has become attached to me." *And I'm a victim.* But she didn't say that aloud. No need to tell this unhappy young man that someone was trying to kill her too—or that his girlfriend might have been a hooker.

He looked at her in wide-eyed astonishment. "But that's ridiculous, Dr. Hogan. You didn't have anything to do with it." He paused and then said quickly, "I mean, it wouldn't seem likely that you would. I can't imagine people thinking you are a suspect."

Susan caught his hesitation. Even he was not putting her completely beyond suspicion. "Eric, you need to help me. You need to tell me everything you think is important."

"I think it was—how do they say it? A random act of violence?" he said softly. "I'm sure nobody deliberately set out to kill Missy." He turned quickly back to his books. "And that means we may never know who did it."

"I hope not," Susan said fervently, "I hope not." Then, after a minute, "Do you know Brandy?"

His face clouded. "Brandy was no good for Missy. I think Missy was moving away from Brandy. She and I didn't get along, and Missy knew I thought she was a bad influence." His face darkened when he spoke of Missy's roommate, and he concentrated on his books, moving the cart a space down the shelf, examining the call numbers carefully.

"What about Missy's other friends?" Susan persisted. She was thinking that if Eric Lindler was any other kind of person Brandy would have every right to be frightened. His anger at her was that great. Trouble was, he just wasn't a murderer.

"Well, she didn't have too many. She and I pretty much spent our time together. That's one thing that's hard for me now. I don't . . . I don't have a lot of friends."

"No buddies?" Susan asked, trying to keep her tone light.

"No, ma'am. I'm too busy, and I don't want to go out drinking on the weekends and stuff like that. My roommate, Tony Baldwin, he's about the best friend I ever had, next to Missy."

"Missy's parents said she earned all her own spending money, yet as far as I can find out Missy had no work-study job." Did she imagine it or did he flinch?

"Work-study doesn't earn much." He shrugged ruefully and pointed to the book cart. Then, slowly, thinking while he spoke, he said, "Missy had a good job in Fort Worth several nights a week. She sold clothes in the women's department at Neiman Marcus. She said she didn't mind the commute."

That, Susan thought cynically, was easily checked. In whispered tones, she said, "Brandy said she liked to shop at Neiman's, that she had expensive tastes."

"Huh!" he snorted. "Brandy taught 'em to her. She couldn't afford to shop at Neiman's except maybe on that last day sale or whatever they call it, and then with her employee discount."

Eric put the books down, turned and faced her squarely, and said, "Dr. Hogan, Missy was the only good thing that happened to me ever in my life—except maybe the chance to go to school here at Oak Grove. She meant everything to me, and I'll do whatever I can to help you find out who killed her."

"Thanks, Eric." She reached to shake his hand. "I've got to go now, but we'll talk again. And if you think of anything or if you just want to talk, come see me. My office is in the liberal arts building." She walked away without looking back. Their entire conversation had been carried on in whispered tones, almost furtively, and when she got back to the English department she found herself still whispering.

* * *

Around four o'clock in the afternoon, Susan sat in her office, head drooping over the lecture on F. Scott Fitzgerald she was going to give to the Wednesday seminar. Their papers on *The Great Gatsby* had been dismal and she knew they had no understanding of Fitzgerald's importance.

Ernie Westin strolled by and planted himself against the doorframe, dressed in jeans and a plaid shirt, the kind with a band instead of a collar that was popular more than a few years ago and now looked decidedly dated. His protruding belly ruined the stylishly casual image he apparently wanted to project, but Susan was sure he was unaware of that. In his hand, he held a cup of coffee.

"You'll never get tenure, Hogan," he said. "I had a drink with Scott the other night, and I know the inside scoop."

She heard the smugness in his tone and wanted to ask him what he had told Scott to ensure she didn't get tenure. "Really?" she asked. "Nice of you to care." She turned back to her papers, hoping he'd go away.

Instead he came into the tiny office and plopped himself down on the chair across from her desk. "You've really ruffled Scott's feathers with this murder business, and if he doesn't recommend you, you're out." He grinned at her, and she knew he'd been persuading Scott not to recommend her.

"Where do you want to teach next year?" he asked.

"Right here!" Susan snapped. She felt a sudden sinking that began in her throat and ended in her stomach. She'd been too busy worrying about other things to face the fact that denial of tenure automatically meant she would have to move on, look for a job, perhaps even—God forbid!—live with Aunt Jenny until she found another position. And Jake? He couldn't—wouldn't—follow her around Texas. And what if she had to move beyond the borders of her home state? She'd never thought about living anywhere but Texas.

Susan drew herself back to the unpleasant present and faced her colleague. "I'll be right here, Ernie. Don't get your . . . " She had been about to use an unpleasant phrase that Jake occasionally used. "Don't get in an uproar," she said.

"I sure don't know how you can say that," he said. "Me, I'd be worried to death." He heaved himself out of the chair and left her office.

Susan badly wanted to throw something, anything at him as he left.

Within minutes the phone rang. It was the provost himself in a direct call, not even a secretary saying, "Please hold for Dr. Atwater."

Susan pulled her heart out of her boots and said as brightly as she could, "Yes, sir?"

"Would you have time to see me for a bit this afternoon, Susan?"

"Yes, sir, of course. At your convenience." To herself she was thinking, Okay, this is it. He's going to tell me the school can't stand a scandal, and I'm suspended until the murder is cleared up. I wonder if he's like everybody else and really thinks I did it.

"If it would fit your schedule, now would be a good time. I hope you won't mind coming to my office."

Her palm was sweaty on the telephone receiver. "That's fine, sir. I'll be right there." *Unless I can think of a quick reason to go to the Caribbean or Fiji or someplace far away.*

Susan took time to rub some powder on her shiny nose, comb her flyaway hair, and wish she'd dressed better for the day. Navy slacks and a white cotton shirt would have to do. At least she wasn't wearing jeans and running shoes. Even with her dawdling, she was in the provost's office within five minutes.

"Susan, nice of you to come so promptly." The provost was a large man in his mid-fifties. He wore a well-cut suit but had hung the jacket over the back of the chair behind his desk, so now he was casually attired in rolled-up shirtsleeves and a loosened tie. He was courteous, polite, and careful as he showed her to a padded chair in a conversation area in his mahogany-paneled office. A huge contrast to John Scott's office.

This was to be no across-the-desk confrontation but an informal talk, Susan saw. She looked at him and realized that he was more casual—and more comfortable with himself—than Dr. Scott ever would be. Then her eyes wandered around the room, this being the first time she'd ever been summoned to the provost's office. A small arrangement of fresh flowers sat on the coffee table between her and the opposite chair. The upholstery was plaid, the wood dark, the atmosphere expensive and masculine but not, as she had imagined, particularly intimidating. She perched on the edge of her upholstered chair and waited in desperate anticipation for him to speak.

He picked up the phone, said tersely, "No calls, please, Shirley," and then seated himself across the small table from Susan.

Bad sign, Susan thought. He doesn't want any interruptions as he tells me I can't teach and I'm not eligible for tenure.

"It's been a bad week for you, hasn't it?" he asked, and there was real kindness in his voice.

Surprised at his sympathy, Susan simply nodded in agreement.

"I want you to know that the university is very concerned about this murder"—at least he hadn't called it *an unfortunate affair*—"and we're doing everything we can to clear it up. I've asked Jake Phillips to devote as much attention to it as he possibly can. You know Mr. Phillips, I believe?"

The provost knew perfectly well that Susan and Jake were a couple, and his careful circumlocution would have amused Susan if she hadn't been too nervous to find anything funny. She simply nodded again. Her tongue seemed to be glued to the roof of her mouth.

Atwater made a tent of his fingers in front of his face and stared at them for a long moment. Then he said, "Dr. Scott has been to see me. He seems to have the, ah, unfortunate"—there was that word again!—"opinion that you were somehow involved in this event and that it should affect your tenure review. I wanted you to know that is not an official university position. We think it was a random act of violence and your car was chosen for no reason, at least no reason that had anything to do with you. The tenure review will concentrate on your teaching record and your publications, as it should. By the time it comes around, I presume this matter will be solved. I've told Dr. Scott as much."

Susan nodded again. This time she managed a weak, "Thank you, sir." But she wanted to ask what Scott's reaction had been.

The interview, which had been exceptionally one-sided, was over. Atwater opened the door for her, shook her hand, thanked her for coming. But as she crossed in front of Shirley's desk, he said, "Susan? I do hope you're more talkative in class." His eyes were laughing.

Outside his office, she collapsed against the wall and stayed there for several minutes, until two secretaries walked by and their curious looks prompted her to move on.

* * *

When she got home that evening about five-thirty, Jake was already there, sharing a drink on the deck with Aunt Jenny. Jake was drinking bourbon, and Aunt Jenny was knitting.

"What're you making?" Susan asked her.

Aunt Jenny shook her head. "Afghan squares. I'll never get enough of them, and I hate piecing them. But it keeps me busy."

Jake and Susan exchanged amused looks over her head, and Jake stood to give Susan a quick kiss on the cheek. Aunt Jenny watched them and beamed happily.

Jake brought Susan a glass of Chardonnay and when she was settled in a chair said, "So how was your day? I hear you went to see Atwater."

She stared at him. "How do you know?"

"He called me in earlier. Said to give the Missy Jackson case as much attention as I could. And told me you had his full support. I think what he said was, 'I believe you know Dr. Hogan?'"

Susan, her terror over the interview now behind her, laughed aloud. "He said almost the same thing to me. He's sly; not much gets past him. I was grateful that he seemed to believe in me."

Jake took her hand and played with her fingers. "Why shouldn't he?" His crooked smile testified to his own belief in her.

Susan hadn't meant to tell him about Eric Lindler. She knew he'd disapprove. But it was a sharing kind of moment, and she opened her mouth before she thought. The story of her interview came tumbling out. "I like him," she ended lamely. "He's . . . he's not a murderer. And I'm going to try to keep tabs on him, make sure he's all right."

Jake started with a stern "Susan!" but Susan interrupted him. "He says she had a job at Neiman's in Fort Worth. That ought to be easy to check."

He threw his hands up in the air. "Yes, ma'am, I'll get right on it." He looked thoughtfully at her. "You think that'll prove your theory, don't you?"

Susan nodded.

Aunt Jenny interrupted them in a loud and clear voice. Without ever looking up from her knitting, she said, "He killed her." After a minute, she said, "Reminds you of Shelley North, doesn't it, Susan?"

They both whirled to stare at the older woman.

* * *

Jake Phillips knew that Susan didn't always tell him the whole truth about some of the things she did. Like her lunch with Brandy Perkins. But he didn't think that she knew that he too could skirt the truth. He certainly didn't intend to tell her that he'd invited—ordered?—Brandy to his office for a conversation.

Jake had thought long and hard about Susan's wild assumption that Oak Grove coeds were involved in a call-girl ring. And he wouldn't have told her, at least not yet, but it made sense to him. Especially after he found out that Missy Jackson most definitely had not worked at Neiman's. He hadn't told Susan yet that the Fort Worth branch of the upscale store reported no record of any employee by that name. So what was Missy doing when she told Eric she was going to Fort Worth to work?

He should, he thought, take his information and his suspicions—all right, Susan's suspicions—right to Dirk Jordan. Indeed, that was what Susan expected of him, he was sure. But if he did that, all of this would soon become public knowledge. As far as Jake could see that had two disadvantages: first, it would expose the school to scandal, and he had as much as promised

Atwater he wouldn't let that happen. Second, and more important, if these suspicions became public, the red-haired man and whoever else was involved would be on the alert—and Susan could be in more danger than she already was.

No, Jake had decided he'd best do some quiet sleuthing himself. He recognized the irony: he was doing what he'd forbidden Susan to do.

Jake sent his administrative assistant Barbara, a middle-aged woman who could have been anything from a full professor to a secretary, to wait for Brandy outside Susan's class. He supplied a fairly detailed description of the girl's appearance, based on the night at The City Restaurant but allowing for the casualness of classroom attire. Barbara said she thought she could do it. The challenge was that Barbara had to follow Brandy far enough from the classroom to talk to her without Susan seeing them. Susan knew Barbara well and would have instantly smelled a rat named Jake Phillips. And would have tried to horn in on the interview.

Barbara had to wait outside the classroom twice, first on Monday and then on Wednesday. Brandy was apparently absent the first time, which made Jake wish he could check her attendance and academic achievement records. Damn the privacy of information laws anyway!

The second time, Barbara confronted the girl, and Brandy replied, "I don't have to talk to anyone I don't want to."

"No," Barbara had told her reasonably, "but Mr. Phillips will go to the Oak Grove police if you don't cooperate with him."

Brandy stared at the woman, trying to judge how serious this threat was. Finally, she said, "Okay. But not today. I've got a lot to do. I'll be there at eight tomorrow morning."

Jake groaned when Barbara reported this. He didn't normally get to the office until at least eight-thirty. But Thursday morning he was there at eight sharp, clutching a third cup of coffee in the hope that it would wake him up. Brandy appeared at almost nine o'clock, and it was hard for him to keep from making a smart, sarcastic remark.

"I'm late," she said, sinking into an upholstered chair in his office, "because I almost decided not to come. You couldn't do anything if I didn't." Belligerence stuck out like a bristle brush.

"No," he said quietly, "I couldn't do much. But I'm sure you want to solve Missy's murder as much as I do, and I thought you might help."

"I don't know anything." Her arms were folded across her chest, and she sunk down in her chair, trying to look bored.

Jake could see that every nerve in the girl was strung tight, in spite of her desperate efforts to appear casual and unconcerned. He looked out the window a long minute, giving her time to relax. Then, casually, as though friend to friend, he asked, "You have a good dinner the other night at The City Restaurant?" *Relax, my foot!* he thought as the girl coiled to attention in her chair. Susan was right: Brandy Perkins was scared to death.

"The City Restaurant? What's that? I've never been any place like that."

"I saw you, Brandy," he said quietly. "I was there for dinner myself, and I saw you."

"How'd you know it was me? We haven't met before."

He shrugged. "I'm a cop." This was clearly not the time to tell her he'd been with Susan Hogan, who had pointed her out.

She sank back in the chair. "So I met my brother at The City Restaurant for dinner. So what?"

"Your brother? Which one—the redhead or the older gentleman you didn't appear to have known before." He didn't add, *Then why did you deny it?*

She hesitated, staring at him appraisingly, wondering how much trouble she was in. Finally she said, "The red-haired one. He's not really my brother—we've just been friends since grade school, and we feel like brother and sister. He wanted me to meet his boss."

"Really? What kind of work does he do?"

"Oh," she waved a hand in the air, "airplanes. He's doing really well, and his boss . . . he's a nice guy. Bought me dinner and everything."

"Did Missy know this sort-of brother of yours?" Jake asked.

She shrugged. "Not really. She may have met him a time or two, but she didn't know him."

She's lying through her teeth, Jake thought. *I've got to save this girl before she ends up just like Missy.* "I don't think you're telling me the truth, Brandy, and I'll tell you why I'm concerned. I don't want what happened to Missy to happen to anyone else on this campus, especially not you."

He saw the look of wild fright cross her face, though she almost instantly covered it with a mask. "Nothing's going to happen to anybody. That was just an accident. You know, some crazy guy picked Missy as his target. Didn't know her, didn't have any reason to choose her except maybe that she was pretty."

"So are you."

She let just the briefest flicker of a smile cross her face. "Thanks. But I'm okay, I really am." She stood to leave and reached out a practiced hand to shake his. "What you really ought to worry about is why that crazy guy stuffed Missy in your girlfriend's trunk."

Touche! She left before he could close his mouth.

Later Jake reflected that the only thing that interview had told him was that Brandy Perkins was lying with every word she said and she was scared. Susan's call-girl theory was becoming more plausible every minute.

Chapter Eight

Susan was doing some secret sleuthing of her own. Remembering how strict the registrar's office was about privacy of records, she went to the housing office. Deliberately, she went at lunchtime, knowing the director of housing and his staff took long, leisurely, off-campus lunches.

"Hey, Nellie, how's it goin'?" She breezed in casually and greeted the secretary, a friend ever since the woman's daughter had taken Susan's American lit survey class and gotten an A. Nellie Thetford was a pleasant woman in her late forties who always carried about her an air of subservience, as though she were constantly aware that in the world of academia she was a mere secretary—uh, administrative assistant. This attitude made her obsequious, and she was given to changing her mood instantly, trying to present whatever attitude she thought was expected of her at any given moment.

"Dr. Hogan! How are you?" Her genuine pleasure at seeing her daughter's teacher made Susan cringe, knowing she was about to abuse the poor woman's trust.

"Fine, fine, Nellie. Nothing new . . . 'cept I guess you heard about the poor girl who was found in the trunk of my car." *Well, there's another white lie,* Susan thought. *I'm not fine. I'm scared, and I'm mad.*

Nellie's face grew solemn. "Of course, everyone on campus knows about it. We all wonder why it was your car somebody put her in." She stared at Susan a minute. "You seem to be okay about it. I mean, if it was my car . . . I'd be . . . oh, I don't know, but I don't think I could just keep on coming to work."

Am I getting paranoid? Does she think I'm guilty because I'm at work? Why doesn't she say she knows I had nothing to do with it and what a tragedy that it was my car. Aloud, she said, "It's hard for me to come on campus, Nellie. But I figure I have to help"— She started to say "clear my name" and then decided that was wrong. "I owe it to that poor girl to help find out who put her in my car. I have some responsibility. In fact, I'm trying to find out a few more things about Missy Jackson."

Nellie's face turned stern with disapproval. "Does Mr. Phillips know you're doing that?"

"Oh, of course he does," Susan lied. "That's why I'm doing it." She leaned forward conspiratorially. "And, Nellie, I think you can help me."

"Me, Dr. Hogan?" She beamed with pleasure again. "If you're sure it's all right with Mr. Phillips . . . "

"He'll be grateful," Susan assured her. "All I need is some information about Missy's roommates in previous years."

"Oh, my!" She drew her mouth into a pucker that reminded Susan of Edith Bunker on *All in the Family.* "I don't know . . . student records."

"Well, of course, I'm not asking for grades or anything. Just some names." Susan had decided if she could worm names and majors out of Nellie, she could track down the students herself.

"Well . . . " Nellie looked around as if to see if anyone was listening. The office was totally empty. "I'll just see what I can find."

Susan nearly took a nap, waiting for the woman to return. She drummed her fingers on the arm of her chair, looked at her watch seven times, and wondered what in heaven's name was so difficult. At long last, Nellie came back carrying a piece of paper.

"Two of her former roommates are still on campus. I wrote down their names for you." She thrust the paper at Susan as though anxious to get it out of her hands.

"Great. Thanks, Nellie." As she stood up, Susan asked ever so casually, "You don't know what their majors were, do you? I'm wondering about a connection . . . " She let that absolutely meaningless sentence drift off.

"Well," Nellie said, "just off the top of my head, I remember that Barbara Buckness was an art major. Very unusual girl. She worked in this office for a while, and I . . . well, I found her difficult."

"Thanks, Nellie. I'll tell Mr. Phillips what a help you've been. And give Rosemary my best—how's her first teaching job going?"

"Oh, just fine, thank you, Dr. Hogan. She loves it, and she still raves about all she learned in your class."

Susan's conscience bothered her as she left the housing office, but not too badly. It was twelve forty-five, and she didn't have office hours until two. She headed for the art department.

The secretary in the art department neither knew nor cared who Susan was. She stared at her computer screen for a long time, apparently bored beyond measure, and finally looked up. "Help you?" she said, her voice flat.

"I'm looking for Barbara Buckness," she said, "one of your senior majors."

"Really don't know where she could be." The woman cracked a piece of gum, and Susan winced. There should be a law against chewing gum anywhere on an academic campus. Then she thought she sounded like Aunt Jenny.

"Do you know her?" Susan asked.

"Yeah, she's a sculptor."

"Terrific," Susan said. "Thanks for all your help." She headed for the sculpture lab, which was empty except for Dan Thurman, the teacher. She introduced herself and told him who she was looking for.

"Barbara Buckness? Yeah, one of my brightest students, got a real good career ahead of her. What you want her for?" He was a muscled, short man with blonde hair cut too short. It looked bleached to Susan. He wore jeans, a tight T-shirt, and he exuded the air of someone who thought himself masculine and irresistible.

"Just want to talk to her," Susan said.

"Well, she's working on that piece over there," he jerked his head toward a stand. Whatever stood on it was covered with a drop cloth, "and I expect she'll be in here about four. She usually works in the late afternoon. I try to come help her when I can fit it into my schedule."

Susan wondered if he was one of those male faculty members who were not averse to a little hanky-panky with their students. One was caught a couple of years earlier when the student reported him, and the resulting scandal cost the associate professor his career and blackened the school's name for a while.

"Thanks," Susan told him. "I'll come back."

"Great. What'd you say your name was?" Without shame or embarrassment, he looked directly at her left hand. His words and tone held an invitation that Susan wasn't interested in.

"Hogan," she said. "English." And with that, she was out the door, hoping he would be gone when she came back to meet Barbara Buckness.

"Hogan?" she heard him exclaim behind her. "The one who . . . "

She was out of hearing before he completed his inquiry.

* * *

Like many art majors, Barbara Buckness dressed the part. She wore baggy cotton trousers, a black turtleneck, and a gray smock-like jacket. The only thing missing was a beret. When Susan entered the studio at four-thirty, the girl was alone, intent on using small, fine tools on the clay figure of a young woman's head.

Susan watched a minute in fascination, because the girl's work dealt with detail which her own eye missed. At last she coughed discreetly—at least, she hoped it was discreet.

Barbara whirled and looked at her. "Yes?"

"May I talk to you for a minute?"

"What about?" It was neither a hostile nor impolite answer, just one of curiosity.

Susan decided to be forthright. "Missy Jackson."

Barbara Buckness was visibly startled. "Missy? What about her?"

It was time, Susan decided, to approach the girl, and she strode across the studio toward her. She was almost next to the sculptured head when she realized with a shock that it was a bust of Missy Jackson. Involuntarily she said, "That's her!"

"Yeah," Barbara said. "I can't get her out of my mind since . . . well, you know. So I thought maybe sculpting her would do it. If it turns out okay, I'll give it to her folks." She looked sheepish, as though she'd been caught doing something naughty. But then she raised her eyes, looked directly at Susan and said, "Who are you?"

Boy, Susan thought, *if they don't take English, you're nobody!*

"Susan Hogan, English," she said, offering her hand and receiving in turn a hand moist with clay. "I'm the one . . . it was my car Missy was found it."

"Oh, yikes, that's right!" Barbara stared at her. "Everyone thinks you did it."

"A few mistaken people think I was involved," Susan corrected.

"Were you?"

"No."

"If you'd known her, you would have been, willingly," Barbara said flatly.

"Really?" she was surprised by the girl's boldness. "I came to talk to you because I heard you roomed with Missy your sophomore year, but I guess you sort of answered my questions already."

Barbara ignored the last part of Susan's statement. "I did room with her, at least first semester."

"But you apparently weren't good friends?"

"No, we weren't. I came to dislike her. Missy had, ah, different interests than I did." She was at work again, scraping away a thin layer of clay here, adding another there.

Susan saw that she looked continually at a newspaper clipping pinned on the wall behind her. It was the picture of Missy that had appeared in the newspaper the day after the girl's body had been found.

Susan seated herself on a stool a few feet away from the young girl and watched silently for several minutes. Finally, she said, "You want to tell me more?"

"Not really. My mother told me never to talk ill of the dead." She didn't look up from her work.

"I take it then you have nothing good to say about Missy? Her record on campus makes her seem too perfect to be true." Susan was thinking that this remarkably blunt and self-contained girl might hold the key to what happened to Missy Jackson, if only she would open up.

"You got that right," Barbara said, whirling to face her and apparently speaking before she thought. Then there was a long pause, and finally she said, "All right. If it was your car, you got a right to know. Missy really worked hard to create that picture of the perfect student. She got good grades, she joined the right groups, she did charity work, but that wasn't her."

"What was?" Susan found herself leaning forward, anxious to hear the truth.

Barbara turned back to her work. "She was scheming, selfish . . . she wanted fame, if that's what being an outstanding student on this campus means, and she wanted money. Always said she grew up poor, and she'd do anything never to be poor again. She practically disowned her parents, didn't want anything to do with them."

Susan remembered those grief-stricken parents. "I didn't think her family was that poor."

Barbara laughed scornfully. "I could have told her about poor on a hardscrabble farm in East Texas, but she never would have listened. She wanted to believe her own story about a miserable childhood as much as she wanted to get rich quick."

"Where did Eric Lindler fit in? I mean, if she wanted money and fame, why was she going to marry a preacher?"

"Marry a preacher?" Barbara's voice was scornful now. "She would never have married that poor boy. He was part of her act, like singing in the choir. Eric Lindler was riding for a fall, a big one, and he was too dumb to know it. Or maybe too naive. He's a nice enough guy, but Missy really had him fooled."

Susan thought about the careful way he'd handled the books in the library and that brown shock of hair that fell in his eyes. He was a good kid, and she right then hated Missy Jackson for what she'd been going to do to him and for involving him in a murder. It dawned on her she hated Missy Jackson for involving her, too.

"Dr. Hogan?" Barbara's voice called her back to the present.

"Sorry. My thoughts wandered." Susan decided to ask the most important question. "Did you see her do anything that would bring her lots of money right away?"

"No." The emphatic answer was followed by a softer, "But I've heard rumors since we roomed together. You better talk to Brandy Perkins. I'm not repeating anything I don't know for sure."

Susan considered for a moment, shifting her weight on the stool to relieve her aching bottom. *How do these kids perch on these stools for hours on end?* "Barbara, tell me one more thing: if you disliked Missy, why are you sculpting her head now?"

Barbara turned to look directly at her again. "Because if I can make this work out, she'll stop haunting me. I may not be Miss Perfect, and I've done some things my folks would be ashamed of, but I never did what Missy did. And I feel, I felt for a long time, that I should have somehow helped her, kept her from . . . " She would never say from what, but Barbara Buckness said one more thing, "We are our sister's keepers, aren't we?" Then she turned back to her work, and the set of her shoulders clearly said she was through talking to Susan.

Susan thought of Shelley. She could never tell this girl that she understood perfectly the need to put away the haunting sense that she had failed as her sister's keeper. "Barbara," she said to the girl's back, "thanks for talking to me. And I think you're pretty terrific."

A mumbled "Thanks" followed her out the door.

Susan's thoughts were in a jumble, but she realized that it was significant that she'd just heard the first truthful description of Missy Jackson. Now, how could she convince everyone else, especially Lieutenant Jordan? And did she want Eric Lindler to know this or would it just hurt him?

Thursday afternoon it began to rain lightly just as Susan left campus on Jake's moped. The dark sky seemed to promise more fall rains, for which everyone would be grateful except Susan if she got caught in a downpour on that damn moped. Stuck down in one of the side compartments she had a plastic parka of sorts that went over her head and waterproofed her completely but brought out her slight tendency toward claustrophobia. She had no adequate way of protecting her books and papers and hadn't thought to bring the plastic bag she usually used in case of rain. If she put the parka over the books, she'd get soaked—but that, she decided was probably the best plan, if it rained hard. *Maybe I can beat it home*, she told herself with fingers crossed for good luck.

She had parked at the library, and as she rode down the hill on Main Street south of the campus, Susan eased her foot off the accelerator to slow down without having to brake so hard the moped would skid. To her alarm instead of slowing the moped picked up speed. It was still getting gas, and its acceleration was increased by the downhill slope. Susan felt a sudden panic, gripped the handles of the moped tightly, and looked in the rearview mirror. Behind her, an old Ford driving far too close to her forced a fast decision. Later, Susan thought she would have gone on downhill if it hadn't been for that car, but making a split-second decision, she chose to try for the turn to the right, even though that wasn't the direction she wanted to go. Heart pounding and vision blurry from fright, she made the widest turn she could. The Ford went straight, and Susan was so busy fighting to control the moped that she never saw it slow down to a crawl as the driver looked back in her direction.

With the moped still gaining speed, she braked as hard as she dared. But the combination of speed, wet pavement and loose gravel was too much. Susan's stomach threatened to come up in her throat and her heart stopped for a minute—she would later swear to Jake that it did—when the moped skidded, turned sideways and went down, her right leg under it. A sharp pain in her ankle made her feel instantly nauseated, even though she had eaten nothing for hours.

Shocked, she lay still for a minute, letting the sickness pass and trying to figure out how she felt. She moved her arms gently, shrugged her shoulders, turned her head, and decided everything but the one ankle was intact. But she couldn't move the bike off her leg. And she felt like a trapped animal lying there with her leg caught—it made her think of beaver caught in those awful spring traps that were now illegal.

Within seconds, of course, she was surrounded by spectators, some of them students, who had appeared from nowhere. They shouted a chorus of questions. "You all right, Dr. Hogan?" "Holy cow, how did you do this?" She managed to regain her composure and answer them coherently. In fact, she was sharp with the young man who wanted to know how she did it. "I didn't! The moped did!"

Several students helped her bend her left leg so that they could slowly and carefully lift the moped off her other leg. Just as they were doing that, Seymour, one of Jake's patrolmen, drove up. "Don't move her!" he ordered.

"Wasn't about to," said one student. "Just wanted to get this thing off that leg."

Seymour knelt by her. "You okay, Dr. Hogan?"

She shook her head. The ankle was really throbbing, and she didn't want to cry in front of all these people. A deep breath enabled her to say, "All but my ankle, I think."

Seymour's fingers were surprisingly gentle as he explored the ankle. Even so, that nausea-causing pain shot through her again. "I think it's broken, but it ain't a bad break. Bone's in place. Maybe just a crack, but we'll have to have it x-rayed." He took off his slicker and put it over her shoulders. "I'll just call Jake. He can splint it good enough to take you to the emergency room."

"My books," Susan said through gritted teeth. "Would you see they don't get wet?"

It was raining harder now, and he looked around helplessly. "Soon as the patrol car gets here," he said and began talking into his cellular telephone.

A tall young man with a burr haircut threw his waterproof jacket over her books, and Susan tried to smile at him. "I'd give you an A if you were in my classes," she managed to say, and he grinned and gave her a thumbs-up sign.

"Maybe I'll take one just for that," he said, water beginning to drip from his hair onto his face.

By the time Jake arrived, Seymour had propped her head on a volunteered book bag and was hunkered down beside her, talking softly. Jake was all business.

"How'd you do this?" he asked tersely, and Susan knew the anger in his voice concealed his concern.

"Slid on the gravel," she muttered.

"Going too fast, I bet," he said. Jake went to the Jeep for his first-aid kit. The burr haircut followed him with her books. Jake just nodded and didn't even say thank you.

"Okay, Susan, I'll be as gentle as I can, but it's gonna hurt. Bite on Seymour's hand if you have to."

"Boss!" Seymour yelled.

"Well, at least let her squeeze your hand, would you?" Jake slipped the loafer off her foot and asked, "These good pants?"

"Yes," Susan muttered.

"Damn," he said under his breath. "At least the pant leg's a little wide. I'll see what I can do without cutting the pants."

For just a moment, Susan forgot her pain. "Cut my pants?"

He ignored her. Gently, Jake pulled her pants leg up as close to the knee as it would go and then pulled a blue plastic tube over her leg. Then somehow he inflated the tube—Susan could feel it put slight pressure on her lower leg. "There. You can run a race now," Jake said.

"Thanks," she muttered.

"That'll keep it from moving till we get to the hospital," he explained, "but don't walk on it. Let us help you."

She was helped to her feet ever so carefully. Then Jake picked her up and carried her to the back of the Jeep where she could stretch out. "The moped?"

"I can probably fix it," Jake said. "Don't see any major damage to it."

That wasn't what she'd meant. He probably could fix the damn moped easier than her ankle would be fixed. "We can't leave it here," she said.

"Seymour'll take care of it."

Then she voiced her next worry. "Aunt Jenny."

"I'll call her. Susan, would you stop worrying and let me take charge. Please?"

She lay back on the carpet in the car and felt the vehicle begin to move. Jake drove even more carefully than usual so as not to jar her ankle. She heard him punching buttons on his car phone.

"Aunt Jenny? Jake. Nothing serious, but Susan's had a little accident . . . Yes, it was on that blasted moped, but it's not serious. I think it's a broken ankle. Yes, I've had a little emergency med training. Have to for my job. Yes, ma'am, we'll have a real doctor look at it and x-ray it. I'll call you from the hospital. What? Sure, chicken soup would be a good idea when she gets home." He punched the "end" button and said over his shoulder, "I don't think she trusts me."

"She's always been a worrywart," Susan said.

"I bet you gave her lots of cause to worry too."

"Some," she admitted. Then, "Jake? Is this . . . is this like someone trying to run me down with their car?" She didn't want to tell him how scared she was. It wasn't the pain. It was the idea that someone was deliberately trying to hurt—or kill—her.

"Nope," he said with confidence. "It was too much speed on a wet road."

"I took my foot off the accelerator," she said slowly, "but it didn't slow down."

"Mopeds don't react like a high-performance car," he said.

Susan decided to give up the conversation, but she wasn't reassured.

At the hospital they gave her pain medication that made her goofy. Jake's face swam in front of her as she lay on the gurney, and she clutched his hand to make the room stop spinning. He stayed by her side every minute except when they actually took the x-ray. In seconds after that he was back, accompanied by a doctor who said, "Nice, clean break. Lower portion of the fibula."

"My ankle?" Susan asked.

"Not really," the doctor said cheerily. "The lower portion of the smaller bone in your leg. But it's not badly swollen—that's the good news—so we can go right ahead and cast it. I'll just cut the cast a bit so it'll have some give and take. I'll have to cut your pants off."

Susan opened her mouth to protest but Jake beat her to it. "Doctor, can't we slide them off. They're good pants, and she'll yell like a banshee if you ruin them."

The doctor looked at him. "You her husband?"

"No, but I know her well enough to help you take those pants off."

The doctor grinned, and together they eased the pants down without jarring the leg.

Then Jake asked, "You said no swelling was the good news. What's the bad news?"

Groggily, Susan realized that they were talking about her as if she weren't there—or were a half-wit. She opened her mouth to protest but nothing sensible came out.

"She'll be on crutches for several weeks," he said.

Now Susan wanted to shout, "Then why are you so damn cheerful?" But she couldn't form those words either. At least her leg didn't hurt so badly any more.

Casting the ankle or leg or whatever seemed to take an hour, but finally the doctor gave Jake instructions about keeping her off her foot, out of the shower, and making her use crutches when she had to move about. "Much as possible, she should keep the foot elevated."

She began to recover her speech. "I can't do all that at school," she wailed.

"You're not going to school," the young doctor said, his voice still irritatingly cheerful, "for at least three or four days. Then we'll see."

Susan thought he was probably an intern. She opened her mouth to protest but was stopped by one word from Jake.

"Susan!" He said it firmly, like an order, and she was reminded for the second time that day of *All in the Family*, when Archie Bunker used to say, "Stifle, Edith."

"Take one of these every three or four hours as needed. Fewer you have to take, the better. And practice walking on those crutches while he's around." He jerked his head toward Jake. "More people hurt themselves falling off crutches . . . " On that note, he was gone.

* * *

Aunt Jenny greeted them with great solicitation for Susan, effusive thanks for Jake, and the news that good hot chicken soup waited on the stove. Susan sipped at small spoonfuls of the soup, grateful for its warmth but not really hungry. Her hazy mind was trying to figure out how to arrange for her classes, notify Dr. Scott—all the things that had to be done to keep her daily world going while she was immobilized. And beyond trying to think about practical things, Susan was wondering what had happened to the moped. She knew, she just absolutely knew, she had been driving carefully.

Jake's mind was on practicalities. "I'll call Ellen, and she can notify Dr. Scott. Just tell him you broke your ankle in a freak accident. No need to tell him it was on the moped." Jake also knew that it would sit badly with the English department chair if he himself called. "I'll get your books out of the car. You can get a lot done on that Zane Grey stuff," he said cheerfully. When he returned he plopped the books on the table and said, "Okay, let's get you ready for bed."

"It's only seven o'clock," Susan protested.

"You're going to take another of those pills, and you'll sleep through the night," he assured her.

With Jake's help, Susan was up on the crutches. The doctor was right—they were awkward and scary, as though they might slide away beneath her. She remembered once seeing a newborn colt trying to take its first steps—that was how she felt.

"Take Aunt Jenny with you to the bathroom," Jake said. "And brush your teeth and do everything you have to now, 'cause you're not getting up again."

"Jake Phillips," she said, "you're bossy!" But she did as she was told.

"You're not going to sleep in that T-shirt and underwear, are you?" Aunt Jenny asked aghast. "Jake is still out there in the hall."

"It's better than the blanket I had wrapped around my nether portions when I came home from the hospital," Susan yawned. If Aunt Jenny hadn't been there, Jake would have helped her out of her clothes himself, but there was no sense upsetting her aunt with that revelation.

Jake did carry her from the bathroom to the bed—pretending to struggle under the weight—and tucked her into the covers as though she were a child. Then he handed her a pill and a glass of water.

She took them obediently, and as Jake predicted she was out in minutes. He sat by the bed with her until her even breathing told him she was deep asleep. Then he went into the kitchen in search of Aunt Jenny.

"She'll probably sleep much of tomorrow. Just kind of try to get her to eat, and watch out if you hear her head for the bathroom in the night. She's too big for you to hold up, but you might steady her."

Aunt Jenny's hands were on her hips. "She's not too big at all. I can still take care of that girl!"

He laughed. "I'm sure you can, Aunt Jenny. And I'm glad you're here to help her now." Actually, a hidden corner of him wished Aunt Jenny weren't around so he could stay with Susan. A thought occurred to him. "Maybe I should sleep on the couch?"

"Go on with you now, Jake. You get out of here. I can take care of things."

"I'll call in the morning," he said, and then he planted a quick kiss on Aunt Jenny's cheek.

She watched him go, her hand on that spot on her cheek and a smile on her face. "I like him," she said softly to herself. "How can I let Susan know that without making her rebel?" Jake Phillips wasn't the only one who understood Susan Hogan.

Jake ran to his truck with his chin tucked down to his chest to avoid the rain that was still coming down fairly hard. He never saw the old Ford that sat a half block from Susan's house.

Chapter Nine

Susan slept most of the next day, drifting in and out, but it was not a peaceful sleep. She fought to consciousness frequently to wipe out images of cars coming at her and mopeds turning over. Missy Jackson's face kept surfacing before her eyes, and once she saw Dr. Scott with his arm around Brandy Perkins. Awake, she managed to make the bathroom on her crutches without accident and to go into the kitchen for more of last night's soup. "Aunt Jenny," she asked, childlike, "would you make meatloaf and mashed potatoes for dinner?"

"Comfort food?" her aunt asked. "I surely will. I'll just go to the market this afternoon while you sleep."

"Can you find it? It's . . . if you go north on Main toward the campus, you'll come to Albertsons. Or you can take Park to Broad, turn left and go to Winn-Dixie. That's not what it's called now, but . . . "

"I can find a store," Aunt Jenny said firmly.

Susan was sound asleep and never knew that Aunt Jenny's trip to the grocery took over two hours. If confronted, Aunt Jenny was prepared to explain that she had just taken a little sightseeing tour to get out of the house and then the market didn't seem to have what she wanted—not the right brand of ketchup and the potatoes were awful so she had to pick carefully and . . .

Actually, she went straight north on Main to Subie's Café on the square. There was only one waitress, and Jenny presumed she was the Margie Jake had mentioned. She ordered pecan pie, and when Margie brought it, Jenny started a casual conversation, since there were few patrons in the restaurant at two in the afternoon.

"I'm just in from Wichita Falls, visiting relatives," she said. "and I want to explore Oak Grove. But I'm so horrified about what happened to that coed. Is this town safe?"

Margie gave a harsh laugh. "Sure, the city's safe. Someone just was after that girl, and I bet it was that Dr. Hogan from the university. That's what the police think too. I know her well," Margie said. "Her and Mr. Phillips, they eat in here all the time. Chicken-fried steak for him and a hamburger for her." Margie apparently had forgotten that she told Jake she thought no one was safe in their beds anymore, and Aunt Jenny didn't know about her earlier opinion that she had apparently narrowed down.

"That so?" Aunt Jenny asked, pretending a certain level of disinterest. "My, this is such good pie."

"We make them ourselves," Margie beamed. Then, conspiratorially, she said, "You know, I like Dr. Hogan. She's, well, she's different, doesn't act like I think a university professor should, but . . . "

Jenny Hogan groaned inwardly at that assessment of her niece. "But what?" she asked.

"But it's so hard to realize that she killed a student. I just can't imagine what could have made her do it."

"You sure she did it?" Jenny asked.

"Who else?" Margie shrugged. "The police are sure. I hear they're goin' to arrest her any day now. We get lots of cops in here and . . . you know . . . I hear things. You want some more coffee, hon?"

Jenny had heard too much of Margie's talk. "No, thanks," she said, "but, my, that was good pie. I'll be back."

"You do that, hon."

Actually, Jenny thought the piecrust was tough and the pecan filling too syrupy. Her own pecan pies were much better. On Main she passed Albertsons and thought she might just as well do her shopping there. She found what she needed, though she didn't think the ground beef was up to her standards, and made her purchase.

She was still so flustered and worried about the possibility of Susan being arrested that she drove right past Susan's house, ended up in the country, and had to backtrack for a mile. When she got to Susan's house, she was relieved to find her niece still asleep.

Back in Susan's kitchen, she set about mixing ground meat, cracker crumbs—she had no idea how to work the Cuisinart and laboriously crumbed the crackers by putting them in a plastic bag and beating on it, softly of course, with a rolling pin. Then she added egg, a little tapioca to make it hold together, ketchup, Worcestershire, mustard, and onion for flavor. Then she patted it all into a pan. Next she carefully peeled the potatoes, the peel so thin that it was transparent—Aunt Jenny didn't believe in wasting potato but neither did she like those newfangled mashed potatoes with the skins still on them. And all the time she worked, one question sang in her head: "What if they arrest Susan?"

Susan woke to delicious smells wafting through the house, and she knew that she was hungry, even famished. She also felt more awake and normal than she had since the accident. A look at the clock told her it was nearly five. Jake would be coming soon to check on her—and no doubt expected to stay for dinner. Aunt Jenny would be scandalized if she greeted him in a T-shirt and panties, no matter how long the shirt. She couldn't manage jeans, she hated her only terrycloth housecoat unless the temperature had dipped below freezing, and she was darned if she was going to put on a dress. A denim split skirt solved the problem, the wide legs slipping easily over the cast. A clean T-shirt, and she was ready for the world. She made her way to the kitchen on crutches.

"Susan! You should have called me. It's a wonder you didn't fall and break the other ankle."

"Thanks, Aunt Jenny," Susan said dryly. Then, "Dinner sure smells good."

"I've fixed the meatloaf and mashed potatoes you wanted, beets and greens—who'd have thought I'd find beet greens in the market?—and frozen corn." She shook her head sadly. "It's better than the canned. And I fixed an apple pie. Apples are so good right now."

Jake arrived with news that Susan's classes were being taken by Ellen, and she'd be by the next day to bring papers for Susan to grade. Dr. Scott had taken the news of Susan's accident with a muttered, "I told her not to ride that thing to school" and said no more. Ernie Westin was sneering about the moped and probably, Ellen reported, went straight to Scott with the story. The provost had called Jake to make sure Susan was all right. He couched the call in strictly impersonal terms.

"I understand one of our faculty members had an accident on campus, and you helped care for her, Jake. What can you tell me?"

Jake gave him an equally impersonal report. "It wasn't technically on campus, sir. It was on Main Street, so the university has no liability. Susan's leg has been set, and she'll be on crutches a while, but she'll be okay." The provost hung up reassured.

Susan wasn't sure who ate more or faster at dinner—she or Jake—but the meatloaf was delicious, moist and meaty with just enough cracker crumbs to bind but not enough to overwhelm the meat. Aunt Jenny buttered the beets and squeezed lemon over the greens, and she had liberally salted and peppered the corn. Susan thought she detected garlic in the potatoes, which would have been new and trendy for Aunt Jenny, but she didn't say anything.

Jake pushed back from the table. "Aunt Jenny, I can't tell you when I had such a good meal. Certainly not since I've been seeing your niece here." He looked at Susan and grinned.

She started to kick him under the table, but the slightest movement reminded her that her right leg wouldn't do that right now. "I haven't seen you make meatloaf," she said sarcastically.

"'Cause I couldn't ever make it like Aunt Jenny," he replied complacently.

They had just finished their apple pie and were sipping on strong but decaffeinated coffee when the doorbell rang. Jake went to the door.

"Mr. Phillips? I wasn't expecting you."

Susan recognized the boyish young voice—it was Eric Lindler.

"I wasn't expecting you either, Eric," Jake said. "What brings you here?"

"I heard Dr. Hogan was hurt, and she was kind to me the other day, and I just, well, I wanted to come tell her I was sorry, make sure she was all right."

"Eric!" Susan called, ignoring Jake, who was frowning and worrying just a little about how Eric knew where Susan lived. "Nice of you to come by. Come on in."

Aunt Jenny was in the kitchen, piling dishes in the sink. She turned to stare as Eric Lindler entered the house. He went straight to the table where Susan sat and said, "Dr. Hogan, I was really sorry to hear what happened to you, and I just wanted to tell you that. I can, you know, run errands for you or do anything like that."

"Thanks, Eric," Susan said sincerely. "Right now, between Jake and Aunt Jenny, everything's okay. You know Mr. Phillips?"

Eric nodded. "Yes, ma'am. We met . . . Missy, you know."

The two shook hands, and Jake said a sort of mumbled "Good to see you again" even while he wondered what could possibly be appropriate in these circumstances.

"And my aunt, Miss Jenny Hogan," Susan said.

Aunt Jenny came forward drying her hands on her apron. She shook hands with Eric, looked straight at him for a long minute, and then said, "Pleased to meet you, I'm sure."

"Have a seat, Eric," Susan said. "Aunt Jenny, can we get him a Coke?"

"Yes," Aunt Jenny said and promptly appeared with a warm can of Coke.

Jake winked at Susan, took the Coke, and said, "Let me get you some ice, Eric."

"Oh, no, sir, I like it that way. Really I do."

They almost had a tug-of-war about it, but finally Jake filled a glass with ice, poured the Coke into it, and gave it to Eric.

"How are you?" Susan asked.

The boy knew it was more than a casual question. "I'm doing okay, Dr. Hogan. I have ups and downs, but I'm doing okay. My roommate, Tony, he's really been helpful." He brightened a little. "We went to see a movie the other night. First time I've been off campus."

Jake was watching the boy closely. Finally, he asked, "You talked to Lieutenant Jordan lately?"

Eric turned. "No, sir. I figure he'll call me if he finds anything out. I just hope they find out who did it pretty soon. I'm not keeping my grades up like I should and . . . "

Something prompted Susan to ask, "Have you heard from Missy's parents?"

He shook his head. "No, ma'am. They're . . . well, they're strange people. They didn't much think I was good enough for Missy. And I think they're grieving so hard they can't reach out to other people."

Both Jake and Susan were astounded just then to hear Aunt Jenny demand in a stern voice, "Young man, have you had dinner?"

Eric looked up, startled. "Uh, no, ma'am. I'll go to the Main when I get back to campus."

"I'll just fix you a plate," Aunt Jenny said, leaving no room for further protest. And fix she did—a huge plate of all the good home-cooked things they'd had for supper. She sat at the table long enough to watch with satisfaction while Eric cleaned his plate.

Having eaten rapidly, he stood up to take his plate to the sink. "Miss Hogan," he said, "I haven't had food like that since my grandma cooked for me. I thank you, I really do."

"You're more than welcome, son," Aunt Jenny said, and her voice softened some.

Eric made his farewells almost as soon as he finished eating, making Susan promise to call him if he could run errands or do anything to help.

After he left, Jake and Susan both stared at Aunt Jenny, who had gone back to the sink and was washing dishes. Susan had tried to get her to use the dishwasher but she snorted and said it only spread germs around. She preferred the tried-and-true method.

"What was that about?" Susan asked. "One minute you're sure he's a murderer, and the next you're feeding him."

Aunt Jenny turned to face them, wiping at her forehead with a soapy hand. "I didn't say I changed my mind. He killed that girl, but he still has to eat. And he's sort of pitiful. I may take it on as a project to fatten him up."

"For death row?" Jake asked sarcastically.

"Don't you make fun of me, Jake Phillips," she said sternly. "I hope to heaven that nice boy won't end up on death row. I think he'll plead temporary insanity when this is all over. What is it they say, a crime of passion?"

Jake sat down beside Susan. "I've thought of that," he said. "I've thought a lot about it. But someone who kills in a passion just simply kills. He doesn't go to all the planned-out trouble that this killer did to hide the body and yet make sure it was found. That's premeditated. It suggests a mind that's thought things out."

Susan was inclined to believe Aunt Jenny's theory. If Eric Lindler had been the murderer, it was a crime of passion—but that wouldn't explain why someone was still after her, leaving dead kittens and causing moped wrecks. No, she was sure Aunt Jenny was wrong—the redheaded stranger was the real murderer.

Susan's mind was whirling with the possibilities the two of them had brought up, and she slept badly that night, especially since she had refused to take another of the pills that made her so fuzzy. This time, her dreams were filled with Eric Lindler and a baseball bat and a redheaded stranger. When Aunt Jenny commented the next morning that she looked tired, she said she'd slept fitfully because of the pain medication. But when Aunt Jenny went out on the deck to knit in the late fall sunshine, she called Jake at home since it was Saturday.

"Eric didn't do it," she said, without even saying "hello."

"Nice to talk to you too, Susan," he replied. "I can't guess what's on your mind."

"You've got to find out about that red-haired stranger . . . or go to Jordan with the story."

"Susan, there you go again. I'm working on it, and to tell the truth, I'm not going to Jordan because it would cause a scandal for the school."

"You're withholding evidence," Susan said, her voice rising in alarm.

"No," he replied patiently, "I'm withholding your wild suspicions." He paused, and Susan could hear him take a deep breath. "Susan," he said slowly, "Dirk Jordan is talking about a search warrant."

"What's he want to search?"

"Your house and your office."

"My house? For a baseball bat?" Susan was furious. "He should be out finding out who the killer is, and he's wasting time looking at me?"

"You're not the only one who thinks he should be finding out who the killer is," Jake said wryly. "He's been getting pressure from the girl's parents and Eric Lindler. Jordan says Lindler is pushing him about the search warrants."

"Eric? I thought he was my friend. I thought he was indignant that any suspicion was cast on me."

"I thought so too," Jake said, again speaking slowly, as if he were thinking and talking simultaneously. "I can't quite figure it all out. Anyway, this is Saturday, so they probably won't be there until Monday. I don't figure Jordan thinks it's a rush."

"Well, they better search Eric's dorm room too," Susan said and slammed down the phone.

Jake winced on the other end. Second time this week she's shot the messenger, he told himself.

Susan made her way on crutches to the deck to join Aunt Jenny. While the older woman chatted about Indian summer and how she thought she'd try going to the Oak Grove Christian Church this Sunday and whether or not Jake would like chicken or pot roast better for dinner, Susan stared into space.

* * *

Aunt Jenny told Susan the next morning that she'd not only attend church services, but she'd go to the seniors Sunday school class. "If it's a bunch of boring old people, I won't go again."

Susan noticed her aunt dressed with care in her best suit-dress, an avocado-green affair with brass buttons that had made Susan bite her tongue as she said, "How nice you look, Aunt Jenny," remembering the days when Aunt Jenny wouldn't dream of going to church without white gloves and a nice small hat. Aunt Jenny picked up her practical brown handbag—which did not go with her practical black shoes with one-inch heels—and headed out the door.

"I'll be back right after church," she said to Susan. "You'll be all right?"

"Of course," Susan said. "Jake will come by before you get home, I bet."

Aunt Jenny smiled benevolently and went out to the street where her car was parked. When she put it in gear and stepped on the gas, she took off with a squeal that made Susan wince.

Jake came over about noon, expecting Aunt Jenny to fix lunch.

"She should be home any time," Susan told him. "She just went to church."

"I'll make tuna sandwiches," he said.

Jake was the only man Susan had ever known who not only liked tuna salad, but he made a great version. This time he put a thick layer of tuna between slices of good rye bread, added pickles on the side, and served the plates with a flourish—and a beer for him and white wine for Susan. They ate on the deck, but Susan began to fret.

"Where could Aunt Jenny be? Did she get lost between here and church? Jake, church has been out for an hour."

He was unconcerned. "Aunt Jenny can take care of herself. And if she needs us she'll call."

"That's another thing. She doesn't have a cell phone. Calls them newfangled gadgets. What if she's lost on some highway out in the country? She has no way to call."

"Susan," he sighed patiently, "stop worrying. Aunt Jenny will be here when she's here. If she doesn't come in time to cook dinner, I'll go get steaks."

It was almost two-thirty in the afternoon when Aunt Jenny breezed in and found them still on the deck, Susan on her second wine.

"Where have you been? I've been frantic with worry. How can you take four hours to go to Sunday school and church?"

Jake, still occupied with the Sunday paper, wished he could disappear. Susan made a strangling noise when she saw a man behind Aunt Jenny.

Aunt Jenny gathered her courage and said, "John, this is my niece, Susan Hogan."

Susan turned so that she could hold out her hand, but John Jackson was staring at her.

"Susan Hogan?" he asked. "The one who's all but indicted for killing that girl?"

Red spread across her face as Susan said, "I guess that's me."

He stared at her a long time, as though measuring her. Finally, he asked, "You do it?"

She stared back and saw a man she could respect and trust. "No, sir, I did not."

"Didn't think so," he said, "but they've sure got to pin this one on someone quick. You watch yourself, girl."

Before Susan could say any more, Jake rose and came forward to introduce himself. When he said, "Jake Phillips, sir, pleased to meet you," the older man replied, "Judge John Jackson, son, and it's my pleasure."

Susan stood with her mouth open. Where had Aunt Jenny found a judge? And why had she brought him home with her? All of Susan's worry and anger at Aunt Jenny's lateness disappeared.

Judge Jackson stayed for a cup of coffee. When Jake offered him a shot of bourbon, he grinned and said, "Wish I could, son, but it's a mite early in the day for an old man like me." Jake had his coffee straight too.

The four of them sat on Susan's deck and talked about everything but the murder, for which Susan was glad. Judge Jackson told them that Aunt Jenny was the first woman with an ounce of sense who had come to the senior class in two years, and he couldn't resist asking her to Sunday dinner. He hoped Susan wasn't too angry.

"Oh, go on with you," Aunt Jenny said, blushing and making a gesture as though to push away his flattery.

Susan assured him it was all right. "Aunt Jenny disappears sometimes," Susan said, "and I worry about her."

"I'll try to see you have no more cause to worry," the judge said gallantly. Then he sobered, "I expect you've got enough to worry about anyway. If I can help you, girl, you let me know." He fished in his pocket and produced a dog-eared business card that had simply his name and phone number.

"Thanks," Susan said, taking the card casually. She didn't expect to need the advice of a retired judge.

After the judge left, Jake looked at Aunt Jenny a minute and then asked her, "Where is your car? Did you forget it at the church?"

Aunt Jenny shook her head firmly. "I did not forget it. I left it there on purpose. I had my own reasons."

Getting Judge Jackson to meet me, Susan thought and was for a moment amazed at the scheming nature of her supposedly dithery aunt. "Aunt Jenny, tell us about church."

"The seniors class was disappointing," her aunt said. "Several old couples, three overweight women who banded together and stared at me, and one lone man who seemed to be sleeping through the lesson on the Minor Prophets. I sat next to him, as far as possible from the three women. Every once in a while, the man nodded, as though agreeing with the discussion leader, and at least twice he stared at me."

Susan sighed. Aunt Jenny's version of the story was long-winded.

"I decided he was not asleep but merely listening with his eyes closed. He looked fairly tall, though hunched down in his chair as he was, I couldn't tell for sure. His hair was silver gray, the kind that must have once been coal black and turned gray nicely, not like mine that simply turned sort of watery yellow-gray. I thought he looked like a nice man to know."

"The beginning of a romance," Jake said dramatically. "Go on. Tell us the rest."

"Jake Phillips, it's not a romance. He's simply a nice, interesting man. And being a judge . . . well, I thought I should explore." Then she hastily added, "Because of Susan, of course."

But Susan caught her unconsciously fluffing her hair.

"After the class," Aunt Jenny went on, "he reached out a hand to welcome me. Told me his name, and I screeched because I thought he was related to that poor dead girl." Her face turned red. "Everyone who was about to leave the room turned to stare at me."

"'And?'" Susan asked. "Tell me he's not."

"No. He said, 'That girl? What girl?' Then finally, he said, 'Oh, the coed that was murdered. No, no relation. Common name, that's all. Why?' I didn't want to tell him so I just said she'd been on my mind. And when he asked my name, I didn't want to tell him the last name because I figured he'd identify me with Susan and it was too early for that. He asked me to sit in church with him, and I was glad for the company."

"So church was out at noon," Susan said, "and you didn't get home until after two."

Aunt Jenny positively beamed. "After the benediction, he suggested lunch at Luby's Cafeteria on the highway. He said he always gets turkey on Sunday, so I got turkey, though I really would have preferred roast beef. Over dinner, he told me that he had lost his wife of fifty-two years some eighteen months ago and was still trying to learn to live alone. But when he told me he'd been a state court judge for thirty years, I really paid attention. He may be of help to you, Susan."

Jake took Aunt Jenny to retrieve the car.

When she came back, Aunt Jenny said, "Oh my, I haven't even thought about supper."

"Steak," Jake said. "I'm on it." And went to the grocery.

Chapter Ten

Ellen Peck was at Susan's house Monday morning when two uniformed officers came, unannounced but not unexpected, with a search warrant. They were followed by Dirk Jordan, who apparently arrived in a separate car. Susan had intended to go back to work that day but the expected search of her house made her postpone her return to campus one day. She called Mildred in Dr. Scott's office and told her she wouldn't be in for one more day.

"You just take all the time you need, Dr. Hogan," Mildred said in a voice that dripped with imitation sugar.

"Who does she think she is, giving me permission?" Susan ranted aloud, though no one was around to hear or to answer the question.

Ellen had arrived waving a copy of the *Daily News*, the student newspaper. "Today's paper," she said, shoving it at Susan. "I figured Jake probably never reads it and wouldn't bring it to you."

Centered on the front page right under the headline was a picture of Susan lying trapped under the moped. In the background a few students could be seen hanging around, and Seymour was kneeling by Susan. Jake was nowhere in sight. A boldface cutline read, "English Prof Crashes." Susan groaned. "So much for not telling Scott how I broke my ankle," she said.

"Oh, he guessed immediately," Ellen said without much sympathy. "And nothing stays secret on a college campus. You know that."

"I guess," Susan said, staring morosely at the picture. "The photographer got there pretty quick. Looks like he beat Jake, but I didn't see him—or her. I guess my mind was pretty well occupied with my leg and getting out from under the damn moped, but still . . ."

"That's how the *Daily News* operates," Ellen said cheerily. "Never there when you want them, always when you don't want them. And they never get the facts straight, unless you particularly don't want them to. Then they're eligible for a Pulitzer."

Susan grinned a little, appreciating Ellen's attempt to lift her spirits. She wondered how much Ernie Westin had to do with the picture getting on the front page of the paper. He was, she remembered, friendly with the journalism professor who directed the student newspaper.

"I taught your women's lit survey class Friday, and just to impress them I took roll. Brandy Perkins was the only one absent."

Susan made a note to check on Brandy. She was worried about the girl—even without knowing that Jake, too, was worried. Meantime, to Ellen, she said, "Great. If you'd take it again today, I'll be back in full swing tomorrow. Got to get this search thing over with."

"What search thing?" Ellen asked, just as the front doorbell rang. Ellen went to answer it, looking out through the glass front door as she crossed the living room. "Susan, what are policemen doing here?" she called out.

"That's the search thing," Susan answered, hobbling behind her. "Jake told me Saturday they'd gotten a search warrant to go through my house and my office. Won't Scott love it when they show up at the English department?" Her light tone masked a deep sense of fear. She knew they wouldn't find anything, but the invasion unnerved her.

"A search warrant!" Ellen's voice was angry as she went to the door and opened it. She stood, hands on her hips, looking at an officer who towered over her.

"Susan Hogan?" The man's voice was tense. "Got a search warrant here."

While Ellen gestured in her direction, Susan said, "I'm Susan Hogan. Show me the warrant." She wouldn't know any more after looking at it than she did before, but she felt she ought to demand to see it.

"Officer O'Donnell, Oak Grove Police Department, ma'am. Need to search the premises, ma'am," he said, handing her the paper. "Lieutenant Jordan will be right here."

Susan pretended to read, though the words swam in front of her eyes. She pictured strange men pawing through her underwear drawer, cataloging the outdated prescriptions in the medicine chest, laughing at the leftovers Aunt Jenny had put in the back of the refrigerator. "Go ahead. Try not to disturb anything." She fought to keep her voice level.

"Yes, ma'am. We'll be careful, but we'll need to ask you to step out of the house." He looked at her crutches. "You need help, ma'am?"

"No. I can make it by myself." Susan was too proud to accept the offered hand.

O'Donnell handed her the crutches and mumbled, "I'm sorry for the inconvenience, Dr. Hogan."

Ellen said, "Let's go have a cup of coffee. My treat."

By now, one officer was busily moving things about in the pantry, and the other was searching the refrigerator. Susan wanted to ask if he really thought he'd find a baseball bat in the refrigerator.

Just then, Aunt Jenny emerged from her room where she'd been making the bed. Susan had forgotten about her aunt.

"What's going on here?" Aunt Jenny demanded, her voice rising into the near-hysteria range. "Get out of my icebox!"

O'Donnell looked at Susan. "Can you take her with you, please, ma'am?"

Aunt Jenny planted herself between the deputy and the refrigerator. "I am not going anywhere. What are you people doing?"

Susan hobbled toward her aunt, realizing too late that she'd forgotten to warn the older woman about the search warrant. "They're searching the house. They have a warrant."

"Why ever would they want to do that?" Aunt Jenny demanded.

"They're looking for the baseball bat that killed Missy Jackson," Susan said as patiently as she could.

O'Donnell threw Susan an alarmed look. Suspects were not supposed to have such specific knowledge about what the police were looking for.

"Well, my goodness, why would it be here? That Lindler boy has it." Aunt Jenny picked up the kitchen towel and began to wipe at her perspiring forehead, even as O'Donnell turned to stare at her in disbelief.

"Excuse me, ma'am, but how do you know this person . . . Lindler . . . has the baseball bat?" The words were barely out of his mouth when O'Donnell was cursing himself for giving away official knowledge.

Aunt Jenny fixed him with a stare. "I just know," she said.

"Ma'am, if you have knowledge you're not sharing with the police . . . " His tone was not threatening, but still a threat hung in the air.

Susan gave him what she hoped was a withering look. "She means she knows by intuition. It's what her heart tells her."

"Oh." The man was humbled but not so much that he didn't turn to Aunt Jenny and say, "Now, ma'am, if you'd just go with these ladies . . . "

She clutched the kitchen counter, as though they'd have to drag her from it. "I am not leaving this house while you people are invading my niece's privacy. We may sue. I have a friend who's a judge."

Susan said a silent prayer of thanks that Jake was not here for this scene. And she bet that Judge John Jackson would have been more than a little disturbed if he knew his influence was being dragged—well, almost—into things.

The second officer, who apparently took orders from O'Donnell, looked to him for instructions and direction. Just then Lieutenant Jordan strode into the house.

"What seems to be the problem here?" he asked briskly.

"Well, sir . . . " O'Donnell was reluctant to admit he was having difficulty making three women, one of them elderly, obey his orders. "They . . . this one"—he jerked his head toward Aunt Jenny—"refuses to leave the house."

Jordan shrugged his shoulders and said, "Okay, let them stay."

"I need to sit down," Aunt Jenny announced. Her face was so red—with indignation, Susan supposed—that even Jordan was alarmed. He helped her to the couch and pulled up the footstool for her.

"You just sit there and relax, ma'am. We'll be out of here as soon as we can."

"I still want that cup of coffee," Ellen announced with determination.

"Me, too," Susan said. "You fix it."

And so the three of them sat in the living area—the two younger women sipping hot coffee and the older one fanning herself with a copy of the journal of the Modern Language Association she'd picked up off the coffee table. The officers were silent, not talking much to each other and certainly not banging and slamming drawers and doors as Susan had imagined. Still, it seemed they were in the house forever.

Suddenly Jordan strode into the room. "Dr. Hogan?" His voice was businesslike.

When Susan turned to look at him, she saw that he was holding a baseball bat. "Where'd you get that?" she asked, her voice rising into a squeak.

"Back of your closet. It's got blood on it . . . and some paint that looks like it came from your car."

"That's absolutely impossible," Susan said. "I do not own a baseball bat, never had one, and there was not one in the back of my closet."

"Susan," Ellen asked, "when was the last time you looked in the back of your closet?"

"Well . . . " Susan chewed on her answer. Sometimes things piled up in the far corners of the closet, and she didn't get to them for weeks at a time. "I don't know . . . not since the murder, I guess." As soon as the words were out of her mouth, Susan wondered if she'd incriminated herself somehow. What she meant was that someone could have hidden that bat at any time since Missy Jackson's death, and she' have never known it.

"Dr. Hogan, you'll have to come down to headquarters with me." Jordan's voice was crisp and authoritarian, and Susan thought she detected just a bit of smug satisfaction in it. "You're entitled to representation, if you want," he added, his tone implying she shouldn't want it.

"Representation?" Susan muttered. "I guess I better call Jake."

"No!" Aunt Jenny interrupted dramatically. "Don't use your one phone call on Jake. I'll call *Judge* John Jackson."

Susan looked at her in amazement. "You can't do that. And besides, I want Jake to be there."

Just as Aunt Jenny said smugly, "John said to call him anytime you need help."

Jordan looked at Aunt Jenny. With obvious dismay, he asked, "Judge John Jackson?"

"That's right," Aunt Jenny said vigorously. "The judge!"

Jordan groaned inwardly. Judge John Jackson was a known stickler for hard facts. Circumstantial evidence never got anywhere in his court. And he could be obstinate, drawing out an argument, challenging the police on every little detail. If he'd said it once, he'd said a thousand times that it was his job to protect the little people. *Susan Hogan,* Dirk Jordan thought, *is not one of the little people. She's an educated, sophisticated woman and for some reason she's killed a young girl. I have to find out why, and that old coot Jackson is going to get in my way.* "Why don't you invite them both," he said to Susan. "I have a feeling it's going to be a big party."

As Susan was led out of the house, she asked Jordan, "Aren't you going to handcuff me?" Her tone revealed both fright and anger.

Jordan ignored her, but O'Donnell answered, with a note of apology in his voice. "Please, Dr. Hogan," he said, "don't make this any more difficult for us than it is."

Jordan looked at O'Donnell and, in true detective-novel style, said, "Cuff her, if that's what she wants."

"Sir, she's on crutches!" was O'Donnell's plaintive reply.

Susan ignored Jordan and hobbled behind Officer O'Donnell to his car. She rode to police headquarters in the squad car with the two officers, while Jordan followed.

Thank heaven they're not blaring sirens and flashing lights! Susan thought. Ellen and Aunt Jenny were behind in Ellen's car, and Jake met them at the station. By then Susan was feeling light-headed from shock.

"Susan, don't say a thing," Jake cautioned. "I'll call a lawyer."

The worry on his face almost consumed her, and she reached for his hand. "Aunt Jenny has called Judge Jackson. He said he'd be here as soon as he could."

Jordan came out of a doorway down the hall where he'd briefly disappeared, saw Jake and ignored him, saying to Susan, "Right this way, please, Dr. Hogan."

"She's got counsel on the way here," Jake said quickly, stepping in front of Susan as though to shield her. "She won't talk until he's here."

Jordan gave Jake a disgusted look. He'd been hoping this would be an open-and-shut, over-with-quickly situation. It was obviously getting more complicated by the minute.

Just as Jordan had dreaded, Judge John Jackson got in his way big time. "You can't hold my client until you have clear evidence that is the bat used in the murder . . . and even then it's circumstantial. There are any number of ways it could have gotten into her house."

"Such as?" Jordan asked.

"Someone planted it there. Seems obvious to me."

"You mind if I ask your client a few questions?" Jordan asked, fixing the elderly judge with a look of distaste.

Jackson shrugged, and Jordan turned to Susan. "Have you ever played baseball?"

"Nope. Too clumsy," she said. Immediately she thought of Jake and his warning not to be flip. Nerves were making her silly. "No," she said more evenly. "I'm not very athletic. Never was. You can ask my aunt."

"That won't be necessary," Jordan said dryly. "If you aren't athletic, why did you have a baseball bat in your closet?"

"I didn't!" Susan's voice rose in anger. "I never saw that bat before, and I sure never put it in my closet. Someone's trying to frame me!"

"Frame you?" Jordan's voice rose with interest. "And why would someone try to frame you?"

Just as Susan said, "Beats me," Jackson held up his hand. "Jordan, you know you can't ask my client questions for which she can't possibly have an answer." His tone was patronizingly familiar, and that irritated the investigative officer even more.

Susan's thoughts tangled in confusion. If Brandy Perkins had told the young man with red hair that Susan was nosing into Missy's murder, then he was probably the one who was trying to scare and frame her—maybe if he could get her convicted of murder, he wouldn't have to kill her. That thought made her giddy for a brief second. The young man didn't know where she lived, but how hard could it be for him to find out? He could have left the kitten and killed the plants, but when could he have put the bat there? With Aunt Jenny visiting, her house was almost never empty. An eerie question popped into her mind: *If he put it there the night of the murder, before I got home, then he did pick my car deliberately. Why?* The thought scared her, but not badly enough that she wanted to tell Jordan about the redheaded stranger. She agreed with Jake: if Jordan knew about that, he'd bulldoze over the entire situation and they'd never get to the truth. And it wouldn't keep Jordan from accusing her of murder.

"Dr. Hogan," Jordan said evenly, "let's go back to the homicide investigation you were involved in fifteen years ago. Why didn't you tell me when I first asked? Surely you didn't forget."

Forget? I'll never forget Shelley lying on that bathroom floor! She wanted to lash out at him for even suggesting that. "I didn't forget, but it wasn't a homicide. We've already been over this."

"But this is an official interrogation. You were considered a suspect, weren't you?"

Susan looked him straight in the eye. "For about five minutes," she said. "I was never . . . what's the word you used? Booked? Or charged? Or anything. I went voluntarily to talk to the police and tell them what I knew about Shelley's drug use." A part of her wanted to cry out all over again with the agony of that telling all those years ago.

"Still," Jordan said relentlessly, "you initially withheld information from me."

"Jordan," the judge said impatiently, "try to be reasonable. You are not interrogating a crack cocaine dealer or a mass murderer here. You are intimidating a woman you've mistakenly accused of murder."

The officer threw him a disgusted look, asked Susan a few more questions, and said in a tired voice, "I'm booking you on suspicion of murder. You'll go before a judge this afternoon"— he looked at Jackson and was tempted to add—"a *real* judge," but he didn't. "Bail will be set. I'm sure it will be reasonable."

"You're arresting me?" Susan asked incredulously. Her thoughts whirled again. This kind of thing didn't happen to people like her. It was . . . well, it was what you read about in books or maybe the newspaper. But it didn't happen to ordinary, everyday people.

"Yes, ma'am, I am," the detective said wearily.

Officer O'Donnell, already embarrassed by the whole thing, took her to an office where she was read her rights—what did they call that? Mirandizing? Bastard English if she ever heard it—and subjected to the indignities of being fingerprinted and photographed. Susan submitted to it all in kind of a daze.

She had not been allowed to see Jake or Aunt Jenny or Ellen again, and when she asked about them, O'Donnell told her, "They've left."

"Left?" Susan had never felt more alone in her life. She didn't know why, but it would have made her feel safer or something to think they were still somewhere in police headquarters. Where had they gone? What were they doing?

* * *

What Jake and Ellen were trying to do was comfort Aunt Jenny. The three of them were back at Susan's house, sitting in the living area, and Aunt Jenny was sobbing loudly, her chest heaving, her face once again alarmingly red. Ellen was more worried about her right now than she was about Susan.

Jake went to the kitchen, and Ellen followed him to whisper, "I almost want to throw cold water on her. You know, shock her out of it."

"Not a good idea," he said grimly, reaching for the bourbon bottle. "This is for medicinal purposes," he said. "You go get a cold rag for her face." Then he poured just a small bit of bourbon into a juice glass and took it to Aunt Jenny with the order: "Sip this."

She stopped sobbing long enough to smell it and make a face. "I don't like spirits," she said, her voice coming with great heaves of her chest that seemed to leave her breathless.

"It's medicine," Jake said, and his tone made it clear he would tolerate no disagreement.

Aunt Jenny sipped, screwing up her face in distaste.

Ellen returned with a cold washrag, which she pressed to the older woman's head.

The sobs subsided, though now the silence between the three of them was punctuated by an occasional hiccup—the aftermath of heavy crying. "I'm so sorry," Aunt Jenny said brokenly. "We need to be worrying about Susan, and I've caused all this fuss. Such a baby"—the word set her off again into tears—"she's my baby. I just can't bear the thought of her in a jail cell."

"She's probably not in a cell at all, Aunt Jenny, and Judge Jackson has gone to arrange bail. He'll need some money . . . " Jake thought he'd just post the bail himself, but then he wondered if it would help Aunt Jenny to be involved.

"My life savings!" she said dramatically. "Whatever it takes, whatever I have . . . it's hers."

"It won't be that much," Jake said kindly. "Probably a thousand dollars. I thought perhaps the two of us—"

"No, no! Susan's my responsibility. I insist." She grabbed her purse and with shaking hands signed a check, the signature barely legible. "Here, you fill out the rest of this. I can't . . . I simply can't."

Ellen stared out the window. "Scott will suspend her now, for sure," she said.

"Suspend?" Aunt Jenny's voice rose as if this were another unexpected blow. "Why would he do that?"

"If she's officially charged with a crime—it's in the faculty handbook or whatever," Ellen said. "But Scott will take such delight in doing it. And Ernie Westin will do a victory dance."

Jake nodded. Then, suddenly, he rose and went down the hall to the bedroom. Ellen could hear him talking softly on the phone. When he came back, he said, "I called Atwater. It's . . . well, it's my duty, sort of, to keep him informed." He paused. "He's coming by to see Susan tonight. I'm to call him at home when she's released."

Ellen nodded. She hoped Susan realized how lucky she was to have Jake on her side.

"Aunt Jenny," Jake said, "what's for dinner tonight?"

Flustered, the older woman ran her right hand through her hair, making it stand on end. "Dinner? Oh, Jake, I can't think about dinner."

"Be the best thing you could do for Susan," he said. In truth, he thought cooking dinner would distract Aunt Jenny.

She seemed to be thinking. Then, suddenly, she burst out with, "Pot roast! That's it. I was going to cook pot roast before all this happened."

"Why don't you cook it now?" he asked gently.

Aunt Jenny pushed herself up from the couch and headed for the kitchen, where she donned an apron and was soon flouring a good-sized piece of beef. As she worked, she hummed a little to herself. She was so busy, she didn't see Jake wink conspiratorially at Ellen.

Still, Ellen and Jake heard her say, "I wonder what poor Susan is doing right now?"

* * *

"Poor Susan" was actually in what Officer O'Donnell called a "holding tank" when he led her there. It was a huge wire cage in an even larger room. There were three such cages in what almost looked like a gym or a temporary building—one cage held two men who looked to be homeless and seedy and undesirable, the next held a sullen, disheveled woman who refused to look up as Susan approached, and the third was empty. Susan was grateful that O'Donnell chose that one. He opened the gate, helped her inside, and pointed to a bench where she could sit. Her leg ached fiercely, and she longed to have something to prop it on as the doctor had ordered, but she refused to ask O'Donnell. He must have seen pain in the expression on her face, because he returned with a straight wooden chair.

"Here, prop your foot on this," he said.

If Susan had been herself, she'd have recognized that he was a really kind man. Now, all she could do was mutter, "Thanks."

She sat staring into space, trying to sort out what had happened to her in the last few hours. She had been sitting in her own home, quietly tending a broken leg, and now here she was—an accused criminal booked on suspicion of murder. *At least,* she thought with irony, *nobody can kill me in here.*

"What's somebody like you doin' here?" The sullen woman in the next cage had come close and was staring at her belligerently. Susan was glad wire walls, no matter how flimsy, separated them.

"You'd never believe it," Susan told her.

"They said I beat my kid," the woman said in a monotone. "Took her to the hospital and brought me in here. It ain't right, I tell you. I never hit that child." Fumes of alcohol drifted toward

Susan, and she realized that even before noon the woman was drunk.

A thousand questions raced through Susan's mind. How old was the child? Boy or girl? How badly hurt? *Don't,* she told herself, *get involved in someone else's troubles. You've got enough of your own.* "Sorry," she muttered and turned her back.

It was the longest four hours of Susan Hogan's life, and she knew now why you saw movies with people frantically shaking the bars of their jail cell. It was all she could do to keep from pressing her face against the wire cage, getting as close to freedom as she could. Panic seemed to lurk just beneath the surface of her consciousness, and she had to remind herself sternly that she was not claustrophobic—at least not much.

People came and went from the area all the time, every single one of them staring at her in curiosity. No one spoke. The men in the far cage could be heard muttering, even shouting at each other occasionally, and the woman closer to Susan moaned, groaned, and finally threw up on the floor. The stink wafted Susan's way, making her almost as nauseated as she'd been when she'd felt the bone in her leg break. Eventually the mess was cleaned up, but Susan thought the odor lingered.

At noon, they gave Susan a small carton of milk, a bologna sandwich (which she could not eat), and an apple. At two, O'Donnell came for her. "Judge's ready for you, Dr. Hogan."

"Doctor?" screeched the woman in the other cage.

Susan hobbled out of the cage, with O'Donnell carefully helping her.

Judge Jackson acted as her appointed counsel. Obviously he knew the judge on the bench, for there was a familiarity between them, even given the protocol of the courtroom. Susan sat behind a table, facing the judge. Behind her, in the spectator seats—is that what you'd call them?—she saw Jake, Ellen and Aunt Jenny, the latter wearing the most worried look Susan had ever seen.

When the judge asked her how she pled, she raised her head and said clearly, "Not guilty." In spite of the strength of her answer, she felt detached, as though this were all happening to someone else, and she, Susan Hogan, was watching it from a distance. She opened her mouth, thinking maybe she should explain to the judge why she couldn't have murdered Missy Jackson, but Judge Jackson laid a firm hand on her arm, signaling her to be quiet. Jake would have said, "Shut up, Susan!"

Beginning with "Your Honor," Judge Jackson launched into a litany of Susan's virtues, her position at the university, the fact that her aged aunt—did he really dare say that?—was living with her, all of which made her unlikely to flee the court's jurisdiction.

The judge, a bespectacled man of sixty or so in a dull gray suit, asked, "Dr. Hogan, are you planning to leave this county any time soon?"

Dumb, Susan thought. *If I were, would I tell you?* Aloud she said, "No, sir, I have to stay here and prove that I did not murder Missy Jackson."

The judge pounded his gavel, announced bail set at $100,000 and said, "Next?"

Absolutely overwhelmed, Susan sank back down in her chair. Knowing she could never come up with $100,000, she envisioned herself sitting forever in that wire cage. But Judge Jackson handed her the crutches and said, "Let's go home."

"Home?" she echoed vaguely.

"Home," he said. "Your aunt has already arranged bail."

Susan's voice squeaked. "She doesn't have a hundred thousand. I . . . she can't do that."

Patiently the judge explained how bail bondsmen worked. "She only had to put down a fraction of the money, and you can only cost her money if you run. I know you won't do that."

When she passed through the swinging half-door that separated the court participants from the spectators, Susan found herself in Jake's arms. And the next thing she knew, she was sobbing harder—and louder—than she ever had in her life.

As they left the courtroom, they passed Dirk Jordan, who looked none too happy. Susan was sure he wanted her locked up, with the key thrown away. But Jake held out his hand to Jordan and said, "Dirk, anything you can do to soft-pedal this in the newspaper will be appreciated."

"You know I have no control over them," Jordan muttered. "I'll see what I can do."

* * *

When they got back to Susan's, Jake settled her on the couch and said, "I have to go make a call. I'll be right back."

Knowing that he was going to call Dr. Atwater, Ellen said, "I better be going. I've . . . well, I've missed the whole day."

"Yeah, you have," Susan said, "my classes and yours both. Scott'll be fit to be tied. But, thanks, Ellen, for being with me today. You're a good friend."

Ellen came over and gave her a hug. "Sure, Susan. I wouldn't have done anything else, Dr. Scott be darned."

"Do two more things for me?" Susan asked, and when Ellen nodded, she said, "Check on Brandy Perkins. I don't care if she's not coming to class—well, I do but I don't—but I want to be sure she's all right." She didn't add, "And not missing mysteriously." Then she said, "And tell Scott I really will take my classes over tomorrow."

Ellen's mouth flew open in alarm at Susan's last words, but she managed to say calmly, "Sure, Susan." Then she left in a hurry.

Jake came back into the room to announce, "Dr. Atwater's on his way over. All right if I give him some of my bourbon?"

Susan's stomach drew itself into a knot. The provost didn't visit faculty at their homes, and she could think of only one reason for his coming here. "You told him, didn't you?" It was an accusation, and there was almost a tone of bitterness about it.

Jake met her gaze steadily. "Yes, Susan, I told him. I wanted him to know before Dr. Scott found out. I thought it was in your best interest. If I'm wrong, I apologize."

Susan put her head in her hands. "Sorry, Jake," she mumbled. "I'm so touchy, so scared."

He was beside her on the couch in an instant, his arms strong around her. "Susan, Susan, you mustn't be scared." He stroked her hair and murmured, "I promise I won't let anything bad happen to you."

But you may not be able to stop it, she thought. She wouldn't have said that aloud for anything.

From the kitchen, Aunt Jenny watched them and tears slid down her cheeks.

Chapter Eleven

Dr. Atwater arrived about five o'clock. "Susan," he said, approaching the couch where she still sat, "so good of you to let me come by at a time like this."

Susan was taken back. He had the shoe on the wrong foot. It was good of him to come by, but she didn't know how to say that. And she was afraid, knowing what he'd come to say, she'd break down and cry any minute. "Jake wants to share some of his bourbon with you," she said as lightly as she could.

Jake made the introductions between Dr. Atwater and Aunt Jenny, who eyed him with suspicion. Then Jake poured shots of bourbon neat for himself and the provost and Chardonnay for Susan. "Aunt Jenny?" he asked.

She shook her head. "Jake Phillips, you're trying to make an alcoholic of me. Bourbon in the middle of the day."

Dr. Atwater looked startled, and Susan, upset as she was, giggled. "Did you really, Jake?"

He nodded to indicate he really had given the older woman bourbon in the middle of the day. But he didn't add that it had helped calm her down.

Atwater pulled the footstool close to the couch, so that he could look directly at Susan. "You know what I've got to tell you, don't you?"

She nodded, biting her lip.

"Do you also know how difficult this is for me? How much I want to make it happen some other way."

"I think so," she managed to quaver.

"The suspension is only until this . . . this *damn* mess is cleared up. Then you'll be reinstated at your same rank. Meantime, you'll continue to receive your pay. And, Susan, by my authority,

I'm postponing your tenure review one year."

Her voice was shaky. "Can you do that?"

He pretended offense. "Of course I can. I'm the provost." Then, more seriously, he said, "This whole thing is out of control, and I want it cleared up as soon as possible. You're one of our best teachers, and I want you back in the classroom. I trust Jake here to help me accomplish that."

By then, Susan was so overcome she could only mutter, "Thank you."

Atwater and Jake talked about the legalities of the case, but Susan barely heard them. After a few minutes, the provost came over to her, put his hand on her shoulder, and said, "Let me know what I can do to help, Susan. I'm on your side."

She looked at him. "Will you tell Dr. Scott you talked to me?"

He fought to hide a grin, which indicated to Susan that the provost understood only too well the nature of his English department chair. "Yes," he said, "I'll do that first thing in the morning. You get some rest—I suspect you need it." Then, too heartily, to Jake he said, "If I could spare you some vacation time, I'd suggest you take this woman to the Caribbean. But sorry, Jake. I need you here right now."

Jake grinned. "The Caribbean doesn't sound bad. Maybe over Christmas break."

"It's a deal," Atwater said, "and I'll buy you dinner for two wherever you decide to go."

Jake walked the provost out to his car, while Susan sat stunned on the couch. Her car was wrecked, someone was trying to kill her, she was charged with murder, and she had lost her job. And, at the lowest point in her life, Jake could talk about a Caribbean vacation.

* * *

When Jake came back into the room, he stood staring at her for a long time. Finally, he spoke softly. "Feeling sorry for yourself?"

"Why shouldn't I?" she asked bitterly. "What else could go wrong?"

He shrugged. "Not much, I guess. But the Susan Hogan I know and love doesn't go much for self-pity. What're you going to do now? Spend all your time sitting on the couch thinking how unfair life's been to you?"

Susan shifted uncomfortably, and when she spoke her voice was defensive. "I can't move around much, and you have forbidden me to do anything that would even remotely seem like I was trying to investigate the murder on my own."

Jake grinned ever so slightly. "Can't you work on your Zane Grey book, go for drives with Aunt Jenny, do the things that lots of women do."

The prospect haunted Susan. She could see days dragging into weeks when she had nothing to do and woke every morning wondering in desperation, "What can I do today?" That, she realized, was the one thing that could make things worse.

"I have to find out who killed Missy Jackson and why," she said with sudden, fierce determination. "Otherwise, I'll do just what you're warning me against. I'll sit around and feel sorry for myself."

Jake looked straight at her. "A couple of promises," he said. "Promise me you won't take chances, and promise me you won't do anything against the law." It never occurred to him that he should make her promise not to lie to him.

Susan nodded. "And I won't tell you anything I'm doing."

"I don't know about that," Jake said. Warning bells were playing a concerto in his brain.

"Pot roast is ready," Aunt Jenny called. "Dinner's in ten minutes. Susan, dear, you feel like eating after all that's happened to you today?"

"I'm hungry, Aunt Jenny. Got to keep my strength up."

Aunt Jenny gave her a puzzled look.

Just as they sat down for dinner, Eric Lindler knocked on the door.

As he got up to let him in, Jake muttered, "The kid's got radar that tells him when food's on the table."

"Tsk, Jake, you be kind now," Aunt Jenny remonstrated. She got up from the table to set an extra place.

"Oh," Eric said as Jake stood back by the open door to let him pass, "you're eating dinner. I'm sorry. I've come at a bad time."

"No, no," Aunt Jenny said, putting down silverware and a plate. "You just join us, young man. I bet you could use some meat and potatoes."

Eric grinned charmingly. "If you're sure it's not an imposition . . . well, yes, I could. But I didn't come at dinnertime on purpose."

"Of course not, Eric," Susan said. If she was surprised that he had the nerve to come here after insisting the police search her house, she hid it well. "Why did you come?"

"I . . . I wanted to apologize, Dr. Hogan. I hear you've been charged with Missy's murder, and I feel it's my fault."

Eric Lindler, she decided, *was a much more complicated young man than she thought at first.* "Why is it your fault, Eric? Because you insisted they search my house? After you told me you knew I had nothing to do with the murder? That doesn't make sense to me."

Jake shifted uncomfortably in his chair and reminded himself that in a way he'd given Susan license to explore. He just didn't know she'd start right in front of him at the dinner table or that she'd start with Eric Lindler—everyone pretty much agreed that Eric was innocent.

Eric didn't hesitate. "The police, well, they're after me every minute, and I never know what to say to them. I mean, I've told them everything I know, and they still want more. So, finally, just to get rid of them, I said, 'Oh, go check Dr. Hogan's house.' And that's just what they did."

"Why'd they arrest you?" Eric asked. "I'll go to Lieutenant Jordan and tell him I know you're innocent."

"They arrested me because they . . . " Susan hesitated. "Because they think they found incriminating evidence in my car." She started to tell him they'd found the baseball bat in her closet and then thought better of it. Later, she would realize that Jake was careful not to mention that too, and she prayed Aunt Jenny would keep silent. And only much later did it occur to her to wonder how Eric knew the police had been there.

"And, Eric, you can't tell Lieutenant Jordan I'm innocent, because you don't know that unless you know who killed Missy. Do you, Eric?"

Even Susan's questions didn't faze his appetite. He took another bite of pot roast, chewed it, and then looked at Susan with that youthful, innocent expression. "No, ma'am, I don't know. I really don't."

"Eric, do you know a young man—older than you—with wavy red hair?"

Eric seemed to think a long time, meanwhile filling his mouth with carrots and potatoes. At long last, he asked, "Can you tell me his name or anything more about him?"

"He's been seen on campus," Susan said. "I wondered if Missy knew him. Brandy Perkins does."

Instantly, Eric was alert. "Brandy has a lot of friends I don't approve of. They're evil. And I warned Missy to stay away from them. But I don't know any of them by sight—I just know what Missy told me. So I guess I don't know the one you're describing, Dr. Hogan."

"Susan, your dinner is getting cold. Let the poor boy eat in peace, and you eat, too," Aunt Jenny said, and Susan devoted herself to her meal. Apparently no one else could think of anything to say, and the dinner became a silent one.

Eric finally broke the silence. "I have no idea what kind of evidence they found, Dr. Hogan, but I'll do everything I can to prove that you're innocent. And, again, I'm sorry. I never meant them to think you had anything to do with Missy's murder. I was just . . . well, I guess I lost it. I was so desperate to get rid of them."

Jake watched the young man carefully. "Eric," he said slowly, "desperation shouldn't make you change your behavior, say things you don't mean. As long as you know you're innocent, you should be able to put up with the constant official attention."

Aunt Jenny sat at the end of the table, her mouth frozen open, a bit of roast on her fork held halfway between her plate and her mouth.

"I know that, Mr. Phillips, and I . . . I guess it's a weakness in me. I've prayed to the Lord for strength, but I'm still so confused. At any rate, I really am sorry I seem to have pointed them in your direction again, Dr. Hogan. I know you didn't have anything to do with Missy's death."

Aunt Jenny recovered herself, put the bit of meat back on her plate and said, "There, there, young man. We know you didn't mean to harm Susan. You just eat that dinner, and you'll feel better."

Aunt Jenny's solution to anything, Susan thought, is to feed people.

After dinner, Eric offered, indeed almost insisted, on doing the dishes, and eventually Eric and Jake did dishes, while Susan and Aunt Jenny sat in the living area. It was too cool for the deck.

"I never did believe in letting men do dishes," Aunt Jenny said, patting her hair into place and smoothing her apron. "They won't get them clean, and I'll just have to wash them again tomorrow."

"Jake will get them clean," Susan assured her.

After Eric left, Susan said, "Aunt Jenny, I was afraid you'd tell him they found the baseball bat here. Somehow . . . I don't know why, I don't think we should tell him . . . if he doesn't already know."

"He knows," Aunt Jenny said. "He put it here, so he'll be able to guess they found it. And now he knows you're lying to him. I don't know who that redheaded man you mentioned is, Susan, but he didn't put the bat there."

Oh, yes, he did, Susan thought, *and he tried to kill me.* But she wouldn't tell Aunt Jenny that. She hadn't even told Jake her suspicion that the bat was placed in her house the night of the murder, which meant her car was chosen deliberately. Why still remained a great mystery to her.

* * *

Next morning, Susan was up before Aunt Jenny. She started a pot of coffee and made her way to the deck to retrieve the newspaper, spreading it open so she could see the front page. Dirk Jordan had indeed done his best. An article in the lower right-hand corner of the page, with a modest headline, proclaimed "Murder Weapon Found." No pictures, nothing to draw attention, no indication in the headline as to what murder. Only when you read the two-column short piece did you learn that a baseball bat had been found in the home of Dr. Susan Hogan, that the police had charged her with murder, and that she was free on bail.

"Damn!" she said, throwing the paper across the deck.

Midmorning, she called Ellen Peck in her office to tell her about the suspension.

"I already know," Ellen said. "So does everyone in the department. Scott posted a memo first thing."

"Damn!" Susan said for the second time that morning. She told Ellen about Dr. Atwater's house call and said, "Atwater promised it would be handled tactfully, that he'd talk to Scott. What's the reaction in the department?"

"Just what you'd expect," Ellen told her. "Most are shocked, and some have spoken up in your defense, saying it's ridiculous and so on. Lucy Hernandez and Jim Hofstadter both offered to be character witnesses for you. But others are keeping noticeably quiet—and avoiding me."

"And Ernie Westin?" Susan asked.

"Gloating, of course," Ellen said.

"What he doesn't know is that Atwater put my tenure review off for an entire year."

"Really?" Ellen said, and then quickly added, "That means we'll both come up at the same time."

"Yeah, but we won't be in competition, like Ernie is with the world—and specifically me." She paused a minute. "Ellen, I didn't call to talk about tenure. I need some things from my office. Can you get them for me? I'm not supposed to set foot on campus."

Ellen giggled. "You can't set foot anywhere—except on crutches. But, yeah, I'll get whatever you need."

"Good. I may have a plan by the time you get here."

"Why do I think I should be worried?" Ellen asked. "I expected you to go into a deep depression over all this, and you sound . . . activated."

"Thank Jake for that," Susan said.

* * *

Ellen came by in the afternoon, carrying a cardboard box full of Susan's Zane Grey research, her Rolodex, and some other personal items she'd requested.

"So, what's your plan?" she asked.

Susan shrugged. "I haven't got one yet, and that's really frustrating me. I know, Ellen, I just know this all hinges on that redheaded stranger, but I don't know what to do about it."

"I suppose," Ellen said, "you'll let me know when you decide?"

Susan looked at her and saw that she was laughing. "Well," she said ruefully, "I won't call Jake, that's for sure."

"I am worried now," Ellen said. She stayed to drink iced tea with Aunt Jenny and let the older woman quiz her about her background, her boyfriends—none at the moment, which made Aunt Jenny shake her head in despair.

"Well," Ellen said a shade defensively, "it's a pretty small campus. Unless I want to go out with Ernie Westin . . . "

"That awful man!" Aunt Jenny said. "He's been almost as unkind to Susan as that terrible Dr. Scott. Now I like that Dr. Atwater that was here the other day . . . "

"He's married already," Ellen said.

"Oh, my, I didn't mean that. I just meant that he's a nice person."

"Maybe," Ellen said mischievously, "I could steal Jake away from Susan."

Aunt Jenny frowned again. "Oh, no, my dear, you mustn't try that! Jake's the best thing that's ever happened to Susan." She glanced sideways at her niece to see if that offended her, but Susan was paying no attention to their conversation.

Ellen covered Aunt Jenny's hand with her own. "I was just teasing, Aunt Jenny. I think Jake is wonderful for Susan."

Susan finally tuned in on them. "I'm not so bad for Jake, either," she said.

"Penny for your thoughts," Ellen prompted.

"Redheaded strangers and cars zooming backward toward me," Susan said. "I don't know if I'll ever be able to think about anything else."

As Ellen left, Aunt Jenny warmly urged her to come for dinner one night, and Ellen bit her tongue to keep from asking, "With Eric Lindler?"

"I just don't feel I can cook tonight," the older woman said. "I'm . . . you know, I'm so upset by all this."

Ellen hugged her. "Don't be upset, Aunt Jenny. I'm betting on Susan."

* * *

When Jake arrived, Susan announced, "Aunt Jenny doesn't feel she can cook tonight."

"Subie's Cafe?" Jake suggested.

"What?" the older woman demanded, trying to sound puzzled. *What if that Margie person recognizes me?*

"Come on, we'll give you some old-fashioned Texas café cooking," Jake said, gallantly offering his arm to Aunt Jenny and leaving Susan and her crutches to fend for themselves. Susan gave him a black look, but she knew that he had done that deliberately.

"Looks like the Pioneer Restaurant in Wichita Falls, only worse. Greasier. And smaller," Aunt Jenny said when they drove up. "Let's just go home. I'm feeling better. I'll fix you all a *good* dinner."

"Now, Aunt Jenny," Susan said, "we're here, and we're hungry now. Just wait. It's your kind of food." She was too hungry to put up with going back to the house and listening to Aunt Jenny flutter over what to cook.

"But not," Jake muttered under his breath, "her kind of cooking."

They sat at a booth, and Jake handed Aunt Jenny a plastic-coated menu. She perused it with a frown on her face. "I bet the chicken-fried steak is tough," she said.

"It isn't," Jake agreed, "and I'm going to order it. Always do."

"The hamburgers greasy?" she asked.

"How can you have a non-greasy hamburger?" Susan asked. "That's what I'm having. A greasy hamburger with greasy fries."

Aunt Jenny sighed. "I guess I'll have the meatloaf. How can your ruin meatloaf and mashed potatoes?"

Jake and Susan exchanged long looks.

As luck would have it, Margie came to take their order. She stared long and hard at Aunt Jenny. "You been in here before? Didn't I talk to you just a couple of days ago?"

"Oh, my, no," Aunt Jenny said. "You must have me mixed up with some other old gray-headed lady."

"Guarantee, she's never been here before, Margie," Jake said.

Aunt Jenny noticed that the whole time she took their order, Margie avoided looking at Susan. When it came time to take her order, the waitress said curtly, "Same as always, Dr. Hogan?"

"Yes, please, Margie," Susan said.

After she left the table, Susan said, "Jake, she's ignoring me. She knows I'm almost a convicted murderer."

"Maybe she reads the newspaper," Aunt Jenny said, reaching across the table to take her hand. "Now, Susan, you can't go assuming people think you're guilty. That will . . . well, it might convince them. You know what Dr. Norman Vincent Peale said . . . "

"Not now, Aunt Jenny. I'm in no mood for Dr. Peale's brand of positive thinking. I'm more for positive action."

Jake bit his tongue so hard he almost said "Ouch!"

As it turned out the meatloaf was almost up to Jenny's standards—"a bit too much green pepper in it," Aunt Jenny said. But the mashed potatoes were satisfactory. Aunt Jenny enjoyed her meal. She told a white lie and said she liked her pecan pie. "Nice, flaky crust. Bet they used lard. Only way to have a light crust."

Susan thought she might gag at the idea of eating lard. She was glad she had decided against dessert.

As they left, Margie said, "I could swear you was the woman ate pecan pie the other day. But she didn't know Dr. Hogan." Suspicion laced her voice.

"Well, I know her," Aunt Jenny said distinctly. "She's my niece."

They left Margie standing with her mouth agape and went to pay at the cash register.

"I hope you didn't leave a big tip, Jake," Aunt Jenny said.

On the way home, the three of them jammed into the cab of Jake's pickup. Aunt Jenny said with determination, "That settles it. I'm cooking for you two as long as I'm here."

"Won't get any argument from me," Jake said, "but I feel like we ought to give you a break. Tell you what, we'll take you to The City Restaurant in Fort Worth next weekend."

Susan knew he said it spontaneously, but the mention of The City Restaurant conjured up a vivid image of Brandy and the red-haired stranger. And then it gave her an idea—an idea she wouldn't dare tell Jake.

"The City Restaurant?" Aunt Jenny asked in a puzzled voice.

"Sure. Aunt Jenny, I'll treat you to the finest steak you've ever eaten."

"Oh, my, steak," Aunt Jenny said in a high quavering voice. "But you've cooked such good steaks for us, Jake. I don't need one at fancy restaurant prices."

"You're worth it, Aunt Jenny," he said. Jake reached across Susan to pat Aunt Jenny's hand. "It's settled. I'll make reservations for Saturday night."

Susan fidgeted. She had to talk to Ellen as soon as possible.

After Jake had kissed her demurely and left, Aunt Jenny said, "Susan Hogan, you best marry that man. Maybe you should let him spend the night occasionally."

"Aunt Jenny!" Susan said with amazement.

Then she went to call Ellen and slammed down the phone in frustration when there was no answer.

That night, Susan lay in bed wide-eyed. Jake's unexpected mention of The City Restaurant had given her the clue she sought all day. The answer to the whole mess lay at the restaurant. She was convinced of it. Somehow, if she was to clear her name, she had to corner that redhead. And she sure couldn't do it with Jake and Aunt Jenny in tow—and her own foot in a cast. Nor could she wait until Saturday—this was only Tuesday. She'd try Ellen again first thing in the morning.

* * *

"Ellen? Susan." Susan called as soon as she thought Ellen would be in her office. It was eight-thirty.

"I'd have never guessed," Ellen replied over the phone.

"Can we meet for lunch? I don't want to go to the Main, but"—she lowered her voice to a whisper—"I don't want Aunt Jenny to hear what we talk about."

"Wow! Now I'm really curious," Ellen said. "My classes are at ten and two. But you can't drive—I'll pick you up at eleven-thirty?"

"Done," Susan said. "I'll be ready."

"I'll see you at eleven-thirty. I have a feeling it will be an interesting lunch."

It will, it really will, Susan thought.

Once they were seated in a far corner of the only tearoom in Oak Grove, Sweet Tea, Ellen said brightly, "You can even have a glass of wine with your lunch. You don't have to go to school, and you can sleep all afternoon. Besides, you deserve."

"You joining me?" Susan asked.

The other woman shook her head. "Can't. I have a class and some student appointments this afternoon. Wouldn't do to breathe wine on them while I try to explain the Victorian mind."

"Who can explain that to anyone?" Susan grumbled. Then she said, "Ellen, want to go have a drink tonight?"

"You're having a drink now, Susan." Ellen regarded her friend with amusement. "You can't drink your way through this suspension."

"I know, I know, and I don't even want wine now. Tea will be fine. And it's not that I want a drink tonight. I need your help to do some, ah, investigating on my own."

"And Jake doesn't know."

Susan shook her head. "He wouldn't want to know." What she really meant was he would ask her not to go—and then she'd be in the awkward position of doing something Jake specifically asked her not to do. Jake never gave her orders, and he so seldom asked her to do things his way, that he would expect her to abandon this plan.

Ellen thought for a minute. "Sure, I'm always game. Where're we going?"

"The City Restaurant."

The arrival of the waitress with their sandwiches stopped Ellen from echoing "The City Restaurant!" in a high-pitched voice. When the waitress left, Ellen asked dramatically, "Why did I know you'd say that?"

"Because that's where I saw that red-haired man . . . and that's who I want to see again tonight. And I want you to see him."

Ellen's voice was filled with caution. "Why? And why me?"

Susan outlined an elaborate plan which essentially involved the two of them sitting at the bar, ordering drinks, waiting for the red-haired man to show up. When he did, Ellen was to go up to him, strike up a conversation and pretend interest in the business opportunity she'd turned down before.

"I don't know, Susan," Ellen said hesitantly. "I know what you think . . . and if you're right, it could be dangerous. If you're not right, we could look like damn fools. Either way, we lose."

"Ellen, you've got a lot less to lose than I do, and I understand that. But I don't mind looking like a damn fool, and I guarantee you, if I'm right about him, I'll be right there, and I won't let anything happen to you."

Ellen looked skeptical until Susan said, "Ellen, it's the only way I see to clear my name. I've got to prove that red-haired man killed Missy."

"If my mother knew I was mixed up in a murder," Ellen muttered, and then, "All right, I'll do it. But Susan, if it goes wrong, I'll never forgive you. And I think you should tell Jake."

"Can't." Susan shook her head vigorously.

They ate chunky chicken salad, with just a touch of curry, on croissants, and Key lime pie for dessert. Susan drank three glasses of tea and knew the caffeine would keep her from napping. But she was too wired to nap anyway.

"Oh, by the way," Susan said as Ellen pulled up to her house, "the graduate seminar has papers due today. You collect them, and I'll read them."

"Thank heaven," Ellen said. "I'll see you about five."

When Jake called about three to ask what she was doing, Susan crossed her fingers and said, "Grading seminar papers. Just because Ellen has to teach my class doesn't mean she has to grade the papers too."

"You going to do that tonight?" He asked, and she could hear him yawn.

"Yeah, I got to so Ellen can give them back."

"Then, if you'll make my apologies to Aunt Jenny, I think I'll skip dinner tonight. I'm bushed. Gonna stay home and read."

"She'll understand," Susan said sympathetically. And when they hung up, she almost let out a howl of relief.

Chapter Twelve

At five-thirty, Ellen pulled up to Susan's house. She wore a dark brown silk dress with a matching jacket, gold jewelry (well, gold-plated) and shiny bronze pumps that matched a small purse she carried.

Susan hobbled forth wearing a black faille pantsuit, with legs fortunately wide enough to accommodate her cast, and carrying a demure black purse. "Aunt Jenny, Ellen and I are going for cocktails. We . . . we have some school stuff to talk about, and we just thought we'd treat ourselves. We should be back in a couple of hours." Susan felt she had to invent a reason they weren't asking Aunt Jenny to go with them.

Aunt Jenny was not fooled. She made a harrumphing sound. "Jake know you're going?" she asked.

"No," Susan said. "This has nothing to do with him. Ellen and I just want to go for a little ladies' night out. We thought we'd splurge and go to Fort Worth."

"All the way to Fort Worth? Couldn't you stay closer to home? You know I worry about you on the highway." She stood, wringing her hands, and then with a sudden change of subject said, "Guess I'll call Jake and fix dinner for him," she said.

"Uh, Fort Worth is a special treat," Susan answered. "You fix supper for Jake." She reasoned that by the time Aunt Jenny got Jake, she'd be long gone and out of his reach.

Ellen and Susan drove toward Fort Worth almost without speaking, both seriously aware of the risk they were taking. Neither could enjoy the passing country nor the beautiful fall night. Occasionally, Ellen looked at her friend and wondered why she had let herself in for this. Then, of course, she told herself it was to help the best friend she had at Oak Grove. Susan, on the other hand, looked at Ellen and wondered if Ellen realized how big her problems were—didn't Ellen always turn things into a joke?—and how much danger they were in. Vaguely Susan remembered her promise to Jake that she wouldn't do anything risky, but she pushed it out of her mind.

By the time they got to The City Restaurant, they were neither talking nor looking at each other. Ellen gave the car keys to the valet, and Susan, crutches and all, led the way into the restaurant.

"Do you ladies have a reservation?" The hostess was most polite.

"No," Susan said. "We just thought we'd have a drink."

"Of course," the hostess said smoothly. "The bar is right this way." She pointed them to the bar, which lined the wall to the left as they moved out of the entryway. They took seats on stools at the bar. Susan leaned her crutches next to her.

The bartender was solicitous. "Madam has hurt her leg?"

"Madam has broken her leg," Susan said tartly, resisting the urge to add a "damn" to the description of the leg.

"For that," he said, "a drink on the house. What will you have?"

"Chardonnay. A dry one, please."

"But of course, and for you, mademoiselle?" He turned toward Ellen, while Susan was left fuming over the fact that he called her "madam" and Ellen, "mademoiselle." That damn young look of Ellen's again! Then she remembered that the very young look was what had brought them here tonight.

"A frozen margarita," Ellen said with a certain air of self-confidence that Susan greatly admired and coveted.

The drinks arrived, and Susan looked around the bar. There was no red-headed young man.

* * *

Brandy Perkins had made the most meticulous toilette of her young life that afternoon. She showered, shampooed, slathered her body with lotion, did her nails with a dark, almost chocolate-brown polish—feet and hands both—dried her hair and put it on giant hot rollers for body but, perish the thought, no curl! Her makeup was carefully applied—just a hint of blush and a light dusting of powder, more attention to the eyes where she used taupe shadow and white highlighter, brown pencil, and deep black mascara. She outlined her lips in a sort of chocolate-brown red and filled them in with a gloss.

At last she chose a black dress, long and not particularly slinky but close-fitting enough to be suggestive. Pawing through her jewelry box, she chose silver—an elaborate American Indian silver necklace, a wide band for a bracelet, silver rings on both hands, and the earrings that dangled just a bit and had just a hint of turquoise—the earrings that Susan had noticed in Subway, although Brandy didn't know that. Anyone else, she thought, would have worn gold with this black dress. It pleased Brandy to do the unexpected, to be different.

She threw keys, a little money, makeup and driver's license into a small black purse with an elaborate silver clasp, grabbed a smart short black coat with a faux fur collar, and locked her dormitory room behind her. Down the hall she knocked on another door.

"Y'all ready? We're late," she called softly.

"I'm ready," a voice called, "but Vicky's having second thoughts. Come on in."

Vicky Lawson sat on the bed, dressed in a black mini-dress with white collar and cuffs. *She looks fantastic,* Brandy thought with a twinge of jealousy. The child of an African-American father and a Greek mother, Vicky had tawny dark skin, great huge dark eyes, and black hair that she pulled smoothly back from her face. Right now, that face was troubled. "I don't think I want to do this." She was about to pick at her perfectly polished nails, but Brandy reached over and pulled her hands apart.

"Don't be silly," Brandy said. "It's not anything you haven't done before."

"Not for money," Vicky said. "My daddy, he would be so mad at me . . . "

"He'll never know, and you'll be two-hundred dollars richer. And you'll get a good steak dinner."

"And," Sallie Cornell said, coming out of the washroom they shared with the adjoining room, "you'll probably like the guy. These airline pilots are cool."

"It's too late for doubts," Brandy said, grabbing the girl by the wrist and pulling her to her feet. "You promised. You made a date."

"Okay," Vicky said, "but I'm not promising I won't bolt and run."

Brandy drove, with Sallie in the back seat and Vicky in the passenger seat, where they could both keep an eye on her and encourage her. Brandy drove her Honda Accord too fast all the way to the city, and Vicky was so preoccupied with clinging to the armrest that she spoke little.

Once, she asked, "Isn't this dangerous? I mean, some guys . . ."

"Beat you up?" Brandy asked bluntly. "Never happens. Kenny screens his clients real carefully. He doesn't want us hurt."

Nobody mentioned what happened to Missy and that Vicky was taking Missy's place, but the knowledge hung in the air. Brandy, for one, didn't believe that a client had killed Missy; she knew in her heart that Kenny had done it—and she wondered why she hadn't shared that knowledge, why she was going to meet Kenny tonight. *Living on the edge,* she thought.

* * *

Susan Hogan saw the red-haired stranger look at his watch as he sauntered self-confidently into The City Restaurant. Six o'clock. He tossed a wave at the hostess, walked past the few people seated at the bar, and took a place on the last bar stool. Without a word, the bartender brought him a Scotch.

At the other end of the bar, Ellen said softly to Susan, "That's him. Damn! I was hoping he wouldn't show up."

"Go on," Susan said. "Nothing bad can happen in a place like this."

Ellen took a deep breath. "I'm not used to picking men up in bars," she said.

"Never know. A little practice, and you might get good at it."

Ellen pushed herself off the stool, picked up her drink, and strolled slowly to the other end of the bar. The redhead watched her approach, admiring her, thinking she looked vaguely familiar.

"Hi," she said, "We met at Oak Grove in the Main the other day. You offered me work."

"Oh, yeah, I remember." He stood up. His mother had taught him manners, after all. He grinned engagingly. "You turned me down."

"Yeah, but I've thought about it since, wished I'd taken your card. May I have one now?"

Something made Kenny a little cautious. "Sure," he said, reaching inside his pocket. "But how did you know to find me here?"

"Here?" Ellen looked around the restaurant. Then she shrugged and said, "I didn't. That's pure coincidence. But when I saw you come in I decided it must be fate. I was meant to meet up with you again."

Susan wished she had extrasensory hearing so she'd know what they were saying, but she saw Ellen shrug as she answered a question.

"Friend and I have been to a meeting at the Worthington. Decided to treat ourselves to a drink, and we'd heard The City Restaurant was a pretty toney place. Can't afford to eat here, but we could at least have a drink."

Whatever she said, the redhead seemed to accept it. "Well," he said, "you work for me, you can pretty soon eat dinner here."

"Sounds great," Ellen said, pocketing the card. "Nice to see you again." She held out her hand and they shook, and then she headed back to Susan. She felt pretty proud of herself—she'd actually carried it off, and she had his card in her purse.

Walking the length of the bar, Ellen faced the entrance directly. When she was about halfway back to Susan, the three Oak Grove girls came into the restaurant, Vicky dragging reluctantly behind the other two.

Brandy saw her instantly. "Dr. Peck!" she exclaimed. "What are you doing here?" Her voice carried the length of the room.

Susan cursed, and Ellen walked toward the girl and said softly, "Having a drink, Brandy. What are you girls doing here?" Her eyes took in all three girls, the clothes they were wearing, the carefully applied makeup. *Susan is right*, she decided, *they're call girls.*

Brandy didn't answer, but in the second it took her to compose her thoughts, she saw Susan at the bar. "Dr. Hogan!" She didn't hesitate a minute but went right up to Susan. "I told you to stay out of this. You'll only make things worse."

"Brandy," Susan said wearily, "for me they can't get any worse." She didn't feel obliged to give the girl a catalog of her troubles.

"Don't bet on it," Brandy said.

"Is that a threat, Brandy?"

"No, a warning."

Just then the redheaded man walked up to the knot of five women gathered at the front end of the bar. "Hey, what's goin' on here. You know these two?" He directed his question to Brandy, and he was distinctly displeased. The good manners his mother had taught him had disappeared.

"They're faculty from the university," Brandy said. "That one"—she jerked her head toward Susan—"is the one whose car Missy was in."

Surprise and panic both showed on his face. He stared at Susan and Ellen, both of whom avoided his look. Finally, he said to the three young girls, "You all go on upstairs and wait for me. I'll be right there." Brandy led the way, and the other two followed her, but Susan saw the dark-skinned girl throw a frightened look in her direction. She interpreted it as a plea for help.

"Look, ladies, I don't know why you're here or what your game is, but I think you best be moving on now. You'll just cause trouble here."

"You don't own this restaurant, twerp," Susan said. "You can't kick us out." But then she saw that the bartender had quietly collected their drinks. With all the dignity she could muster, she said, "We're leaving anyway. Tell Brandy . . . " She started to tell him she'd see Brandy in class Friday, but then she realized that wasn't true. She wouldn't be in class. Anger boiled through Susan again, and she resisted an urge to slap this red-haired man whom she felt she knew so well, even if she didn't yet know his name.

The man had made one serious mistake: he forgot that Ellen had his card. He sauntered back to the other end of the bar, trying to appear casual even though he was thinking fast and furiously. While Susan and Ellen waited for their check, not daring to say anything to each other, they watched the bartender and the redhead whispering together at the far end of the bar. At long last, the bartender came toward them, and said, "Drinks are on the house, ladies, if you'll please just get out of here."

So much, Susan thought, for a toney restaurant. We aren't bringing Aunt Jenny here Saturday.

They waited an extraordinarily long time for their car. The last weekend had seen the time-change from daylight to central time, so even just before seven it was almost dark—and with the dark came the chill of October nights. Both women shivered.

"You think they parked your car in Dallas?" Susan asked, trying to make a joke.

"At least in North Fort Worth," Ellen replied. "Damn, it's cold!"

Ellen Peck never swore, and Susan, who had under duress been accused by Jake of swearing like a trooper, stared at her. Ellen, she decided, was scared and angry, both at the same time.

At long last Ellen's Mitsubishi roared up to the curb and a young man jumped out, full of apologies about taking so long. "Got the wrong car the first time, ma'am. Sorry."

Ellen gave him five dollars and hoped to heaven he'd turned the heat on already. He hadn't.

They were silent as Ellen maneuvered through Fort Worth's downtown streets. Instead of heading toward Forest Park, she turned north on Throckmorton.

"Where are you going?" Susan asked.

"I have this strange feeling," Ellen said. "I just want to be sure no one is following us."

"Oh, for Pete's sake, Ellen, this isn't a grade B melodrama," Susan said crossly.

"You sure?" Ellen asked. "I'm beginning to think it is."

Susan was silent for a minute. Then she said, "We don't know any more than we did before—all we got out of that was a couple free drinks."

"At those prices, that wasn't a bad deal. But, Susan, we do know a little bit more. I've got that man's card in my purse. Here, fish it out and see what it says." She took the purse from the side of her seat, where she always kept it, and handed it to Susan.

Susan pulled out the card and read, "Kenny Thomas. At your pleasure. 817-332-4557." She sighed. "Well, it's a downtown Fort Worth phone number. Doesn't tell you much else. We have no proof he's running a call-girl ring."

"We've certainly got instincts, though," Ellen said. "If I ever doubted your story, Susan, I apologize. It's obvious what he's doing . . . and what those girls are doing."

"Did you see that one?" Susan asked. "She looked terrified. I wanted to run and grab her, save her."

"Might've been the best thing you could have done for her."

Susan was already blaming herself for not having taken more action. Ellen's words didn't help, and she stared out the window, lost in thought.

"Susan?" Ellen's voice had a real edge to it. "The car behind us is really tailgating. Pushing me hard." They had turned off Throckmorton and were now on the part of Forest Park that followed the river and was almost like a four-lane country road. The only car around was the one behind them.

Susan turned and saw headlights blazing at them, not inches from the back of their car. "Can you pull off?"

"No place here. And I'm afraid to slow down, afraid he'll ram us. I've picked up the speed some, but so did he."

"Why doesn't he just pass us?" Susan asked. "No other cars on the road."

"That's what's worrying me," Ellen said. "It's like he wants *us*."

"We're about halfway to the freeway," Susan said. "If we can make that, we'll be back in traffic."

"Yeah," Ellen said grimly, "if we can make that."

"Ellen, drive as fast as you can." The car behind them kept pace with them.

"Susan . . . " It was a wail for help from Ellen, but it was too late.

The car turned as though to pass them, then slowly began to crowd them off the road. Susan was afraid they would tumble down the embankment into the Trinity River, and she began to review everything she'd ever read about escaping from a sunken car. The momentum of speed Ellen had built up carried the car. It flipped once and landed upright, lodged against a small tree, the motor still running. The car that had forced them off the road sped off into the night.

If it weren't for that tree, Susan thought, we'd be in the river. God must be looking after me, in spite of all.

They sat in total silence in the darkness, too stunned and scared to speak. Susan moved every part of her body just a bit and thought, *It's like the night the car tried to run me down and the moped wreck, only worse.* This time, nothing new seemed broken—a miracle if she'd ever heard of one. "Thank God for trees," she said. "Ellen?"

"What?" Ellen's voice was hoarse and strained.

"You okay?"

"No. I've got the most tremendous pain in my side that I've ever had in my life. It hurts bad, Susan."

"Okay, let me think. We've got to stay here for a bit, not moving, make sure that whoever it was doesn't come back to see if he did what he wanted to do. I'll call Jake." She fished in her purse for her cell phone.

"I can't move anyway," Ellen said and began to sob.

Jake didn't answer at his house, and no one answered at her house. Susan had a vision of Jake and Aunt Jenny, sitting happily on the deck, ignoring the phone because they couldn't hear it.

"Don't even think of getting out and walking. You can't leave me here."

"I can't walk either," Susan reminded her.

Ellen gave a giggle that verged on hysteria. "We're a great pair. I can barely breathe, and you can barely walk."

Susan was more concerned about Ellen's pain and raspy breath than she wanted her friend to know. She dialed 911 and in as businesslike tones as she could muster told them where they were and what Ellen's condition was.

It seemed hours that they sat there, Ellen breathing hard and Susan shaking from cold and fear, but it was probably only minutes until they saw the flashing lights of a police car. Then an officer waving a flashlight made his way down the embankment to the car. "Anybody in there?" he called.

"Yes," Susan answered in a loud, strong voice. "Two of us. The driver's hurt."

He jerked open the driver's door and knelt beside Ellen. "How're you hurt?"

"Pain right here," Ellen panted, pointing to her rib cage, "and it hurts to breathe."

"I'll call an ambulance, but it sounds to me like a broken rib. You okay, lady?"

"Yeah, didn't even rebreak my broken ankle," Susan said. She had gotten in the habit of telling people it was her ankle rather than the lower part of whatever bone it was. It required less explanation that way.

The officer asked where they were headed and what had happened. When they told him a car deliberately ran them off the road, he shook his head. "Lot of kooks on the road these days. No telling what you did to make him mad."

Susan knew exactly what they'd done and who it was, but she didn't want to go into it with this officer. What she wanted, she realized with a lurch, was Jake.

"How'd you know to look for us?" she asked.

"Funny thing," the officer said. "'Bout the time your call came in, we also got an anonymous call about a car run off the road on Forest Park."

Susan shuddered. Whoever did this hoped they were dead. "Would you radio security at Oak Grove University and have them tell Jake Phillips what happened? Ask him to meet us at the hospital."

"Jake? Sure, I know Jake. Went to police academy with him. You a friend of his?" The officer's face was lit with a smile.

"I may not be for long," Susan muttered.

* * *

Jake got to the hospital about an hour later, having broken every speed limit. The ambulance had transported Ellen, who was in the emergency room. Susan sat in the ER waiting room doing just that . . . waiting. She felt like she was waiting for her fate. Jake's mood was neither comforting nor loving. "What in the hell have you been doing?" he demanded.

"Ellen and I just went for a drink . . . "

"Come on, Susan, I'm not stupid. You went to The City Restaurant . . . and you went to check on that red-haired stranger. And you lied to me."

"He has a name. Kenny Thomas. And, Jake, I know I'm right. Brandy came in with two other coeds from Oak Grove. That's how he found out about us, who we were. And that's why he ran us off the road." The words tumbled out as Susan tried desperately to convince Jake that she had not been merely willful and foolish.

"He ran you off the road? Did you see him? Can you testify against him?"

"Well . . . no. It was dark. I don't know that it was actually him. But, Jake, it was deliberate. That car tailgated us, kept forcing Ellen to go faster, when it had every opportunity to pass us . . . It's a wonder we weren't killed."

"I've thought of that, Susan," Jake said dryly. "Don't try to play violins for me now. I'm glad you're all right, and it sounds like Ellen has a broken rib and maybe a collapsed lung. Painful but not serious."

Susan hung her head. "Okay, so I put Ellen in danger, and we didn't get anything for it."

"Sounds that way to me," he said. "Could easily have just been some drunk ran you off the road."

Susan noticed that he had deliberately kept his distance from her. Where, she wondered, was that protestation of love she'd heard—what? not twenty-four hours earlier? "Aunt Jenny?"

"I was at your house when the call came in. She called and invited me to supper. When I got there, she said you'd gone for a drink with Ellen, which sounded uncharacteristic to me—the two of you drink at your house if you want to share confidences."

"I've caused her all kinds of worry, haven't I?"

"Yeah, you have. Not to mention me. You made me a promise, you know—nothing risky." For a minute, he thought she'd tell him she was sorry, but she didn't. "And I never thought you'd lie to me. I guess that's the worst of it."

Susan couldn't look him in the eye. Finally she tried to turn the conversation in another direction. "There is one bit of good news," Susan said, fishing in her purse. "Ellen got that Kenny Thomas' card. We have a phone number."

"But not proof he's doing anything illegal, from running a call-girl service to running cars off the road," Jake said. "It's probably all coincidence, but I'll give this to Jordan. With the police finding you tonight, this thing's public."

"Nobody else was doing anything," she protested. "I've made progress."

Jake stared at her so long and hard that she dropped her eyes again. Finally, he spoke. "Susan, there's something else. I took the moped to a repair shop, just to have it checked. Someone had tampered with the accelerator. It was stuck—that's why you couldn't slow down."

"Stuck?" she echoed him in amazement. Then she said softly, "Kenny Thomas. I think he was the one who tried to run me down that night. I'm convinced of it. But why me?"

Jake shrugged and looked her squarely in the face. "Susan, your life is in danger. Someone's tried to kill you three times. And to frame you for murder."

"And scare me to death with wilted plants and dead kittens."

"I think that's someone else," he said. "I don't know how the two link up together."

"We better solve this murder quick so I can get my life back." He didn't have to try to scare her—she was scared enough without any help.

Jake drove her home but declined to stay and eat the shepherd's pie Aunt Jenny had kept warming in the oven.

"It's not your cooking," Jake assured Aunt Jenny. "I'm just not hungry tonight." He turned toward Susan and was almost formal when he said, "I'll take you to the doctor's office day after tomorrow."

Later Susan sat at the table, her unfinished meat pie before her. Finally, she raised her glass of wine and took a sip. "Great dinner, Aunt Jenny." She was really thinking that, once more, things had gotten worse. Now she'd made Jake mad—and who knows when, if ever, she'd hear from him again. She doubted he'd just walk out of her life, but that possibility terrified her.

Aunt Jenny read her mind. "I think you've pushed him too far, Susan," she said, her hands on her hips as she stood before her niece. "Call him and apologize. All that man wants to do is protect you and love you."

Susan knew her aunt was right, but the depression that had settled on her was so great she couldn't face lifting the receiver, figuring out what to say. "I'll call in the morning," she said.

She went to bed exhausted in mind and body. When the phone rang, she fumbled with it groggily, putting the mouthpiece to her ear, then finally righting it and managing a sleepy, "Hello."

The clock said three, which made Susan more alert. No one would call at that hour unless it was an emergency. Had something gone wrong with Ellen?

A high-pitched voice, obviously disguised, whispered into her ear, "Die, Susan Hogan. You must die."

"Who is this?" she demanded, clutching the phone tightly.

There was a giggle, in the same high-pitched tone, and then the phone clicked in her ear.

Whoever ran us off the road is telling me he'll try again, she thought in panic. *I should call Jake—but Jake is mad at me.* Sleep would not come again, and she lay in bed crying from terror and a terrible sense of loss—the loss of her life. She muffled her sobs in the pillow, so Aunt Jenny wouldn't hear. Susan didn't want solicitous care right now—she wanted to be miserable. It was nearly dawn when she finally closed her eyes, and even then she slept fitfully, her dreams full of headlights racing at her . . . and Shelley.

Chapter Thirteen

With the morning sun streaming into her bedroom, Susan stretched tentatively . . . and realized that every muscle in her body was an aching mass of knots. For a minute, she was puzzled, and then it came back to her: the accident, the car that ran them off the road, Ellen in the hospital with a broken rib and a punctured lung, Jake angry with her, the threatening phone call in the night. She lay still a moment, knowing she had nothing to do the whole day, indeed could do nothing, and yet feeling a compelling urgency to get up, to get on with finding Missy Jackson's murderer. She had to make this living nightmare end.

Sitting up in bed, she was aware of soft voices in the kitchen. *Jake must be here for breakfast,* she thought with relief. *He's not going to stay mad at me.* She threw her ratty old terry-cloth housecoat over the T-shirt in which she had slept, smoothed her hair knowing that the comb alone would never fix it and it needed washing. *At least I don't have to pretend for Jake.* She did brush her teeth.

Clomping into the kitchen on her crutches, Susan was amazed to see not Jake but Eric Lindler calmly seated at the table eating breakfast.

"More eggs, Eric?" Aunt Jenny asked.

"No, thank you, Miss Hogan. This is plenty. I'm not used to such good food in the morning. The dorm food . . . it's not like this."

"Eric!" Susan's sharp voice cut through their pleasantries.

He jumped to his feet, almost stumbling over his chair. "Dr. Hogan! I came to see if you were all right."

Suspiciously, she asked, "Why did you think I wouldn't be?"

He reached across the table, grabbed the newspaper and brought it to her, with the headlines showing prominently: "Teachers Roll Car in Fort Worth."

Susan groaned as she took the paper and hobbled to the couch. The article described how the two very specifically identified Oak Grove faculty members had been "returning from downtown Fort Worth"—*why didn't they just say we'd been for drinks and be done with it?*—and their car left the road, flipped once, and landed against a tree. "No reason for the accident has been determined as yet."

"No reason! Somebody ran us off the road, that's the reason! Damn!" Susan threw the paper across the room.

Eric was back at his plate, slathering ketchup on Tater Tots. "Ran you off the road?" He stopped, fork in midair. "Really, Dr. Hogan?"

Susan stared at him. His surprise was genuine, she thought. No matter what Aunt Jenny thought about him, he wasn't the one who had tailgated them last night. Susan would have bet on that. "Yes, Eric, ran us off the road." She thought for a moment. "Can you think of any reason someone would do that?"

As Eric protested that he absolutely could not, Aunt Jenny interrupted. "Now, Susan, you leave this boy alone. He's still grieving."

Susan thought seriously of telling Aunt Jenny to shut up, especially when she saw Eric grin, but her love of the old woman was too strong—and so were the manners that Aunt Jenny had drilled into her. Before she could think clearly what to ask Eric next, there was a knock at the door. Susan looked up, still expecting Jake, but saw instead the face of Judge John Jackson.

"It's the judge," Aunt Jenny said, wiping her hands on her apron.

"Let him in," Susan suggested.

"Oh, my!" Aunt Jenny's hands went to her hair, probably with the intent of smoothing it, but they accomplished just the opposite. "Oh, my, what's he doing here at this hour?"

"Maybe he's hungry," Susan said, "but Aunt Jenny, he's looking straight at you through the glass panel in the door. Go let him in."

Eric sat spellbound by the whole scene.

"Judge!" Aunt Jenny said, "What a surprise."

"Hope I'm not too early," he said, walking right into the room. "Came to see about Susan."

"Join the party," Susan muttered, and then she wondered all the more why Jake hadn't joined the party. Sure, he knew she was all right, but was he so mad at her that he wouldn't come to see how she was this morning?

Instead of coming over to Susan, Judge Jackson stopped in front of Aunt Jenny and in a soft voice asked, "How are you this morning, Jenny?" He grasped her hand and held it just a shade longer than a handshake.

"Oh, me? I'm fine. It's Susan we're worried about." Nervously, she pulled her hand away.

"Of course." Turning toward Susan, the judge found himself staring at an unfamiliar young man, eating a hearty breakfast. "Son, I don't believe I know you."

As Eric rose, held out his hand to introduce himself, Aunt Jenny fluttered, "This is Eric Lindler. Susan and I have adopted him, sort of."

"Eric Lindler." The judge rolled the name on his tongue and considered for only a second. "You're the boyfriend of the murdered girl."

He doesn't miss a trick, Susan thought.

Eric looked appropriately upset. "Yessir, I'm afraid I am . . . er, was."

"And Dr. Hogan has adopted you?" Disbelief was in the judge's voice.

"Well, actually, Miss Hogan has been feeding me regular, says I need fattening up. But I came this morning just like you, to check on Dr. Hogan."

Clever, Susan thought, he's placed himself in the same category of caring friend as the judge.

"I got to go to class now, though," Eric said. "Dr. Hogan, if I can run any errands for you, you just let me know. Pleasure to meet you, sir. And, Miss Hogan, thanks much for the breakfast."

After he left at a dead run, Aunt Jenny said, "He didn't even finish his breakfast."

"No," Susan said, "he didn't. Maybe the judge made him nervous. Aunt Jenny, tell the judge what you think about Eric."

"Why," Aunt Jenny fluttered her hands in the air, "I think he murdered that poor girl and put her in the trunk of Susan's car."

"You do?" The judge was incredulous. "Then why," he asked, "do you keep feeding him?"

"Well, partly because he keeps showing up here to check on Susan . . . and partly because if he stays around here long enough and gets comfortable enough, he'll let something slip."

"Jenny Hogan," the judge said, "I wish I'd had you on the bench with me sometimes. You'd have out-tricked most lawyers I know."

"Go on with you," she said, going back to the kitchen. "Can I give you some breakfast?"

"Just coffee, thanks. Never could stomach breakfast before about ten o'clock. Now, Susan, tell me about last night."

Susan told him every detail she could think of, from Ellen's first approach to Kenny to their time in the emergency room.

"Jake's right," the judge said, "Jordan will want to see you. And with good reason. I'll go with you."

"You don't have to bother . . . " Susan began.

"Bother? An old man like me hasn't had this much fun in years," he said with a laugh. "Jenny, where's that coffee? Does a man have to serve himself around here?"

"Oh, no, coming right up, John."

Susan noticed that her aunt said "John" and not "Judge."

* * *

Jake called about nine-thirty, by which time Susan had talked to Ellen on the phone. The hospital wasn't sure when they were releasing her—maybe not until the next day. Her first comment to Susan was, "Scott will have a hissy. Now he's got two faculty members out—from suspicious causes."

"I hope he has to teach the classes himself," Susan said, "but he'll probably give them to Ernie, who can't wait to tell everyone what happened." She couldn't help laughing at the idea of Ernie Westin teaching women's lit.

"Yeah," Ellen said. And then, "My car?"

Susan told her it was towed to a garage and quipped, "I know where you can borrow a good moped."

"Don't," Ellen said. "It hurts to laugh."

"I don't feel much like laughing anyway," Susan muttered. "I'll call you later today."

Susan breathed a sigh of relief when Jake called, since she had been putting off calling him in spite of Aunt Jenny's urgings. She simply didn't know what to say to him.

He was not at a loss for words. "Sorry, we had a heck of a night on campus after I left you. Seems a coed got hysterical in her room—still don't know why, but she began throwing things and screaming. Paramedics had to medicate her on the spot, and she's in the hospital now."

"What's the girl's name?" Susan asked, even as she was thinking that there was something different about Jake's voice, something clipped and businesslike.

"Lawson, Vicky Lawson. You know her?"

"No. What's she look like?" Foolish question—as if she could tell one coed from the other by a telephone description!

"Hard to tell, state she was in. But I'd say she's part African-American, probably good-looking when she's not going bonkers."

"Jake! She was at The City Restaurant last night. She really was!" Susan gripped the phone intently.

"Susan, are you sure?" His voice was very controlled now.

"I am. She was with Brandy—and she looked scared to death."

"Might go along with your theory," he said reluctantly. "I'll keep you posted on what happens." He hung up without asking how she was or saying anything about coming to see her.

Aunt Jenny's right. I've pushed him too far.

Dirk Jordan called in the late morning. "I need to talk to you."

Judge Jackson sensed who it was and grabbed the phone, "Jordan, this is John Jackson. You want to talk to this girl, you'll do it in my presence . . . and not over the phone, where you could, for God's sake, be running a secret tape."

"That's illegal," the officer said clearly.

"Wouldn't stop most cops I know," Judge Jackson said. "What time do you want me to bring her downtown?"

They settled on two in the afternoon, which led the judge to say, "Lunch at Subie's Café, my treat."

"Oooh," Aunt Jenny said.

"What's the matter, Jenny? Don't you like the café?" His voice was almost disapproving.

"Oh, my, yes. They have wonderful pie. It's just . . . well, I could cook something here." Aunt Jenny did not want to face Margie again.

"Nonsense. It's settled. Susan, you call Jake and have him meet us there."

"I'm sure he's busy," Susan said testily.

The judge gave her a wry look. "Then I'll call him. Most officers, even private duty kinds, are seldom too busy for a judge . . . maybe for an English teacher but not a judge." He winked at her.

Susan left the room to get dressed. As she dressed slowly and carefully—*how can you pick clothes out of the closet while balancing yourself on crutches?*—she heard peals of laughter from Aunt Jenny and an occasional deep chuckle from the judge.

"I was just telling Jenny some courtroom stories," the judge explained when she came back into the room.

At lunch—where Jake did not join them—Susan thought she caught the two older people holding hands under the table. She wanted to be happy for them, but she was too distracted by her troubles. And, she grudgingly admitted to herself, she was jealous. She wanted Jake to be sitting next to her.

* * *

Dirk Jordan was not disposed to be either kind or understanding. "Dr. Hogan, you seem to be Johnny-on-the-spot when it comes to being around serious incidents—a body in your car, a moped wreck, a car run off the road. That's an amazing record for an educated woman in—what? Slightly over two weeks? Can you explain it? Plus, of course, that . . . ah, earlier incident."

Susan looked at the lieutenant, staring at her so insolently, and shook her head. "No, I can't. I'm very tired of it myself. I wish you'd do your job and find out what's happening."

"Do my job?" His voice rose almost an octave in indignation. "How can I do my job when you hide things from me and sneak off to do your own detective work? Who knows what else you've done?"

Susan knew then that Jake had talked to him and told him about Kenny Thomas. There was no use dissembling, not that she'd meant to, but she was tired of the way the officer kept playing cat and mouse with her. "What do you want to know about Kenny Thomas?" she asked.

He almost jumped. Susan saw the impulse race through him and knew that he'd worked hard for years to control any visible expression of surprise. "Everything you know," he said tersely.

So Susan repeated, mostly telling him what she'd told the judge earlier in the day. She was, as a matter of fact, getting tired of telling this story over and again. Jordan was relentless, pressing her for details she didn't know, couldn't know. "How does Brandy Perkins know this Kenny Thomas?" "What was his connection to Missy Jackson?" "Why were those girls there last night at The City Restaurant?"

Susan wanted to tell him to use his imagination, but the judge put a gentling hand on her arm. "I can only tell you what I suspect," she said for the third time. "I have no definite knowledge, no proof of anything."

Then the subject turned to Eric. "Why do you befriend him?"

"I really don't. My aunt does."

"Why?"

"She'd befriend you. She's pretty all-encompassing in the people she adopts." Susan didn't feel like sharing Aunt Jenny's convoluted logic at that moment.

Judge Jackson coughed, and Susan managed a small laugh. "Doesn't include you, Judge."

"Do you think Eric Lindler killed Missy Jackson?"

"What does it matter what I think? What matters is what you can prove. No, I probably don't think he's capable of murder, but something about him makes me nervous. Do I think Kenny Thomas is capable of murder? Yes, I'm quite sure of it."

It seemed to Susan that she was in the sheriff's office for a day and a half. When she and the judge emerged into daylight, she blinked, expecting it to be dead night. But they had only been there two hours.

And Jake never even showed up, she thought unhappily. I suppose the judge told him he'd take care of everything, but still—I wanted Jake there, even though I would have told him not to come. She realized she was being contradictory and probably unfair to Jake.

"You did well, Susan," the judge said. "But he still thinks you know more than you're telling him."

* * *

Jake didn't come for dinner that night. By nine o'clock, he still hadn't called, and she called him at home.

"Susan? Yeah. I'm just drinking a beer, hanging back."

"Aunt Jenny expected you for dinner. She made smothered steak, says it's better than chicken-fried."

"Tell her I'm sorry I missed it. I . . . well, I just had a long day."

"It's okay. The judge ate your helping."

"Oh . . . good." There was a long pause. "Susan, I just had to have some time away, some time to think." He took a deep breath. "I love you, and I'm more worried about your safety right now than I can make you believe. But I . . . I don't know how much you care about me if you'll lie to me and do the one thing I asked you not to do."

At a loss how to tell him how scared she was, how much she needed him, Susan was silent.

Jake Phillips put the phone down and stared into space, his beer growing stale and warm. He knew he was attracted neither by Susan's intellect nor her beauty but by the fact that she insisted on swimming upstream. If there was a difficult way to do something, Susan Hogan would stubbornly find it. Not that Jake didn't find Susan attractive. Tall and thin, she wore her light blonde hair—he had seen the dark roots—in a boyishly short cut. Her smile was wide and quick and her eyes were brown under incredibly dark eyebrows. At thirty-five, Susan could still make heads turn, and Jake was proud to be seen with her.

But now, she'd stepped over some kind of line in his mind. She refused to listen to reason, to his concern for her safety. She kept taking off on her own, swimming upstream again. Could he live his life with this? Yet, he couldn't imagine his life without her.

At the other end of the line, Susan hung up the phone, grabbed her crutches, and clomped to the bedroom without a word to Aunt Jenny and the judge, who both stared after her in dismay. In her bedroom, she peeled off the outer layer of clothes, threw herself on the bed, and cried herself to sleep.

* * *

Brandy Perkins had been doing some hard thinking. Wednesday night, when Vicky went bananas in her room, Brandy had done everything she knew to calm the girl down, mostly because she couldn't stand to see anyone so upset but partly because she was afraid the reason for Vicky's screaming hysteria might become public.

At first, Vicky had tried to run, but Kenny barred the door and threatened her with physical violence. Brandy heard him, and it wasn't pretty. After that, Vicky had managed to make it through dinner with the airline pilots. The guy who was her date, Stan, was a nice enough guy, but Vicky acted like she was a statue made of stone.

When Brandy went down to the hotel lobby, hours later, she found Vicky sitting quietly in one of the plush chairs. On the way home she refused to talk about what happened, and Brandy didn't push her. But when they got back to the sorority house and in Brandy's room, the girl fell into hysterics.

Sallie left the room in disgust. "She's a whiner, and I don't want any part of this."

"How can you just walk away from her? We did this to her."

"Not we, Brandy, you. And I can walk away easy, 'cause I've got two hundred in my pocket, and I think she's stupid."

Brandy only stared after her a second because her attention was called back to Vicky, who was screaming, "My daddy, my daddy! He's gonna beat me within an inch of my life."

"Vicky," she whispered soothingly, "he's not going to know. Nobody's going to know." Brandy tried hugging, holding the girl tight so that she wouldn't thrash about—but the screaming kept on.

It was a girl down the hall who called the campus cops. When they got there, they called the ambulance, and Vicky was sedated before she left the room on the stretcher.

Foggily, Vicky mumbled, "Brandy?"

"I'm right here, Vicky." She reached for the girl's hand and squeezed it.

"Don't tell anybody, pullease."

"I won't, Vicky, I won't." *This means she won't tell, unless they give her so much sedation that she talks in her sleep.* She was grateful that the paramedics were so busy taking care of Vicky that they didn't hear her desperate plea.

Brandy spent a long, mostly sleepless night. When sleep did come, she fought major battles—yelling at Kenny, trying to save Missy, who mysteriously came back from the dead, hugging a sobbing Vicky. During all those battles, she thought she was awake and only realized she wasn't when she awoke in a drenching sweat. But by morning she'd made a decision.

She went to Dr. Hogan's contemporary lit class the next afternoon, expecting to find Dr. Hogan returned as she'd promised. Brandy had counted on a private word with her. She wanted to confess, as it were, what she knew and tell her of the decision she'd made. It had taken four cups of coffee to give her the strength—though her hands shook from the caffeine and the lack of sleep.

But instead of Dr. Hogan or even Dr. Peck, she found a note on the board that said simply, "Class cancelled."

With a need to know that went beyond curiosity, Brandy went to the English office. "How come Dr. Hogan's class was cancelled?" she asked Mildred.

Mildred looked at her from her privileged position as the secretary to the chair of the English department and said, "Surely you've heard."

"Heard what? No, I guess I haven't." A sinking feeling started in Brandy's stomach and worked its way upward, making her think she might throw up.

"Drs. Hogan and Peck were in a bad automobile accident last night. Dr. Hogan is all right, but Dr. Peck is hospitalized."

Nobody had to tell Brandy that they'd been run off the road. She knew it without hearing.

But Mildred told her—or repeated Dr. Scott's version. "They *say* they were run off the road by another car," she said, her voice clearly suggesting doubt.

"That son of a bitch!" Brandy exploded, leaving the office on a run.

Mildred stared after her in surprise and then picked up the phone to dial Ernie Westin. He'd love to hear that, she knew, even if what the girl said didn't make sense.

Wearing the sweatshirt and jeans she'd gone to class in, Brandy got in her car and headed for The City Restaurant. By four-thirty, she was drinking a beer.

Kenny Thomas came into the bar early, close to five.

Brandy saw him and stood up.

"Brandy, sweet," he said, giving her a peck on the cheek. "What are you doing here tonight . . . ah, dressed like that?"

"Don't sweet-talk me, Kenny. I have business on my mind."

"So do I, my sweet, always."

"Not that kind. I want out, now! I know what happened to Missy, and I don't intend to be next. I'm not going out with your pilots ever again. And I'm not going to have anything to do with you. You cause me any trouble, and I'll tell the cops everything I know. Believe me, it's a lot." She didn't realize she was raising her voice.

"Shhh, baby, you're upset. I heard about that Vicky girl's problem—believe me, I heard from Stan—but it won't happen again. Let's go upstairs and talk." He took her arm and all but dragged her up the stairs.

Upstairs, he punched the button and said, "Bring Brandy a martini, and a Glenlivet straight for me" Then, turning to lean over her, "You look like terrific, baby, even in jeans. I want you for myself."

She hadn't thought of that possibility, but she didn't like it any better. Kenny Thomas was the man she was afraid of. "No." She backed away.

When the drinks arrived, he pulled a chair up so that Brandy was almost sitting in his lap, "Now, baby, tell Kenny what's the matter."

Maybe it was the three beers she'd consumed in rapid order, nervously waiting for him to appear, but something made Brandy bold—and foolish. "I think you killed Missy," she said, "and I don't want to end up like her. I don't want to work for you anymore." She took a swallow, too big a swallow, of the martini and nearly choked.

Kenny patted her on the back. "You okay?" he asked solicitously.

"Went down the wrong pipe," she said, taking another swallow to ease the tickle in her throat.

"Baby, I'm not into killing, 'specially not beautiful women. They're my stock in trade. I swear to you, I did not kill Missy Jackson, Boy Scout's honor." He raised his right hand in the traditional Boy Scout sign of a pledge. "Besides," and now he grinned charmingly at her, "how would you buy all those pretties if you quit letting me help you." Kenny preferred not to think that the girls were "working for" him.

"I can do without them," Brandy said. Somehow she was losing her resolve. Kenny looked a little fuzzy, and the room had begun to swim before her eyes.

He reached across the table and took her hand. "Now, sweetheart, you know I only have your best interests in mind. I wouldn't let anyone hurt you. Any of those airline pilots I fix you up with get out of line, I'll have their hides."

The last thing Brandy Perkins remembered was Kenny Thomas leaning across the table and kissing her, hard, on the mouth.

Chapter Fourteen

By Sunday morning, Brandy still hadn't called, and Ellen called Susan to say Vicky was worried. Vicky, desperate when she was about to be dismissed from the hospital, called the only person she could think of—Dr. Peck, whose class she'd liked so much. Only then did she find out that Dr. Peck was just out of the hospital too and recovering at home. Ellen, knowing she needed help at home, suggested Vicki stay with her a couple of nights. So Vicki was staying with Ellen, partly to help the injured teacher and partly because she was embarrassed to go back to the dorm, though she knew she'd have to some time.

"Is it unusual for Brandy to disappear for this long?" Susan asked.

"Apparently so. Vicky's called everyone, asking who last saw here. Nobody remembers seeing Brandy lately, but nobody has missed her either—she had no roommate to keep track of her comings and goings. Since we didn't hold class Friday, we don't know if she was there or not."

"Bring Vicki over here," Susan said, "and I'll call Jake."

"Susan," Ellen was being her most patient self, "I have no car. I can't bring her anyplace. And her car is on campus."

"I'll have Jake come get you," Susan said, sure that he would agree no matter their personal differences.

Susan decided she would tell Aunt Jenny as little as possible, just that this girl was scared and that Missy Jackson's roommate was missing.

"Eric doesn't know anything about that," Aunt Jenny said.

Startled, Susan said, "How do you know?" And then she knew the answer would be just what it was.

"I just know."

Jake was less distant than the night before when Susan told him why she was calling. "Is Vicky willing to talk? She might know enough to help us."

"I think she's willing. From what Ellen says she's still fragile emotionally but she's really worried about Brandy. She seems to think Brandy is her one true friend and that she tried to help her."

As usual, Aunt Jenny enveloped Vicky in a hug when she, Ellen, and Jake arrived. "Child, are you hungry?"

"No, ma'am, thank you. Dr. Peck, she's been feeding me."

"Yeah," Ellen said, "a piece of toast and a Coke for breakfast."

"Oh, my," Aunt Jenny said. "Let me scramble you an egg quick before I have to go to church. I have a chicken roasting—well, actually I did two chickens, so there will be plenty, and I'll make John . . . er, the Judge . . . come back here for Sunday dinner. No Luby's today."

"Judge?" Vicky repeated in alarm.

"He's a good friend," Susan said, putting her arm around the girl. "He's defending me every time they ask about Missy's murder."

Vicky stared at her in alarm. "Missy! And you're the one everyone thinks killed her." She drew back a little.

"Not everyone," Aunt Jenny clucked. "We know better."

"Kenny did it," Vicky said. "He threatened me, and he scared me so bad."

Jake listened intently to everything the girl said.

As Aunt Jenny gathered herself together to leave for church, she said, "Jake, I left dirty dishes in the sink and chickens in the oven. Will you take over the kitchen? The judge and I will be back right after church. And, young man, don't you stay away from us so long again."

Jake could do nothing but laugh and say, "Yes, ma'am."

He was gentle with Vicky, pulling out details about the evening at The City Restaurant that they hadn't heard before, about airline pilots and a steak-and-lobster dinner. With a flush and a hasty look at the two teachers, Vicky confessed her failure to satisfy her date and said he was pretty cool, paid her, and told her not to try that again. "Kenny will beat me if I ever see him again," she said.

Ellen gave the girl a gentle hug, all the while protecting her own sore chest. "You won't ever have to see him again, will she, Jake?"

Jake wished she wouldn't make promises he wasn't sure he could keep, but he'd do his darndest to protect this child. "Now what about Brandy? Are you sure she's missing?"

Vicky began to cry, her sobs punctuated by hiccups. "No one's seen her since Thursday. I'm pretty sure Kenny did something to her . . . and . . . and I keep thinking about Missy."

"I'll get right on it," Jake said. "If she's really been gone that long, Jordan needs to know."

He strode out to the deck, pulling out his phone, and was gone for maybe five minutes. When he came back, he said, "Jordan will put out a missing persons report and get the school to notify her family after they verify she hasn't been seen." He turned quickly to Vicky, "Not that I don't think you're right, but they have to deal with official sources. I've also called my office and asked them to look into it." Without another word, he turned toward the kitchen.

When Aunt Jenny and the judge arrived, the table was set for six, salad was made, dishes were in the dishwasher, and roast chicken and potatoes were coming out of the oven.

While the judge asked, "Are we having a party?" Jake said, "You want to make the gravy, Aunt Jenny? It's not one of my skills."

She threw off the shawl she'd worn to church, flinging it onto the living room couch as she passed by, and donned an apron. Then she mixed cold water and flour in a small Mason jar and began to shake vigorously.

Judge Jackson came forward. "Can I do that for you?"

"Oh, my, no thanks. I'm used to it, and I know just when I've got the consistency I want." Then she turned to Jake, "If you'd move these chickens to the carving board . . . "

He did so quickly, and then they all watched as she skimmed grease off the pan drippings, slowly poured in the flour-and-water mixture, stirring over low heat all the while, added salt, pepper and a bit of something called Kitchen Bouquet.

"What's that?" Jake asked, peering over her shoulder.

"Gives it a bit of color and maybe a tad more flavor," she explained.

Judge Jackson smelled the bottle and said, "Anchovies?"

"Go on with you. There will be no anchovies in my gravy."

Vicky watched all this as though they had taken leave of their senses and totally forgotten about Brandy, which she couldn't do for one minute.

At last Sunday dinner was on the table—chicken, gravy, potatoes, and salad. As they ate, the others filled Aunt Jenny and the Judge in on the story of Brandy Perkins.

"Eric Lindler has nothing to do with this," Aunt Jenny said, "but that poor girl is in terrible danger."

With a scream of "Oooh," Vicky bolted from the table and ran for the bathroom, closely followed by Ellen.

There was a lot of leftover food and a lot of plates left half full that noon.

Gloom descended over the group. When Vicky and Ellen returned, they all avoided talking about Brandy and made small talk instead. Was Vicky going to go back to school the next day? She didn't know. Was Ellen? Yes, she was going to try. All right then, Vicky would try too. Susan, of course, could not go back, and she was frustrated. She wanted to confront John Scott and Ernie Westin.

Dirk Jordan called Jake about two o'clock, and Jake again went out on the deck. When he came back, he announced solemnly, "No one can find a trace of her since someone saw her get in her car early Thursday afternoon, wearing a sweatshirt and jeans."

"I suppose Dirk Jordan will call me, since he thinks I'm involved with every suspicious event that happens," Susan said.

"Yeah," Jake said, "he probably will. Be straight with him, Susan."

"I'm never not, but I don't have any idea where she could be," she said. "I care what happens to that girl."

Dirk Jordan didn't call—to Susan's surprise, as they sat by the phone all day, waiting for word on Brandy. The judge went home, and eventually Jake took Vicky to get her car on campus and then took Ellen home, where Vicky met them. When he came back to Susan's, Aunt Jenny had cooked a pot of chicken soup that smelled heavenly. Jake ate heartily, but Susan found it tasteless, her mouth dry and sour, as though she'd been on a binge.

"Susan Hogan, you've got to eat!" Aunt Jenny's voice took her back in time twenty-five years or more to the days when Susan had been a reluctant eater.

"Do I have to go straight to bed if I don't?" she asked, but there was little humor in her voice.

Jordan called about eight, and Jake took the call. Susan listened to him say, "Yes," and "Where?" and "What do you think?" and nearly screamed because she could make no sense out of his questions. When he hung up, he turned to her. "Jordan found Brandy's car—and her purse—parked near the railroad yards in Fort Worth."

"Near The City Restaurant?"

"Near enough that Jordan went by there to talk to Thomas, but the place is closed on Sundays. He traced the phone number on Thomas' so-called business card, but it goes to a service. His phone bill goes to a box number. Gotta give that kid credit—he's clever. Jordan put out an APB, but the guy could be in California by now."

"It's not a good sign, is it, Jake? I mean, finding the car."

"Nope, it's not."

"Jordan needs to ask Vicky Lawson where to find Kenny Thomas."

"He did. Called her at Ellen's. She knows nothing except The City Restaurant."

He grabbed his car keys. "Jordan's got to talk to that Sallie Cornell, the third girl who was with Brandy and Vicky Wednesday night. You know her?"

Susan shook her head. "Not at all."

"I feel I ought to go. You be all right?"

"Yeah, go," Susan said. "But call me."

"I will."

He called within an hour. "We didn't learn anything. Boy, that girl's a hard case. I think she's mad 'cause she's out of work." He tried to laugh a little.

Susan missed his feeble attempt at a joke. "I'll call Ellen," she said.

"No need. She already knows. Remember, Jordan had to talk to Vicky."

At ten, Aunt Jenny went to bed, with a hug for Susan and a reassuring, "None of this is your fault, dear. You mustn't think that."

"Brandy warned me I'd only make things worse," Susan said.

"You have to protect yourself, clear your name. And you can't turn away when you know something's wrong."

"I guess so." Susan turned out the lights and prepared to follow Aunt Jenny's example and go to bed. But she knew she was in for a night of tossing and turning. She pulled off her wide-legged pants, put on her sleeping shirt, and then wrapped her old terry-cloth bathrobe around herself and hopped on one foot back to the couch.

Sitting in the darkness, she tried to figure out how all that had happened was connected, what Eric Lindler's relation was to Kenny Thomas, why she had been drawn into it—and then had drawn poor Ellen into it. Vicky Lawson had unwittingly drawn herself into it. And Brandy Perkins—what could one think about her? *Poor Missy Jackson,* Susan thought, *you've been all but forgotten in all this.* Indeed, she could barely summon the details of Missy Jackson's photo in her mind's eye.

At one o'clock, Susan was still sitting on the couch, still lost in thought, when Aunt Jenny padded into the room in her chenille slippers. "Susan, was that you?"

"Was what me, Aunt Jenny?"

"I thought a heard a noise, almost like a noise under the house. But maybe you moved something in here."

"I haven't even moved myself, Aunt Jenny, but I didn't hear anything. Guess I was lost in thought."

"Well," the older woman said, "I was asleep, so I guess I'm not clear about what I heard. Maybe the wind blew a branch across the roof."

Under the house doesn't sound like on the roof, Susan thought. She didn't remind her aunt that there was no wind that night to blow a branch. Maybe a possum or something had crawled under the house, but Susan didn't think so. Once again she had the eerie feeling that they were not alone, that someone was watching. She put a hand on the phone to call Jake and tell him she thought she knew where Kenny Thomas was—right under her house—but then she decided she was letting her imagination run away with her. Struggling with her crutches, she checked to be sure the bar was in the sliding glass door and then went from window to window making sure all were bolted. "Should have gotten that alarm system Jake recommended," she muttered.

After Aunt Jenny's scare, Susan had secured the house as best she could, but she still didn't feel safe. She lay in bed, listening for noises, the phone at her pillow for ready access. When it rang, she was startled out of sleep, though she'd have sworn she had not slept at all.

"Hello?"

That same high-pitched voice said, "Die, Susan Hogan. You must die."

This time Susan really did not go back to sleep, and morning found her exhausted.

The phone rang again about six in the morning. Tensely, Susan answered it, steeled against that falsetto voice and its chilling threat. She didn't speak for a minute, as though by listening, she could tell who it was. Finally, she said "Hello?"

"Susan, it's Jake. They've got a Jane Doe at the Wise County hospital up north. Sounds like she could be Brandy. I'm going up to Decatur to try to ID her."

"I'll be dressed in five minutes," Susan said, suddenly alert. "Bring me coffee on your way. Black."

"Susan, I don't want you to go. I know Brandy or at least what she looks like well enough, and . . . well, it'll be pretty unpleasant. This girl's been beaten within an inch of her life. Some hunter's dog found her in a ditch on a way back road, covered with leaves. Whoever left her there didn't mean for her to be found."

"She's alive, isn't she?"

"Barely."

"Come get me, Jake. It's my responsibility."

Hanging up the phone, Jake muttered, "You and your damn responsibility to everyone but me!" But he stopped for black coffee at McDonald's and was at her house in twenty minutes. He'd have been there sooner, but he'd called Ellen Peck too.

Wearing her sweat suit with the leg split to go over her cast, no makeup, her hair still tousled from sleep, Susan stood on the porch. "I left Aunt Jenny a note," she said. "Should we go see if Vicky Lawson wants to go?"

"I called there," Jake said, "after I called you. When Ellen told Vicky what we think happened, Vicky went hysterical. It was a repeat of the scene in the dorm the other night—crying, sobbing, screaming."

"Is she all right?"

"Ellen says she can take care of her, and I think she can. Your friend Ellen is pretty tough."

Susan wondered if he said that to other people about her.

* * *

The "Jane Doe" lay in a cubicle in the Wise County hospital's intensive care unit. An officer was posted at the door to the cubicle.

Susan approached the bed and stared at the limp body. The girl's face was puffy, her eyes swollen shut, her color more purple than anything else. "Bruises just beginning to heal," the nurse said. "She has a slight concussion, and a broken arm and a fractured elbow, both of which have been set. She was badly dehydrated, but we're fixing that with IVs. We don't think she has internal injuries, but we're watching."

"She's unconscious," Susan said, stating the obvious. She stared at the girl and was glad she'd had no more than the one cup of black coffee that morning. Even that rose in her throat.

"Yes," the nurse said, "but her vital signs are fairly strong."

"Why is she unconscious?"

"Probably," the nurse said, "there's something too painful for her to wake up and face. Happens in more cases than you think. If we can find out who she is, we can begin to talk to her, call her by name, bring in her family. All of that can draw a person back to reality." She fixed them with a long look. "Do you know her?"

Susan shook her head. "I don't know. What color's her hair?"

"Dark, almost black. Longish . . . or it was, before we cut it."

Jake shook his head in despair. "She's so disfigured, I can't tell. I really can't. I think it's her, but . . . "

Susan turned to the nurse. "Was she wearing earrings?"

Jake said, "Susan! Earrings?" and the nurse looked startled, but she said, "I don't know . . . but we can check the few belongings that were found on her." She went to a locker in the corner of the cubicle and pulled out a brown paper bag that looked like a small grocery sack.

Susan wanted to laugh hysterically. You nearly die, and they put your belongings in a grocery bag!

The nurse pulled out jeans and a sweatshirt, both bloody and soiled beyond repair and musty smelling. Then she held up a small white envelope and emptied its contents into her own palm. Two silver earrings, dangle style with a bit of turquoise, tumbled out, followed by a silver ring, also with a bit of turquoise.

"Those are Brandy's earrings," Susan said with conviction. Suddenly she felt she'd done something, some small thing to give Brandy her life back, to make amends for meddling in it.

"You sure, Susan?" Jake was incredulous.

"Yes," she snapped, "I'm sure. Call that blasted Dirk Jordan and tell him you've found her." Then she moved closer to the bed and grasped the hand that wasn't in a cast. "Brandy," she spoke softly, "it's all right. Everything will be all right. You're safe now." *What kind of a person can this Kenny Thomas be to have done this,* she wondered. *And what will he do to me if he gets the chance?* She shuddered.

"You okay?" the nurse asked.

"Yeah, just upset. I mean that anyone could do this to her . . . "

"Why didn't you tell her your name?" the nurse asked.

"She thinks I'm responsible for part of her trouble . . . or all of it," Susan said humbly. "I don't guess mine is the face she'd want to wake up and see. We've got to call her family."

"Already done," Jake said. "I called the office when I learned about her. Didn't want to get their hopes up, but they'll have to back up your ID."

Susan and Jake stayed in Decatur most of the day. Brandy's parents proved to be a college psych professor and his psychologist wife. They arrived mid-afternoon, having driven straight and hard from Oklahoma City, and Susan both liked and pitied them immediately.

Linda Perkins took one deep breath when she saw the battered condition of her daughter and then went immediately to the girl's bedside. Holding Brandy's uninjured hand tightly in one of her own, she used her other hand to lightly stroke the swollen, bruised face, barely touching its surface and yet transmitting through her fingers a great love for this girl. "Brandy," she crooned softly, "it's me. You're okay, sweetheart, you're okay. I'm here . . . and I won't leave."

Ned Perkins spoke to his daughter too, his tone soft and encouraging, but he hadn't the endurance of his wife, and after a few minutes of reassuring the comatose girl of his love, he had to step into the hall.

"Hard, hard," Susan said. "I'm so sorry."

Ned Perkins shook his head. "You don't know the half of it. She's the baby of the family—three older brothers and two sisters, and she's the only one who was always . . . I mean *always* in trouble. Linda and I have asked ourselves if psychologists' children are like the cobbler's child, but that's not it. The others are fine. And Brandy was the most loved of children . . . I don't know what unhappiness drives her."

Susan realized he didn't know the full story of what had happened, what Brandy had been involved in, and she wasn't about to tell him. It wasn't her place. That duty, she thought wryly, belongs to Dirk Jordan, in spite of his clear lack of compassion.

Linda Perkins had brought a bag of things—an apparently beloved stuffed bear, a tape deck and some tapes that she played softly for her daughter, slippers and a robe so that she herself could comfortably spend the night at her child's bedside.

"We'll move her to Fort Worth to the medical center tomorrow," Ned Perkins said. "They tell us she'll get more sophisticated care there."

Susan and Jake left for Oak Grove about five, begging the Perkins to tell them if and when Brandy recognized them.

"We will," Linda said simply, "and thank you for all you've done for our daughter."

Susan was struck as though by a knife. All she had done for Brandy was stir up trouble. But then she thought of the Jacksons, Missy's parents, and their very different reaction to tragedy, their instant accusation rather than appreciation.

Not knowing Susan's insecurities, Linda went on, "Brandy's favorite older brother will meet us in Fort Worth tomorrow, and the sister she's closest to. I think between us, we can bring her around."

Neither Susan nor Jake spoke on the long drive back, both lost in the enormity of what had happened to Brandy. At Susan's house, Jake came in to see what Aunt Jenny had for supper. "Nothing," the older woman said. "I had no idea when you'd be back. But I can scramble some eggs and fry some bacon."

"Do it, woman," Jake said, trying to lighten the moment.

Susan stared at him as if he'd lost his mind, but Aunt Jenny began to cook, and they were all three soon eating breakfast for supper, none of them speaking, except Aunt Jenny, who from time to time muttered, "That poor girl. Who could have done that?"

"Kenny Thomas," Susan said with conviction.

About nine, Jake yawned ostentatiously and said he guessed he'd better go home. Aunt Jenny excused herself to go to her room, and Susan knew she was giving them some privacy. She also knew Jake wasn't interested.

"I'll call first thing in the morning," he said, brushing her hair lightly with his hand in a gesture of affection.

Several awful possibilities of what could happen between now and morning flitted through Susan's head, but she pushed the thoughts aside.

Once he was gone, Susan again had that spooky feeling of being watched. She called Ellen, both to report on Brandy and to check on Vicky.

"She slept all day," Ellen said. "I called the hospital, and they sent an intern over with a shot of something that put her out like Lottie's eye. She'll be better when she wakes, and I can give her sort of good news. Susan?"

"Yeah?"

"Get some rest. Is Jake there?"

"No, he went home. I told him we'd be all right."

Chapter Fifteen

Jake called so early the next morning even Aunt Jenny wasn't up, and Susan was grumpy as she answered the phone, fearing that high-pitched voice again. Instead, Jake began talking a mile a minute. Kenny Thomas had tried to kill Brandy in the hospital and had been arrested.

"Whoa, slow down. What happened?"

"Jordan put out word that Brandy was conscious and talking . . . "

Before Susan could rush in with "Wonderful" or any such, he went on. "It wasn't true. It was a trap, and Thomas fell for it. Snuck into the hospital, stole some scrubs, and went in pretending to be, oh, I don't know . . . intern, resident, orderly. Anyway, he dismissed the mother and the nurse and thought they'd left, so he talked to Brandy for a minute. Can you imagine? He's about to kill an unconscious girl, and he talks to her? Then he tried to smother her with a pillow. The nurse, who was really a lady cop, cuffed him and read him his rights on the spot. He's charged with the murder of Missy Jackson and the beating and attempted murder of Brandy Perkins."

When she should have been grateful and relieved, Susan was angry. "I wish you'd told me last night. I might have slept."

"You can sleep now, Susan, safely," Jake said patiently, pushing aside his own anger.

"Is she awake?" Susan asked.

"No, but they think that will come soon. I . . . I gotta get to work. I'll talk to you later."

Susan hung up the phone slowly. It was over. Jake thought it was over. But she knew it wasn't.

* * *

Brandy Perkins's parents were at her bedside when she first began to show signs of regaining consciousness. Linda Perkins stroked her daughter's forehead and murmured gently to her.

"Mom?" the voice was weak and faint.

"I'm right here, sweetie. So's your father. Everything's going to be all right."

Brandy drifted back into unconsciousness, and her parents kept their vigil.

Dirk Jordan, notified that the patient had spoken even if ever so briefly and softly, came directly to the hospital. Ned Perkins met him in the hall.

"Didn't you ask her who beat her?" Jordan demanded, the expression on his face showing clearly that he couldn't imagine that wasn't the first thing Ned Perkins said to his daughter.

"No," the father said calmly, "we told her we love her."

"I've got to see her," Jordan said, turning toward the door to Brandy's cubicle.

Ned Perkins put out a restraining arm. "She's asleep again. When she wakes and the nurses feel she's capable, we'll ask her."

Jordan clamped his teeth together, his mouth forming a straight line. "I'll wait."

It was late afternoon before Brandy was awake long enough to answer any questions. Even then, the doctors insisted that her parents might ask about the attack, but Jordan could not be in the room. "You're a stranger to her, man," the doctor said. "We can't have her frightened at this point."

But when asked who beat her, Brandy whispered, "Kenny." Then with a wail, she added, "Why did he hurt me so much?"

"He won't ever hurt you again, Brandy. He's in jail. Forget about him for now." Linda Perkins was alarmed by the sudden strength of her daughter's reaction. Ned Perkins reported the answer to Jordan, who seemed satisfied for the moment.

"I'll need to talk with her at length as soon as that's possible," he said.

"Days," the doctor told him, "days from now. Not soon."

* * *

Susan was home alone that afternoon, sitting in her usual place on the couch in the family room, staring at the five o'clock news. The room was almost dark, Susan apparently having refused to turn on the lights. A knock on the door and then Jake slid open the door to the deck. Since she was supposedly no longer in danger, she hadn't locked it.

"Susan? May I come in?"

"Of course," she said.

"It's over, Susan. Brandy's conscious, and she named Kenny Thomas as the one who beat her. Jordan's dismissed all charges against you."

"Doesn't a judge have to do that?"

"That's a formality. You're cleared, Susan. It's over."

"Did that Kenny confess to killing Missy?"

"No, but Jordan says he's the right man, just like you always said." Jake shifted from one foot to the other, as though uncomfortable that he had not believed her all along.

"I guess," she said but her tone lacked conviction. It seemed too sudden, too hard to believe. The turmoil that had disrupted her life couldn't end so suddenly and much more quietly than it had begun. Something in the back of Susan's mind was sending out warning signals—she just couldn't make sense of it all.

"Where's Aunt Jenny?" Jake seated himself in the overstuffed chair but sat on the edge.

"Judge Jackson took her to that new B&B in Mineral Wells for dinner. She left something in the oven for me." Susan paused a moment, then "They'll be late getting back."

"I got to go back to the office," he said lamely. "You be all right?"

"Sure," she said dryly.

He stood up and took two steps to her side, leaning down to kiss her on the forehead. "Tomorrow, we'll talk. We'll go someplace . . . maybe for dinner, and we'll talk."

"I'm never going to The City Restaurant again," she said emphatically.

He almost grinned. "Me neither. Just remember," he said as he left, "it's over." On his way out the door, he flipped the switch to turn on the outdoor floodlight. "At least you'll have a little light from outside," he told her.

After a while, Susan hobbled to the kitchen and poured herself a glass of wine. Then she turned off the television and sat back down on the couch, still not turning on any lights. It grew dark, and she sat there, puzzling. If it was over, why didn't she feel relieved? Well, there was still Jake to worry about—what would happen when they talked? And tenure—she hadn't thought about Zane Grey or even about teaching for a week or more. Could she just call up Dr. Scott in the morning and announce she was coming back on campus? Not likely. Probably the suspension would have to be formally lifted.

When the phone rang, she lifted it hesitantly. If Kenny Thomas was safely in jail, this shouldn't be another threatening phone call. But if this was that same voice telling her she had to die, then it meant Kenny Thomas wasn't the one. Her hand on the phone, Susan knew why she felt uneasy: she didn't believe it was over, no matter what Jake and Dirk Jordan thought.

"Susan Hogan," she said, putting as much force into her voice as she could muster.

"Ernie Westin here, Susan. Just wanted to see how you are."

Caution crept into Susan's voice. "Fine, thanks, Ernie. And you?" Surely Ernie isn't part of a plot against me. No one would take academic rivalry that far. Not even toad Ernie.

The real reason for his call came out. "I hear they arrested someone for the murder of Missy Jackson. Just wanted you to know how relieved I am. 'Course I always knew you didn't do it."

Then why, she wanted to ask, did you work so hard to make Scott think I was guilty? She thought a long minute and then gave up on tolerance, forgiveness, patience, and good manners. She knew this call was prompted by Ernie's need to get himself on the right side of any problem . . . and he'd been on the wrong side all along. "Ernie, you know you wished all along that I did do it, that I'd be gone from Oak Grove. And you did everything you could to make me look bad with Dr. Scott."

There was silence at the other end of the phone, so she went on. "You probably put yourself on the wrong side, Ernie, because Dr. Atwater believed me all along. I suspect he'll have something to say to Dr. Scott . . . and perhaps Scott will pass it along to you."

After a long pause, Westin replied in a voice that clearly reflected anxiety. "Susan, you ... you misunderstand. I have always supported you ... "

She hung up the phone, tired of listening to him. Remember, she told herself, about forgiveness and letting go. Carrying a grudge against Ernie Westin isn't going to do you any good. You've got more to worry about—like who really killed Missy and what you can do about Jake.

It was now full dark, but still she resisted lights and wasn't interested in Aunt Jenny's dinner. She sat on the couch, every once in a while hearing a car go by outside on the distant street. Once she thought she heard that same noise that had frightened Aunt Jenny but she told herself it was her imagination.

When the sliding glass door was eased open, she knew it wasn't her imagination.

"Dr. Hogan?" Eric Lindler asked.

Susan knew immediately why it wasn't over. Aunt Jenny had been right.

"Eric? What are you doing here? There's no crisis, nobody missing—in fact, they've found Missy's murderer. And Aunt Jenny's not cooking tonight. And me? Frankly, I'm not in the mood for company." She was babbling.

"It's not over, is it, Dr. Hogan? Mr. Phillips was wrong." His voice was cold and distant, lacking that boyish enthusiasm with which he had always filled Susan's house.

She decided it would be better to stand up. She wasn't going to be a willing victim to a baseball bat while cowering on a couch. She turned toward him, reaching for a crutch at the same time. It would be her only weapon of defense.

Eric was faster than she was. He crossed the room in a flash and with one well-aimed, deliberate kick at her good leg, knocked her to the floor. Then, with a cruelty that she couldn't believe, he stepped—hard!—on her broken leg at the ankle.

Susan heard the bone crack, felt an incredible wave of pain accompanied by nausea so strong that she was sure she going to throw up right there on the floor. In spite of her effort to be quiet, she whimpered—she knew she did.

"Sorry, Dr. Hogan," he said, but there was no apology in his voice. "I had to be sure you wouldn't be trouble."

After a few minutes, the pain had not subsided but she had become more steeled to it—or maybe greater fear had lessened her concentration on the pain. She couldn't move much without jarring the ankle and reawakening the pain that was not to be stood, but she could turn just enough to see Eric.

He had seated himself at the table, as though he were waiting for dinner. In one hand he held a butcher knife, but she saw no baseball bat.

She wondered vaguely which was worse—bat or knife—and decided, almost with a hysterical giggle, that it didn't matter. "What are you going to do, Eric?" she asked, knowing the answer to the question full well.

"I'll have to kill you," he said simply. "You and your aunt. Where is she?"

"Gone," Susan lied. "She's gone home, back to Wichita Falls."

"That's not true," he said calmly. "She's gone to Mineral Wells with the judge for dinner. Don't lie to me, Dr. Hogan, or I'll kick your ankle again."

"How do you know where she's gone?" Susan asked, curiosity for a moment overriding fear.

He grinned, looking proud of himself. "I have a spot in the crawl space under your house. I spend lots of time there, listening to what's going on."

"That's how you always knew to appear when something had happened?" *And that's why I always felt we're being watched!*

"Right." He nodded in satisfaction and began tossing the knife back and forth in his hands.

Susan watched in horrified fascination as the beam from the outdoor floodlight occasionally glinted off the knife. The blade was long, tapered, and looked very sharp.

"Eric, if you kill me and Aunt Jenny, then what? You can't stay here and go to school and pretend to know nothing about it. Everyone will suspect you."

"No, they'll think that man that Missy worked for did it. I know about him."

"He's in jail right this minute, Eric."

He advanced toward her. "I told you not to lie to me again, Dr. Hogan."

She almost winced, feeling another blow to her ankle coming, but she kept her voice calm. "No, Eric, call the Fort Worth jail. He's there. He was arrested yesterday, and Brandy identified him as the man who beat her."

"Brandy identified him?" His voice raised in interest. "They'll think he killed Missy, too."

"You killed Missy," Susan said flatly.

He got up, agitated for the first time, and began to pace the floor. "Yes, I had to. She was dishonoring herself, going against the strictest of the commandments. 'Thou shalt not commit adultery.' And she was selling herself—selling herself"—his voice rose in hysteria—"I had to do it. I followed her to Fort Worth one afternoon, watched while she went into a hotel with a man. I hotwired your car—I know how to do lots of things like that—and I took my baseball bat with me because I knew what I was going to find. When she came out of that hotel, I convinced her to get in your car. Then I pulled her behind the hotel, hit her in the head with the bat and just kept hitting and hitting. I remember feeling I had to beat the evil out of her. I had to do the Lord's work."

"Where was the man?" Susan decided to do anything she could to keep this frenzied young man talking.

"What man? Oh, the one in the hotel. Who knows? Probably sound asleep after satisfying himself—with my fiancé!" His voice rose in anger again.

Okay, Susan, keep him talking but try not to let him get worked up into a rage.

"Did you choose my car deliberately?"

"Yes. I knew it was your car. Then I drove back and parked it just where you left it. You didn't know for two days."

"Why didn't you dump Missy on a road somewhere? Nobody would have found her, and you'd have been a lot safer."

"No! She had to be found. The world had to know that she'd been punished, just like Brandy's been punished. I was going to stop Brandy next because she corrupted Missy just like you did. But she was so evil, someone else did it for me."

"Why me, Eric? Why did you choose my car?"

"Because you corrupted Missy too, Dr. Hogan. She was . . . well, different, after she took your class. She told me she didn't have to do what I told her. She wasn't even sure she wanted to be a minister's wife! And she said it was because you made her think in your class. I didn't want her to think. I wanted her to love and follow me!" He pounded his fist into the table and sat down, as though momentarily dispirited.

Susan's hopes rose, but when he spoke again, she shuddered at his derangement.

"I'm sorry, Dr. Hogan. I'd kill you now and get it over with, but I have to wait for your aunt."

"Why wait for Aunt Jenny?" She almost bit the words off. *What are you trying to do, Susan? Convince him to go ahead and kill you now?*

"Miss Hogan knows too. She's always known."

"Eric, she's fed you, fussed over you. How can you hurt her?"

He spread his hands helplessly. "I don't want to, but I have to. I've heard her say that she knows I killed Missy. She knew I trashed your plants and did all those other things. She hears the devil's voice."

So Eric Lindler had trashed the plants, not Kenny Thomas. It was Eric who tried to frighten her all along. "Did you call me on the phone, Eric?"

"Yes, ma'am. Got one of those things that disguise your voice on the phone. Works pretty good, don't you think?" Again, he swelled with pride.

"And did you put that baseball bat here? The dead kitten? The plants?"

"I did all that," he said, puffing with pride. "Pretty clever, don't you think? I had you scared."

Yeah, Susan thought, *but never as scared as I am right now.* Her mind was working frantically. What could she do when Aunt Jenny came in? How could she save both of them? Jake should be here right now, and this wouldn't be happening. She pictured him, sitting at home, drinking a beer and reading, and she both hated him and prayed for him to walk through the door.

* * *

At the Yellow Butterfly in Mineral Wells, John Jackson sipped bourbon on the rocks, while Aunt Jenny daintily tasted a glass of white Zinfandel. John had assured her it was sweeter than whatever it was that Susan drank—that white wine made Aunt Jenny pucker her lips. They had just ordered their dinners—steak for him, shrimp for her—and were waiting for their salads.

"Isn't this a lovely place?" Jenny asked, looking around the dining room. It was small, with only ten round tables—she had counted them—that held four people each and no more. White linen cloths covered the tables, and there were heavy white linen napkins, real sterling silver, and fresh flowers on each table. The walls were wainscoted with dark wood and above that covered with a flocked, flowery paper. Heavy drapes covered the windows and were swagged at the top and highlighted with gold cord.

"Queen Victoria probably would have liked to eat here," the judge muttered, "but it's a mite fancy for my taste. I'll take The City Restaurant."

"Oh, no, we're never going back there."

He reached out and covered her plump hand with his own wiry fingers. "All right, then, the steak house at Ponder. Or maybe even Subie's Cafe."

"But you're the one who picked this place! If you don't like it . . . "

"I thought you'd like it," he said, squeezing the hand he held, "and it pleases me that you do."

The waitress brought their salads, explaining that they were wild greens dressed with raspberry vinaigrette.

"Raspberry vinaigrette?" the judge echoed. "Give me good old Kraft's Italian."

Jenny Hogan giggled merrily. But just as she took a forkful of greens that she couldn't identify—they surely weren't lettuce, why one was even purple!—Jenny suddenly said, "John, we've got to get back to Oak Grove. Susan's in terrible trouble."

The judge was completely dumbfounded. "Jenny, we've just ordered our dinners."

"Bother the dinners! We've got to go *now!*"

John Jackson stared at this woman who both fascinated and puzzled him, but something told him he'd better listen to her. He would later wonder if he left that steak behind because he believed Jenny about Susan being in trouble or simply because he would do anything for Jenny. "I'll have to pay for the dinner."

Their waitress was puzzled. "You didn't like the salad? I can bring you soup instead."

"No, no," Jenny said, "please just hurry. We have to leave right away."

Still holding the judge's credit card, the young girl looked at Aunt Jenny. "Did you get an emergency call on a cell phone?"

"You might say that," the judge said dryly, rising and holding the chair for Jenny. "Just bring me the ticket right away."

The girl scampered away, and John called after her. "Where's your phone?"

"Who are you going to call?" Jenny asked. "Susan won't answer her phone."

"If she doesn't," he said, "I'm going to call Jake."

"Oh, my," Jenny said, her voice tremulous.

"Jenny Hogan, don't you faint on me." The judge's voice was stern.

* * *

Both Eric and Susan had been silent for a long while, Susan absorbed in pain and Eric in whatever thoughts were tormenting him when the phone began to ring.

"Don't answer it," he said.

"Everyone knows I'm home alone," she said. "They'll worry if I don't answer it." If she could only talk to Jake, she'd find some way to tell him that she was in trouble—real trouble.

"Don't answer it," he repeated.

Grinding her teeth, Susan listened to the phone ring eight times, then grow silent again.

"It won't matter who it was," Eric said. "Nobody can change what's going to happen."

Susan shuddered.

* * *

Jake was spending the evening just as Susan had pictured him—sitting in his favorite chair, reading *The Cattle Killing* by John Edgar Wideman, sipping on a few beers. He felt a certain complacency—the Missy Jackson case was closed, Brandy Perkins seemed to be recovering, Susan was safe and off the hook, and tomorrow he and Susan would have a long talk about what had gone on—or wrong—between them. *After all, he reasoned, crises like they'd gone through were bound to affect even the best of relationships. Maybe Susan hadn't even realized she had lied to him.*

When the phone rang, his first thought was, *Damn! I won't go out again tonight!* "Phillips," he barked into the phone.

"John Jackson, Jake. Don't know how to tell you this, but Jenny is convinced Susan is in serious trouble. And she doesn't answer her phone."

Jake shook his head, puzzling out what he was hearing. "I thought you were in Mineral Wells eating dinner."

The judge sighed. "We are . . . or were. Just about to be served the steak I'd ordered when Jenny announced we have to get back to Oak Grove right away. You know how she is."

"Her intuition, right?" Jake said.

"Right."

"Well, I don't much believe in intuition in police matters, but then again Aunt Jenny . . . " Jake's voice trailed off.

"She won't let me talk any more. She's pulling me out the door. Just go check on Susan, will you, Jake?"

"Sure, right away."

In the car, speeding toward Oak Grove as fast as the judge dared drive over dark country roads, Jenny said, "I signed your credit card slip."

"Forged my name?"

"No, I signed Jenny Jackson." She said it without self-consciousness.

In spite of the situation, the judge laughed aloud. "Did you leave a good tip?"

"Fifty percent. I figured we owed them something extra after leaving the meal."

The judge groaned this time. "We should have asked for to-go boxes," he said.

* * *

As he pulled on his shoes and grabbed a jacket against the cool night, Jake Phillips felt a sudden rise of panic. If something happened to Susan, he'd never forget that he should have stayed there with her this evening, should have overcome his stiff-necked pride. He stuck his service revolver in his belt, checked his flashlight. The truck held rope, handcuffs and anything else he might need.

As he drove, squealing around the corner and speeding down the highway, taking corners at a wide turn, Jake considered whether or not he should have called Dirk Jordan's office or his own people. He decided against it. Any of those calls would have brought cars with flashing lights and would have meant danger to Susan. If there was any trouble, he'd rather handle it by himself.

He parked a block from Susan's house and walked softly along the edge of the houses, cursing the wide spaces between houses and praying no neighbors came out to demand what he was doing. At Martha Whitley's house, he stopped and stood peering at Susan's house. It was totally dark. Jake considered. Then he went back quietly to Mrs. Whitley's front door and knocked softly. When she answered, he explained that he thought Susan might be in trouble and Mrs. Whitley should turn out all her lights, inside and out, and stay in the house no matter what alarming noises she heard. No, she should not call the police unless she heard him yell directly to her to do that.

She was flustered, protesting, until he said, "I can't stand here and talk. Please do as I say."

Jake looked through Mrs. Whitley's flowerbed until he found a good-sized rock. Then he eased down the driveway and standing at the corner of the house, in the shadow of Mrs. Whitley's house, he took careful aim and shattered Susan's outdoor flood-light. The noise echoed through the night but brought no immediate response from inside the house.

* * *

Inside, both Susan and Eric jumped at the sudden sound of shattering glass, but Eric calmed immediately. "Someone's here. But I told you, Dr. Hogan, it won't matter."

Susan wondered if he would simply kill her right now. If so, maybe she should yell a warning rather than lie here waiting to be slaughtered. But if she did that, Eric would come after her for sure, and it would be a question of who was outside and how fast they were. As she weighed her odds, Susan felt her heart pounding.

Eric paced the room, looking out the sliding glass door, then peering out the windows over the kitchen sink, but it was pitch black without the light. He whirled at an imaginary sound, peered where he thought he saw movement, but, in truth, he could see nothing. And it made him furious to know that someone was outside, trying to outsmart him, to stop him.

"We may not be able to wait for Miss Hogan," he told Susan.

Susan had been trying to figure out if it was Jake who knocked out the light. If she had known for sure it was, she could yell and bring him inside in time; if it was Aunt Jenny, there was no hope—but how would Aunt Jenny knock out the light? Or even Judge Jackson? And besides, they were still in Mineral Wells. No, it had to be Jake out there. Besides, Susan truly believed that Jake would always keep her safe. *I just never told him how much I trust and need him,* she thought bitterly. She made up her mind.

When Eric went once again to the kitchen window—with the cooking island and two chairs between him and Susan—she yelled at the top of her lungs, "Jake! Eric! Knife!"

* * *

"Can't you go any faster?" Jenny asked impatiently.

"Jenny, I'm doing sixty now. I know this road but not that well . . . and not at night. I go any faster, we might not get there at all."

"Well, couldn't you have taken the interstate?"

John Jackson was faintly amused. "It doesn't go from here to there, Jenny. Try to be calm. I'm doing the best I can."

"But it's been thirty minutes already. Oh, I'm sorry, John. I'm just so worried . . . "

"Think about Jake, Jenny. He'll take care of Susan."

* * *

Before Susan yelled out her warning, Jake had inched his way carefully to the edge of the sliding door, hugging the side of the house so that anyone looking out the door wouldn't see him. He'd circled the house carefully and heard both voices and movement, so he knew Aunt Jenny wasn't having idle premonitions—Susan was inside and in trouble, and she wasn't alone. Jake's plan was to attack suddenly, surprise whoever was inside.

So he was already poised when Susan made her dramatic choice. And she chose three words that could galvanize Jake

Phillips into action—when she called his name, if he'd have thought about it, he'd have known that she was telling him she needed him and that she trusted him to be there, and when she identified Eric, he knew Aunt Jenny was right. And "Knife!" told him what kind of opposition to expect.

But Jake Phillips didn't really think any of those things as he burst through the door, yelling, "Police. Stop! I've got a gun!" He had a moment of gratitude that he knew where the light switch was inside the door. In a quick gesture, he flipped it on and flooded the room with light.

Susan's scream had caught Eric unprepared. He truly thought he had her frightened into silence. Instead, that loud voice broke through the night—and through his nerves. Knife in hand, he whirled and started toward her, forgetting momentarily the layout of her house. He crashed into the counter that separated kitchen from the family area where she still lay on the floor. He almost dropped his knife.

When Jake turned on the light, Eric had regained the knife but still stood between the sink and the island. Jake, now between Susan and Eric, pointed a pistol at him and said, "Drop the knife, Eric."

"You won't shoot me," Eric said. "I'm a student." He clutched the knife and moved as if to circle the counter and head toward Susan, who lay motionless on the floor.

"Take one more step and I will shoot you, student or no." Jake's voice was tight. If Eric moved around the island, he would be directly facing Jake who stood just inside the sliding glass door.

Susan saw Eric coming toward her, brandishing his knife, and then she heard the explosion of Jake's gun, followed by a scream of anguish from Eric, and a clatter as he and the knife fell to the floor.

"Jake, you didn't—?"

"I shot him in the arm. You all right?"

"No," she said weakly. "He broke my ankle again . . . and it hurts."

For a moment, Jake almost forgot all his professional training. He turned on Eric Lindler in such anger that he raised his fists. Only Susan's cry of "Jake!" stopped him from beating the boy, who was whimpering and crying, "It hurts. Oh, God, it hurts."

"It's all right, Susan. Lie still just a minute more. Eric, sit at the table." He grabbed the boy none too gently and propelled him to the table, where he handcuffed Eric's good arm to the table leg. Then he picked Susan up off the floor, being as gentle as he could, and laid her on the couch.

"How long's he been here?"

"Forever," she said. "Maybe thirty minutes after you left."

"Susan, I am so sorry . . . I should have stayed."

She put a finger to his lips. "Before you call the police and this place turns into a zoo, would you please kiss me?"

He did, a long kiss filled with promise.

Within ten minutes, the small house was surrounded by squad cars with lights flashing.

Chapter Sixteen

Jake didn't get his talk with Susan the next day as he'd planned. Having spent half the night in the emergency room, she slept all day, well medicated to keep the pain down.

"How did you manage to rebreak this?" the doctor had asked impatiently.

"You wouldn't believe," Susan told him through gritted teeth. Now that she was safe and it really was all over, she had given in to the pain.

Jake stayed with her at the hospital, an arm protectively about her shoulders even as the doctor probed with careful fingers and announced that he would be able to recast it that night. "Now," he said ominously, "you'll have to stay off it at least six more weeks."

The pain medication had taken over, and Susan was too groggy to know what he'd said.

* * *

Susan and Jake had their talk two days later. Jake told Aunt Jenny that Susan needed fresh air. He bundled her into his pickup truck and drove her out in the country to a roadside picnic area sheltered by trees. Few cars went by on the highway, so they were essentially alone.

"Why here?" she asked.

"Because it's a pretty place to picnic." He leaned over and kissed her gently.

The day was warm and sunny, a perfect fall day in Texas, and Jake had brought a blanket and a picnic: two small thermoses of his homemade chili, crackers, onion, and cheese to put on the chili, two bottles of beer for himself, and a bottle of wine for Susan. "Wine with chili is barbaric," he said as he poured some into a plastic glass for her. He spread the blanket on the bird-splattered picnic table, since he could hardly ask Susan to sit on the ground, and then he helped her to the table.

"It's over, but it isn't," she said. "There are so many questions. What will happen to Eric?"

"His family's here, and they've hired a lawyer. They'll plead insanity, I'm sure."

"What's his family like?"

He shrugged. "I can only give you first impressions. Father's a physician in Dallas, very sophisticated, very busy, probably never had time for Eric. Mother's a mouse of a woman, completely cowed by her husband. I bet he doesn't spend two nights at home a week."

"How did Eric get so religious?"

"If religious is what it is, I imagine he found it a refuge. A place where there were safe rules . . . and it's probably not insignificant that those rules forbid adultery. Meeting his dad, I guess I know why that was such a big thing for him."

"He won't ever be executed?"

Jake shook his head. "Almost definitely not."

"I'm glad."

"He would have executed you."

She shrugged. "Yeah, but he didn't get to." She picked at the edge of the blanket, then found a small stone at her feet and flung it as far as she could. "Like you, throwing a rock at my outdoor light," she said, smiling at him. "Jake, I owe you an apology . . . lots of apologies. And I owe you my life. I always knew you'd keep me safe."

He leaned over and kissed her. "Let's not have that talk I've been so hard-headed about. I'm glad you're all right . . . and I'm glad I could be the one to save you. Makes me feel like a knight in shining armor. But, Susan, no more lies."

She nodded, and after a long minute, she said, "I don't suppose anything like this will ever happen to us again. We can just go on and grow peacefully old on the campus."

"Sounds good to me," he said, leaning over to kiss her. "Have we got time to stop at my house?"

"I told Aunt Jenny we'd be gone all day," Susan said almost shyly. "Besides, she's probably entertaining the judge as we speak."

"I hope they lock the doors," Jake said.

"Jake Phillips! That's not what they're doing!"

"Why not?" he asked, laughing at her. "That's what we're going to do."

"But she's my aunt! She's not supposed to do that!"

Susan had thought their lovemaking would be frantic and furious, after abstinence and the terror they'd been through. The cast on her leg hindered them, but not much. Still, they moved slowly, as though in a dance, caressing, clinging, tasting each other, slow to rouse but then quick to finish. Afterward they lay without talking, Jake stroking Susan's head, nestled in the curve of his neck. She lay perfectly still and soon her even breathing told Jake that she was sleeping naturally and deeply, probably the first time in two days she'd slept without the aid of pain medication. He let himself drift off, content with his world.

"Jake!" Susan pushed herself up on her elbows and stared at him. "Jake, I've just had a terrific idea."

"About what?" he mumbled.

"My Zane Grey project. I can see where it's going. And Eric, bless his heart, with all his worry about adultery, helped me figure out Grey's attitude toward sex. Oh, Jake, it's terrific. It's going to be so good."

"And nothing," Jake said, "is going to change. You're always going to wake me up with these terrific ideas."

This time they made love like young animals—hindered by a leg in a cast.

* * *

Brandy Perkins elected to return to the dormitory and finish the semester. When Susan and Jake spoke on Brandy's behalf, Dean Atwater had a serious and confidential talk with the girl and then announced she would be allowed to return to school. It was, he explained, part of keeping the scandal quiet. And, besides, she deserved one more chance. He believed, he said, more in individuals than rigid rules.

It was unbelievable to Susan that most of the campus seemed unaware of Brandy's part in Missy's murder or of all that had gone on after the murder. They simply knew Eric had been arrested. Dr. Atwater wanted to keep it that way, and there had been no blaring headlines about campus girls in a call-girl ring. Brandy and Vicky would certainly never tell.

Brandy was dismissed from the hospital the following week, still swollen and bruised but awake and alert. Vicky would room with her.

"We've had conversions before," Ned Perkins said wearily, "and each time I've hoped they were permanent. This . . . this is more dramatic. It may last."

Dr. Atwater's office notified Susan that her suspension was officially lifted, and the faculty was looking forward to welcoming her back to class.

"I'll bet," she said to Jake. Her situation with Dr. Scott and Ernie Westin had only worsened, because she'd triumphed in a sense. She knew, though, she hadn't triumphed over them, and they'd still be trying to sabotage her. Now she was ready for them.

Her first day back, several faculty members came by her office to welcome her with comments like, "I knew you were innocent," and "How's your ankle? Can't believe what happened." Ellen, now mostly recovered, though her chest still ached, ran interference for her and fetched coffee and lunch.

Susan was as gracious as she could be about the welcoming comments—and for her that was a real effort. She knew many of these same faculty members were the ones who had shunned her. Like Ernie, they now wanted to be on the right side. Especially since it was apparent she had the provost's support. Ernie Westin kept his distance, with good reason. He knew what Susan thought of him, and he probably feared her scalding tongue.

She did not have John Scott's support, though he made a show of welcoming her back by calling her into his office.

"Doesn't he know you're on crutches?" Ellen fumed. "Couldn't he come to you?"

Susan just smiled. "This should be interesting."

John Scott stood to welcome her and indicated a chair. Then, very formally, he told her he was glad the matter was resolved and she had been cleared. He did hope, however, that she would get her car back soon.

"It's repaired and cleared, sir. But I can't drive it for six weeks. Jake Phillips will be bringing me to and from campus."

"Ah yes, Mr. Phillips. I believe you're involved with him."

"Yes, sir."

"You know I disapprove of nepotism."

"Sir, with all respect, you'd be fine with it if I dated a faculty member."

He disregarded the comment and moved on. "On another note, I understand Dr. Atwater has postponed your tenure review. I don't approve of such a move and protested it to Dean Brighton to no avail. Your review will be next year, and I will not be chair. I am leaving Oak Grove at the end of this year."

Susan desperately wanted to ask if he'd been asked to move on but she didn't. He was, after all, tenured, but he hadn't covered himself with glory in this whole thing. She left his office as graciously as she could, without expressing regret at his impending departure.

In each of her two classes that day, Susan received a round of applause when she entered the room. Young men gallantly rose to help her to her seat—none of her usual walking around while she lectured. And each period was pretty much wasted, because the students had so many questions. She figured it was their right to know. Brandy Perkins sat in the front row in the women's lit class and actually smiled at her.

When she got home that night, Aunt Jenny had fixed one of her favorite meals: salmon croquettes, stewed tomatoes, and mashed potatoes. Jake came for dinner and said not a word about the menu but ate heartily.

When Susan said, "I can make these," he laughed.

"You may not have to," Aunt Jenny said. "I'm going to move to Oak Grove. I decided today."

"Ah . . . to live with me?" Susan asked tentatively, envisioning a permanent end to her privacy, a long-term restriction on her relationship with Jake, and maybe even eventual frustration with this aunt she now adored.

Even Jake showed a bit of concern on his face.

"Oh, my, no. I couldn't do that. Your house is too small, Susan. You really ought to look for a bigger place. I'll go back to Wichita Falls next week . . . John is going to drive me. Meantime, Sunday I'll roast a turkey. I always think you should celebrate with turkey, and we have a lot to celebrate."

"It's kind of close to Thanksgiving," Susan protested. "What will we have for Thanksgiving?"

"Why, turkey, of course. But I don't know what you'll eat for Christmas. John is taking me on a Caribbean cruise that whole week. You and Jake will have to fend for yourselves."

Susan's mouth dropped open. "I had no idea the Caribbean interested you."

"It doesn't," Aunt Jenny said airily, "but if John thinks it does . . . " She shrugged as though to say, "What else can I do?"

"Aunt Jenny, when you move here . . . you're not going to marry Judge Jackson, are you?"

"Why, Susan, he hasn't asked!"

Susan tried a different approach. "You're not going to . . . ah . . . live with him?"

"Oh, Susan, that's for young people like you and Jake. No, I thought I could live in a small house in town here a lot more cheaply than in Wichita Falls . . . and be close to all of you. John likes the idea."

"I bet he does," Susan said. Then, not all her questions answered yet, she said, "Aunt Jenny, if you knew Eric had murdered Missy and trashed my plants, killed the kitten, and done all that stuff, why did you keep mothering him?"

"Well," her aunt drew the word out, "I like to mother people, and Lord knows that poor boy needed love. But I also thought there had to be some spark of good in him . . . and if I was kind enough to him, he'd finally be remorseful and tell us what he'd done." She hesitated. "I guess I don't understand . . . what's the kind of personality Officer Jordan talked about?"

"Sociopath," Susan supplied, "but I'm not sure that fits Eric. Anyway, he'll probably go to some state or private mental facility."

"And I'll send him cookies and things," Aunt Jenny said.

THE END

Acknowledgments

Sincere thanks to editors/proofreaders Mary Dulle and Lourdes Venard, who both probably have read this more than times than they want to remember. And to Lyn Stanzione, who was patient with my indecision about cover art.

As always I owe a great deal of gratitude to Fred Erisman, who read the first draft and made helpful comments.

And of course thanks to my family who are my biggest supporters. I love you guys!

About Judy Alter

Judy Alter is no stranger to college campuses. She attended the University of Chicago, Truman State University in Missouri, and Texas Christian University, where she earned a Ph.D. and taught English. For twenty years, she was director of TCU Press, the book publishing program of the university. The author of many books for both children and adults, she retired in 2010 and turned her attention to writing contemporary cozy mysteries. She is the author of the Kelly O'Connell Mysteries and the Blue Plate Café Mysteries.

She holds awards from the Western Writers of America, the National Cowboy Museum and Hall of Fame, and the Texas Institute of Letters. She was inducted into the Texas Literary Hall of Fame and recognized as an Outstanding Woman of Fort Worth and a woman who has left her mark on Texas. Western Writers of America gave her the Owen Wister Award for Lifetime Achievement. She is a member of the Texas Institute of Letters and Sisters in Crime and a past president of Western Writers of America.

Alter is the single parent of four grown children and grandmother of seven. She lives in Fort Worth, Texas with her Bordoodle, Sophie.

Also by Judy Alter

Kelly O'Connell Mysteries
  Skeleton in a Dead Space
  No Neighborhood for Old Women
  Trouble in a Big Box
  Danger Comes Home

Blue Plate Café Mysteries
  Murder at the Blue Plate Café
  Murder at the Tremont House